ENDLESS LOVE

A SWEET SECOND CHANCE ROMANCE

TINA NEWCOMB

DEDICATION

*Faith Freewoman (my fabulous editor), you slash my manuscript
with a mean
red pen while filling the margins with encouragement.
Thank you for your time, talent, and wonderful sense of humor.*

CHAPTER 1

*L*ori Maguire shook out her umbrella under the overhang of the office building. Taking a minute to calm her nerves, she pulled out her silenced cell phone and scrolled through the two good luck messages her kids had left. The last time she interviewed for a job happened so long ago, she couldn't remember the kinds of questions they asked.

Inhaling deeply, she entered the building and smiled at a young security guard. "I'm looking for the *Star's* offices."

"Who are you here to see?"

"Dave Stephens."

"His office is on the second floor. Take a left after you exit the elevator."

On the second floor, she opened one of the double doors with *The Seattle Star* etched in the glass.

"Can I help you?" asked a receptionist.

"I have an appointment with Dave Stephens. I'm Lori Maguire."

"I'll let him know you're here."

Lori slipped out of her coat and hung it on a rack near the

door, then smoothed a hand down the side of her dress. Should she have gone with a brighter color? Navy seemed safe. Maybe a little too safe. A brighter color might have— *Oh, stop being silly! The color of your dress isn't going to get you a job.*

Or would it?

Taking a seat, she set her purse on her lap, willing her fingers to stop fidgeting with the strap. At approaching footsteps, she glanced up. A man stopped in front of her and flashed a friendly grin. "Lori? I'm Dave Stephens."

She stood and shook his extended hand. "It's nice to meet you, Dave."

He tipped his head. "Let's go into my office."

As he led her down a hall, Lori's skittery heart settled slightly. His smile and thoughtful dark eyes matched the voice she'd become familiar with over the phone. After they received her resume, she'd had three phone interviews. One with the HR director Pamela East, one with Dave, the deputy managing editor, and the last one with the executive editor, Leland Jensen.

"Please, have a seat." Dave indicated one of two chairs as he rounded his desk. "I have an advantage over you. I brought my wife to one of your book signings here in Seattle last year, which gave me a face to put with the voice on the phone. My wife and daughters love your books."

"I'm glad they enjoy them."

Seven years ago, she decided to follow a teasing, daydreaming fantasy to write women's fiction. To her surprise, her books took off. She now had nine in print, one being released next week, and another with her editor. Still, writing a column for newspapers had always been her first love.

"You didn't mention your books in your resume."

"I try to keep my day job separate from my night job." She folded her hands in her lap to keep them still.

"When is your move to Seattle?"

She smiled. "Last week."

"You've already moved?" he asked with a raised brow.

"The couple who bought my house wanted to move in over Thanksgiving weekend, so I shifted my moving date up a couple of weeks."

"That was nice of you."

She shook her head. She wanted to be settled in her little house before Christmas. "It worked out for everyone."

"I have a couple more interviews." Dave tipped his head from side to side, seeming to weigh his thoughts. "If hired, would you be able to start the first Monday of January?"

Her heart did a little flip. It couldn't be this easy. "Yes."

"Do you have a few minutes? I'd like you to meet the editor."

Don't get your hopes up yet, she told her racing heart. "I have time."

~

*M*att Kelley had been holed up in his office all morning helping his assistant finalize plans for the office Christmas party which was less than two weeks away. Leland hadn't finalized many details before resigning for another job. Matt didn't feel right about dropping the ball on anyone else's shoulders this close to the date, so he and Denise ended up taking over.

When Dave called to see if he had time to do a quick interview, Matt jumped at the chance to escape for a few minutes. Denise was more than happy to take a break. She'd been complaining all morning that she hated party planning.

He and Dave had already eliminated two candidates for

the columnist job. Though well qualified, they hadn't been quite what the newspaper needed. They were looking for a fresh perspective for this particular column. Dave mentioned this interviewee was a woman who'd just moved back to Seattle after living out of state. New blood might be good, and female blood might be even better.

Matt took the stairs down two flights and tapped on Dave's door before walking in. "Hey." And then everything stopped while his heart slammed into his ribs. Sucking in a quick breath, he blinked to make sure his eyes were working correctly while adrenaline flashed through him, leaving him light-headed and hot at the same time.

Lori Maguire, someone he never thought he'd see again, stood up from her chair, her mouth open and her eyes wide —obviously as shocked to see him as he was her.

"Lori." He wanted to say more, to say anything, but nothing came to mind. Instead, he stood, staring like an idiot. A pink blush washed across her cheeks, and memories hit him harder than a three-hundred-pound linebacker.

Dave stood. "You know each other?"

"Lori and I—"

"We went to college together," Lori filled in quickly.

Dave looked from him to Lori. "Small world."

Matt could hear the smile in Dave's voice. He finally willed his feet to move. Ignoring the hand Lori held out, he wrapped her in a hug. The scent of her perfume catapulted him into the past a second time.

She stepped out of his embrace. "I didn't realize you work for the paper." She glanced at Dave and her blush deepened.

"My fault," Dave said. "I forgot you did a phone interview with Leland. He took a job in Atlanta last week. Surprised us all—especially Matt, who was suddenly promoted to executive editor."

Matt stared at Lori, catching only bits and pieces of

Dave's explanation. The girl who captured his heart in college was now a beautiful woman. She wore her strawberry blonde hair shorter now, but her green eyes were just as bright and vivid as they were twenty-four years ago.

A breathless "Oh," escaped her.

"Matt?" Dave cleared his throat. "Would you like me to give you a few minutes in private?"

I want more than a few minutes.

Matt shook his head and gestured to her chair. "I'm sorry. I'm just so surprised to see you. Please, have a seat, Lori." He reached for the resume Dave held out and sat in the chair next to her.

"I attached the letter of recommendation sent from Lori's Chicago editor," Dave said before taking his chair.

Matt flipped to the last page and skimmed the letter, smiling at the editor's comments, then turned to Lori's resume, noting dates and places. His smile dropped away. Both the letter and her resume listed Lori's maiden name at the top.

"So . . ." Dave said, followed by a what's-the-holdup look.

"You've been with the Chicago paper for . . ." His muddled mind couldn't do the simple math.

"Sixteen years," she filled in for him.

"That's the only job you have listed."

"It's the only job I held in Chicago, although I've written articles and columns for other Illinois newspapers and magazines. I can supply those editors' names if you need them."

Matt nodded as he kept his gaze on Lori. She caught her full bottom lip between her teeth and his heart kicked hard. Those lips had first tempted him then, driven him beyond reason many times in college. His attention moved up to the green eyes she often used to warn him when he was about to step over the line. Sometimes he stepped over anyway, just to see that flash of emerald.

Dave cleared his throat, and Matt mentally shook himself. He was gawking. Again. He smiled. "Dave mentioned you moved back to Seattle."

"Yes. Right before Thanksgiving."

He quickly turned a page to see her Seattle address. "Are your parents still in Snohomish?"

"Yes," she said after a pause.

"How are they?"

A slight frown appeared. He'd veered from interview to personal, which seemed to make her nervous. "They're doing well. How are yours?"

"Great. Still in Astoria."

Used to being in control of most situations, he was botching a simple interview, thanks to a thumping heart and sweaty palms. Dave would probably fall off his chair if Matt asked how long she'd been using her maiden name.

Going through the steps of this interview was a waste of time. He already knew that if she met the qualifications they were looking for—and she did, or Dave wouldn't have called him down here—they would hire her. Which meant she'd be invited to the newspaper's Christmas party. He'd make sure Denise got Lori's invitation in the mail along with the others.

His thoughts jumped ahead. He assumed she was divorced, but maybe she'd moved back to town to be with someone. He couldn't think of a way to reword an interview question to get the information he wanted without seeming too obvious.

Dave tapped a pencil on his desk, giving Matt a what-the-heck-are-you-doing? signal.

Matt asked a few questions about her Chicago column, and she answered each with a confidence she didn't have in college. She'd never fully believed in herself or her potential while they dated. Clearly that had changed in a big way.

Dave leaned forward, resting his forearms on his desk. "I

told Lori we have a couple more interviews to conduct before we decide."

None of the resumes he'd looked over matched Lori's experience. "I think we have everything we need." Matt stood.

Lori did the same, and held out her hand, careful to keep her distance—no farewell hug. "Thank you for your time."

He held onto her hand longer than he should have. "It's nice to see you again."

Dave came around his desk and shook Lori's hand. "I agree with Matt. It's great to see you again, Lori."

Matt opened Dave's office door. "Give your parents my best."

She offered a tight smile and walked out. He leaned out into the hall and watched her until she disappeared around the receptionist's desk. When he turned back into the office, Dave grinned.

"When did you meet her before?" Matt asked.

"I took Mary to one of her book signings."

"Her book signings?"

"She writes novels." Dave folded his arms and leaned against his desk "What do you think? She's got a notable resume and the letter of recommendation from her Chicago editor is impressive. She's won several awards for her writing, which he mentions, but she doesn't."

"Lori wouldn't mention awards." Matt glanced at her resume and then the recommendation.

"My wife and daughters rush out to buy her novels as soon as they hit the shelves. She doesn't mention those in her resume either."

Matt walked to the window and peered down just as she pushed through the street-level door. *Is she as rattled as I am?* "She has another source of income."

"Does that matter?"

"Not as long as it doesn't interfere with her job."

"It didn't seem to interfere with her column in Chicago."

"Right."

"What do you think?" Dave asked lowering his hands to the desk.

Matt turned back to the window and watched Lori until she crossed the street and turned a corner, disappearing from view. "I think it would be a shame to let her get away."

Dave snorted. "The newspaper or you?"

Had he been that obvious? Matt dropped into the chair Lori sat in. Her perfume lingered.

"How well did you know Lori in college?"

"Well enough that I wanted to marry her."

"What?" Dave choked out. "I didn't know you'd ever come close to marrying *any* woman."

"Just one. A long time ago."

"What happened?"

Matt leaned forward and set Lori's resume on Dave's desk. "She moved to Chicago and married someone else." He frowned at Dave. "Would have been nice if you'd dropped a name when you called me to come down. I could have been a little more prepared."

"You being tongue-tied was pretty entertaining." Dave pushed off the desk. "If it makes you feel any better, she looked as shocked as you did. In fact, I worried that she might be sick."

Matt frowned. "Yeah, making a woman sick when she sees me makes me feel all warm and fuzzy inside."

Dave laughed.

"Pull up the Chicago newspaper so we can take a look at a couple of her columns." Matt wanted to get this taken care of so he could tell Denise to send out the Christmas party invitation.

"So we're going to offer her the job?"

"Yeah. If she just moved back to town, she may have submitted her resume at other area papers. Let's nab her before someone else does."

Dave circled his desk while Matt picked up Dave's phone and punched in the number for Lori's Chicago editor.

~

*L*ori was shaking so violently; she could barely open her car door. Falling into the seat, she slammed the door shut and dropped her forehead to the steering wheel.

Matthew Jefferson Kelley still lived in Seattle after all these years, and was editor of the newspaper she wanted to work for. She never imagined he would still be in the area. Why hadn't Leland mentioned he was leaving during their telephone interview?

She took a deep breath and let it out slowly. Okay, so Seattle was out, but there were other newspapers in the area. She'd just have to drive a little farther. Maybe *The News Tribune* or *The Olympian* were hiring. She'd find something. If not, she'd venture into writing fiction full time.

Her thoughts tumbled to the first day of her freshman year at the University of Washington. She walked into her Creative Writing class hoping to recognize at least one person besides the professor, who was an old family friend.

High school AP classes, the three prerequisites she'd taken over the summer, plus a few nudges from her adviser had gotten her admitted to this class, which wasn't usually open to freshmen.

Her hopes were dashed when she stopped just inside the door and glanced around. She'd chosen to go to college close to home, and yet she didn't see one familiar face.

Only the guy sprawled in his chair like a cat in the

sunshine noticed her walk in. He fixed his gaze on her, and she could see the intense blue of his eyes from across the room.

Before she could blush, she glanced away and spotted an empty desk down the first aisle.

Professor Hill walked in a minute later. Lori hadn't seen him in a couple of years. He wasn't as lean, and his blond hair had turned a soft shade of brown, but she'd always recognize him by his teasing eyes and contagious smile. He greeted the class, told a joke, and then started calling roll. When he got to the Ms, he stopped, looked up, and scanned the room until he caught sight of her. "Lori Maguire."

She groaned inwardly.

The professor leaned against the front edge of his desk and laced his fingers together. This was how she remembered him—relaxed with a friendly smile that held a touch of mischief. Normally she'd smile back, but she had a queasy feeling the mischief would be directed at her.

"I was sixteen when a beautiful redhead moved in next door. She was inquisitive to the point of annoying, yet too adorable to ignore. Every time I walked outside, she was waiting for me, asking question after question, but I couldn't resist her four-year-old charms."

The class laughed at the twist in his story. She glared at Professor Hill, her cheeks blazing.

When she looked at her schedule a few days before classes started, she wondered if knowing the professor would be a help or a hindrance. Professor Hill had just answered that question. If he planned on embarrassing her with childhood stories, it would definitely be a hindrance.

She spent the rest of the hour with her nose in her book.

After class Professor Hill stopped at her desk before she could duck out and opened his arms.

"You're kidding, right?" she asked with a laugh.

He caught her arm and tugged her into a hug. "Sorry, I shouldn't have done that to you on your first day—*on any day*," he quickly corrected when she slugged him in the chest.

"Is it too late to transfer to another class?"

"Don't. I promise not to tell any more stories, though we both know I have some doozies in my repertoire."

"I'd like to hear more stories," said a voice behind her.

Lori glanced around at the guy with the intense blue eyes. He moved to her side, close enough that his arm brushed against hers. At least a foot taller, he grinned down at her, and she had a hard time pulling her gaze away. She side-stepped closer to Professor Hill and the guy smiled. Her stomach took a nosedive.

"Lori, this is Matt Kelley. He took a class from me two years ago as a freshman but decided to squander his talent on the football field instead. Matt, this is Lori Maguire."

Which makes him a junior.

"I'm definitely more interested in your class this year, Professor. Hi, Lori."

"Hello." She picked up her backpack and slung it over her shoulder, then glanced at Professor Hill. "I'll see you Wednesday if I don't transfer out." She headed for the door.

"You better not or I'll come looking for you. Remember, I know where you live," she heard Professor Hill shout before she ducked into the hall, glad to be swallowed up by the moving crowd.

She saw Matt twice on campus before her next Creative Writing class. Both times he was in the middle of a small crowd—mostly girls. Both times he went out of his way to say hello. And both times she nearly went into cardiac arrest. When she arrived at Professor Hill's class on Wednesday, she found Matt waiting at the door.

"Hi, Lori."

"Hello." She hurried past and took the same seat she sat in

on Monday. Matt took the desk beside her. When she turned a questioning eye his way, he raised a brow and flashed a devilish, completely heart-stopping grin. "I can see much better from here."

She looked down as her cheeks heated.

"You do look pretty in pink," he said on that long-ago day.

Lori lifted her head from the steering wheel and started the engine. She'd been able to shove memories of Matt aside for years, but he'd be front and center now.

Her mind was so busy going over her interview that her ten-minute drive home flashed by in a blur. Disappointment hit her harder than she thought it might. She hadn't expected to get the job, but she'd hoped her experience would help her be a top contender.

Not likely now.

Okay, not a problem. Newspapers, magazines, fiction—she had plenty of other options. A laugh erupted that sounded a bit on the maniacal side. Had she actually thought things had gone too easily thirty minutes earlier?

And why did Matt have to look so great? At six four, he still had a commanding presence. His wheat-colored hair was a little darker and a lot shorter than he wore it in college. He was clean-shaven when they dated. Now he wore several days' worth of stubble, which looked nice, but hid the dimple in his chin. His eyes were still striking blue and his shoulders still football-broad. Twenty-four years, and he could still unnerve her with a look. He'd always been good at that. Among other things.

She wondered if he ever married.

Turning right, she took the driveway around the side of her house and parked near the back deck. Moving from an eighty-two hundred-square-foot house on the shore of Lake Michigan to a twenty-four hundred-square-foot house in Seattle had been quite a change. She'd planned to buy some land close to her parents' house and build something, but after she happened upon this quaint little place, she wasn't so sure she wanted bigger and newer.

She opened her car door just as her cell phone rang. The number wasn't familiar, but she recognized a Seattle area code. "Hello?"

"Lori, Dave Stephens."

That didn't take long. They must not have wanted her to get her hopes up right before Christmas. *Happy New Year to me.*

"Hi, Dave," she said, dialing her tone to happy.

"I know this is fast, but . . ."

She listened in confused silence while Dave offered her the columnist job. She'd left his office less than thirty minutes before. *What happened to the other interviews?*

"That's a generous offer, Dave," she said when he finished. But suddenly she wasn't sure working for Matt would be wise. "Can I take a day or two to think about it?"

"Sure."

She heard his hesitance. "I'll let you know no later than Thursday morning."

"I'll look forward to hearing from you."

"Thanks, Dave."

As soon as she disconnected the call, she grabbed her purse, searching her wallet for the phone number of *The Seattle Star*, and tapped in the number.

"May I please speak to Matt Kelley?" she asked when the call was answered. "Tell him it's Lori Maguire."

CHAPTER 2

$\mathscr{M}$att took the stairs to his office two at a time, thinking the day couldn't get any better. He sat down and spun his chair so he faced the window, work and party planning forgotten for the moment. *Lori Maguire was back in Seattle.*

He held up her resume like reading it again would give him the answers the first six times didn't. Her Chicago editor had nothing but praise for Lori. He hated to lose her but understood she made the move in order to be close to family. She'd been an asset to their office, and her coworkers were going to miss her.

He gave Matt a ballpark figure of what Lori made in Chicago and reminded him that she also did a lot of free-lance work and was a published author. Matt made a few more phone calls and then gave Dave the go-ahead with a salary higher than what they initially planned. The *Star* couldn't match what she made in Chicago, but Lori would have known the circulation was smaller before she sent in her resume.

He swung around in his chair and grabbed his ringing phone. "Kelley."

"Hey, it's Dave. I just talked to Lori, and she asked if she could have a couple of days to think over our offer."

"You offered the amount we agreed on?"

"Yes. She said the offer is generous, but . . ."

"But what?" Matt asked when Dave hesitated.

"I'm not sure money is the part she needs to think over."

"If not the money, what? Do you think she got an offer from somewhere else?"

"No."

"So, what are you trying to say without verbalizing it, Dave?"

"Really? You can't guess?" Dave chuckled. "I've been married a long time, but I can still detect when there's a strong current of electricity shooting between two people. You two must have been pretty serious for you—a confirmed bachelor—to consider marriage."

Matt sat forward. "You think I'm the reason?"

"Yeah, I do."

The idea that Lori was hesitating because of him bothered Matt. He'd been so wrapped up in his thoughts that he hadn't considered how she might feel. The last time they saw each other, they hadn't exactly parted on good terms, but that happened years ago. And this was business—not personal. He didn't want to be the reason the *Star* lost her before they even got her. "Do you think I should call her?"

"Yes. You should tell—"

"Hold on, Dave," Matt interrupted when his assistant tapped on his open door. "Hey, Denise."

"Sorry to interrupt, but Lori Maguire is on line two."

His breath caught. "Thanks, Denise. Dave, I'll call you back. Lori's on the other line."

"Get her to say yes, Matt."

He pushed the blinking light for line two, anxious to hear her voice again, yet afraid she'd called to turn them down. "Lori?"

"Hi." She paused. "I want to apologize for this morning."

"Apologize?"

"I didn't know Leland had left the paper."

"There's no need to apologize. Leland's departure surprised all of us. I don't think our webpage has even been updated yet, so you couldn't have known."

Matt heard Lori draw in a deep breath. "Dave called and offered me the column, but I wanted to make sure you're okay with it before I accept."

Matt smiled as Lori's words tumbled out. She sounded as jumpy as he felt. "Dave wouldn't have offered the column if I hadn't agreed with the decision, Lori." He hoped he sounded calm and more reassuring than he felt. "Does this mean you're accepting the offer?"

Say yes.

"I don't want you to feel obligated in any way. I—"

"Why would I feel obligated?"

"Because we . . . knew each other in college. I don't want you to feel compelled to hire me because of that. My move isn't dependent on this job. When I left Dave's office this morning, I understood he had more interviews to conduct, and he couldn't have completed those before he called."

"Dave and I pulled up some of your columns in the Chicago newspaper, and I talked to your editor. You're more qualified and experienced than any of the other applicants we've interviewed so far. And frankly, we've been looking for something different, a fresh angle. Both Dave and I think you could give us that. We'd be lucky to have you on staff."

He paused for a moment so she could digest the fact that they weren't just jumping into this decision. "I would never hire you out of obligation, Lori. I'm just sorry you'll be taking a pay cut to work for our lowly paper."

"Money isn't the reas—" She left her sentence unfinished.

Dave was right. She'd hesitated because of him. "Both Dave and I think the paper could use someone who can deliver a different vibe. You've been living out of state and can offer a fresh viewpoint regarding this community. Plus, we've never had a woman write this particular column before. That alone will offer a new perspective."

He didn't want to wait until Thursday. He'd go crazy wondering. "Can I tell Dave you accept the offer?"

"Yes," she said with quiet reserve.

"Great. I'll let him know." He glanced up and waved in the reporter standing at his door. "HR will be in touch."

"Thank you, Matt."

"Bye, Lori." He hung up the phone and pumped his fists in the air.

"You look like the Grinch when he came up with the idea to steal Christmas," Phil Cates said, as he took one of the chairs in front of Matt's desk.

"We just replaced Tom."

"I hope you took into consideration that they'll occupy the office next to my cubicle and found someone who smells better than Tom."

"She definitely smells better than Tom."

"She?"

"Yep." He picked up his phone and punched in Dave's extension. "Hey, Dave, we got her."

"What did you have to do to convince her?"

"Just state the facts, but it worked."

"Good job."

Matt swiveled his chair back and forth, feeling like a kid with his favorite candy bar. "Have HR get started on her paperwork. I want her to start on the first Monday in January."

"What about the Christmas party?"

"I'll have Denise send out an invitation today." He hung up and picked up Lori's resume. Her new address put her ten minutes from the office.

Phil leaned back and stretched out his long legs. "A 'she' will be a nice change."

"Yep. Her name is Lori Maguire. She moved here from—"

"Lori Maguire?"

"You've heard of her?"

"I've known Lori since Mrs. Johnson's kindergarten class. We grew up in the same area of Snohomish. My parents live a couple of blocks from the Maguires."

"When was the last time you saw her?"

"Our high school reunion"—Phil held up a hand, ticking his fingers as he counted—"five years ago."

"Was she married?"

"Yeah. I think so, but she came to the reunion alone."

"She listed her maiden name on her resume, and she wasn't wearing a wedding ring."

"Who wasn't wearing a wedding ring?" asked the petite blonde who buzzed into Matt's office. She circled his desk and kissed his cheek. "Hey, handsome."

"Hey yourself, beautiful."

Faith Cates moved back around and dropped into her husband's lap.

"Are you ready for lunch?" Phil asked, patting her behind.

"Yes, I'm starved. Who wasn't wearing a wedding ring?"

"A girl I went to school with is coming to work for the paper."

Faith flashed an indulgent smile. "If she went to school with you, she isn't a girl anymore."

"Aren't you witty today," Phil said with a roll of his eyes.

"Okay, a girl I went to school with, who is now a beautiful woman, is coming to work for the paper, and we were discussing her possible lack of marital entanglements."

"Why?" Faith glanced at Matt. "Surely you're not interested. If she went to school with Phil, she's *way* too old for you. You date women half your age."

Matt blew out a breath. "I don't date women half my age, and I didn't say I'm interested. We were just discussing—"

"Why?" Faith asked again.

"Just curious." Matt glanced at her resume again. "Lori and I dated."

"What?" Phil laughed in surprise. "When?"

"In college."

Phil shook his head. "You couldn't have dated the Lori I know. She went to Northwestern."

"She did her freshman year at UW."

"That's right. I forgot," Phil said. "Sure is a small world."

"It only seems small because Matt has dated every woman in town. What's with the frown? You know it's true." Faith pointed at him. "But that look on your face has aroused my interest. How long did Lori put up with you?"

Matt was used to Faith giving him grief about his dating habits. "Six months."

"Six months? That's like a record for you, isn't it?"

"No." Matt heard the defensiveness in his voice and suspected they did too. "Where are you two going for lunch?"

"I hit a nerve. Matt's trying to change the subject, honey," Faith said. "Tell me more about her."

"You've met Lori," Phil said. "She was at my high school reunion."

Faith frowned. "You expect me to remember her from what—six years ago?"

"Five. Lori had reddish hair, curls everywhere. She's the author you like."

"Lori Maguire? I love her books." She glanced at Matt. "She was sweet and very married to a corporate attorney who couldn't make it to the reunion because of work."

"Back in middle school, Lori used to wear this red skirt that hit about here," Phil said, leveling the side of his hand high on his thigh. He looked at his glaring wife. "What?"

"You remember the color of Lori's skirt from like thirty years ago, but you can't remember our anniversary?"

"I also remember a blue and white polka-dot bikini."

"When did you see her in a bikini?" Faith exclaimed with a frown.

Matt wondered the same thing.

"Her parents have a cool house with this attached indoor pool. Lori used to have swim parties all the time." He glanced at Matt. "I remember a sexy green bikini, too."

Matt had seen the indoor pool, but he'd never seen Lori in a bikini.

"Okay, that's enough remembering, Romeo. Did you date her?" Faith asked, flicking the tip of his ear.

"Ouch. No." Phil put a hand to the side of his face. "We just hung around together. I don't think it ever occurred to me to date her, because we were friends. She was like one of the guys."

Matt couldn't imagine Lori ever being like one of the guys. "What else do you remember?" he asked.

Phil waggled his eyebrows. "I remember when she got her first bra."

Faith flicked his other ear.

"Ouch! Matt asked a question and I answered. A girl getting her first bra is the kind of thing boys in the fifth and sixth grade notice. I remember when Lori got one specifically, because she was small like you. Ouch! Stop flicking! I didn't mean small as in . . ." Phil cupped his hands in front of his chest. "I mean Lori is petite, like you."

Matt sat back and let Phil take the heat. *Better him than me.*

"Anyone under six feet is small to you. And you're a pervert if you remember her getting her first bra after all these years."

"I'm not a pervert. I remember because she and I went for a walk one night—"

"If you tell me she showed you—"

"No. We used to go for walks on summer nights. We'd talk about school and friends and teachers. One night I brought up the first bra thing, she told me she was embarrassed about it and I said she shouldn't be. Heck, she'd be the most popular girl in school for at least two weeks." He laughed. "As I recall, that didn't make her feel better."

"You're an idiot." Faith swiveled around to face Matt.

"Finish your story. You and Lori dated for six months. What happened?"

Matt didn't want to discuss Lori, especially in front of Phil. But he knew Faith would hound him until he did. "She married someone else."

"Why? What did you do to her?"

"Why do you assume I did something?" His defensive tone turned to irritation.

"Because I know you. How serious was your relationship? I mean six whole months. Were you in love with her?"

Matt tipped his head back and stared at the ceiling. "Yes."

"Matt Kelley in love," she said, her tone all swoony. "Did you ever tell her?"

He glanced at Phil, who shot him a glad-it's-your-turn smirk. "Yes."

"Did she love you back?"

"Faith—"

"Did. She. Love. You. Back?" Faith demanded, all evidence of the swoony gone.

"Yes."

"Did you ever talk about getting married?"

"Weren't you guys going to lunch?"

Faith leaned forward, watching him with hawk eyes. Phil looked as eager for an answer as his wife.

"Matt, did you two ever talk about marriage?"

"Sort of."

Phil's mouth dropped open. "Are you kidding me? You and Lori Maguire talked marriage? Why haven't you told me any of this before?"

Before Matt could say *because it's none of your business,* Faith snorted. "How do you *sort of* talk to someone about marriage?"

"It doesn't matter. She transferred to Northwestern and married someone else."

Faith stood and leaned over his desk. "I can't believe you admitted to being in love with someone, and that you were serious enough to discuss marriage. This is huge, Matt," she said waving a hand in the air. "Possibly a breakthrough as to why you can't date women your age. She must have hurt you so badly she stunted your emotional growth."

"Okay. Time to go." Matt pushed to his feet and walked around his desk.

Faith straightened and met him halfway, hands on hips. "There's more to this story. I bet it's all tied together with the reason why you can't commit now. She's the reason you're afraid to love. Am I right? Hot or cold?" She glanced at Phil. "I should have gone into psychology." She turned back to Matt. "Come to dinner next week, and we'll delve deeper into this subject."

"Yeah, I don't think so. I appreciate the invitation to have splinters shoved under my fingernails, but I'll take a hard pass."

Faith wrapped her arms around his waist. "Sorry I pushed."

"No, you're not," Matt replied with a laugh. She harped on this subject every time they got together.

"You're right, I'm not. Want Phil to bring you some lunch?"

"Thanks, but I brought something from home."

Matt walked over to his office window after Phil and Faith left, remembering how much he loved Lori and wishing he'd handled things differently. Back then he was a stupid boy who believed he was a smart man. He let his anger and pride ruin something that could have been close to perfect. He should have stopped Lori from going to Chicago. Deep down he knew he could have, but he waited until it was too late.

It may still be too late. Just because she didn't have a wedding ring on didn't mean she wasn't with someone.

Turning to his computer, Matt searched Lori's name. Her books appeared on several sites, as well as many of her articles. Under images, pictures of Lori at book signings and headshots for book covers popped up. In one photo, she held up an award while posing with an older gentleman Matt assumed was her Chicago editor.

He enlarged an image of her in a rose-colored gown, her arm around a man in a tux, probably her husband. In another photo she stood between two teenagers, a boy and a girl. Zooming in, he could see the resemblance. The girl had Lori's hair color, the boy inherited her eyes and her smile. He clicked the picture and saw a date from two years ago. How old were her kids? Did they move here with her or stay with their dad?

A million questions raced through his mind. He'd tried to imagine her life in Chicago so many times over the years, but he never searched for her. Today was different. He pulled up Chicago records and found an address which he entered into another search. When a picture of her house materialized, his jaw dropped. He added her current address in a street view. Very modest compared to the way she lived in Chicago.

Next, he went to her author website. She had nine books in print, and another flagged to be released next week. He scrolled through the covers and wondered if his mom or either of his sisters read her books, and if so, why hadn't they mentioned them?

Matt closed his laptop. If she attended, the upcoming Christmas party would give Lori a chance to meet most of the newspaper staff. He'd also get to see her again before her January start date. His plus-one was Madelyn, a woman he'd been dating for a few weeks.

For the first time in his life, he wished he didn't have a date.

*L*ori and her sister Tara settled in Tara's family room after their parents left. Tara and her longtime boyfriend, Kevin Diaz, had prepared a congratulatory dinner of beef tips and mushroom gravy served over mashed potatoes to celebrate Lori's new job. Tara also served her family-famous rolls.

Lori spent dinner answering questions about the interview and job offer. Her mom wanted to know if she'd tied her hair up for the interview. Her dad, once he heard how quickly Dave called back, thought she should have held out for more money. Lori left out the part about the new editor being Matt Kelley. Her parents had loved Matt.

"You cooked enough for an army," Lori said, glad she'd worn leggings with a stretchy waist.

"The kids will devour the leftovers."

Tara had three kids with her ex-husband, who was nonexistent in his kids' lives. Kevin had stepped in and filled the role of father when he and Tara started dating ten years earlier. Kevin had asked Tara to marry him more times than Lori could remember, but because of her horrible first marriage, Tara wanted to keep things "as is." Lori couldn't blame her, though Kevin had more than proven he was nothing like Ted.

Kevin walked in and settled next to Tara on the sofa. "We won't have any leftovers after the kids swoop in this weekend."

"Ravenous heathens," Lori joked.

"You would think three kids out on their own could manage to cook once in a while," Kevin said.

Tara snorted. "They'll never learn to cook if you keep giving them all our leftovers."

He tweaked Tara's nose. "We wouldn't be able to fit through the door if we ate all the leftovers ourselves."

"True." Her sister shrugged a shoulder. "Thus the need for ravenous heathens. You skimmed over the surface of how the twins are doing. What's up with Taylor and Megan?"

"They're both doing fine. They spent Thanksgiving with their dad in Chicago, and then they both headed back to school. They'll be here for Christmas."

"Are you excited about the job, Lori?" Kevin asked.

"I am."

Tara laughed. "That's Lori's excited face. You ought to see her when she's unhappy."

Lori tucked her legs under her. She might as well rip the bandage off. Tara would find out eventually. "Do you remember Matt Kelley?"

"That's a name I haven't heard in a long time."

"Who's Matt Kelley?" Kevin asked.

"He's the editor of the newspaper."

Tara's eyes grew huge before a laugh burst out. At Lori's glare, she quickly covered her mouth.

"Mom and Dad don't know yet, and I'd like to keep it that way for as long as possible."

"How did you *not* know that little tidbit before you sent your resume in?"

"The editor I interviewed with over the phone left for another job last week. I didn't know Matt had been promoted to the position until he walked into the managing editor's office today."

"But you knew he worked there," Tara stated rather than asked.

"I had no idea he still lived in the area."

"Who's Matt Kelley?" Kevin asked again.

"He's a hot football player Lori dated in college."

Kevin frowned, then took off his black-framed glasses and held them up to the light. "I guess I don't understand the problem. Why wouldn't you apply for a job just because you dated the editor twenty-five years ago?"

Twenty-four, but who's counting?

When she didn't answer, Kevin mused on. "Seems knowing him would be to your advantage."

Tara turned a comical look on him. "You think knowing *my* ex would be an advantage?"

"Well, no, but your ex is . . . unusual," Kevin said, slipping his glasses back into place.

Unusual was an extremely kind word to use when describing Tara's ex.

"Is Matt still as good-looking as he was in college?" Tara asked, waggling her eyebrows.

Lori pressed her lips together.

Tara laughed again. "He is. I can tell by your blush."

Lori blew out a breath. "Give me your honest opinion. Do you think taking this job will be a mistake?"

"I don't know, but it could be really fun finding out," Tara joked.

Lori shook her head at her sister's goofy expression. "You're not helping."

Tara was a vivacious extrovert, a quality Lori wished she possessed. Her older sister was comfortable in any situation, and if she wasn't, you'd never know. They looked and behaved nothing alike. Most people in school had been surprised to find out they were sisters.

Lori glanced at Kevin. "Do you think Matt hired me because he felt obligated?"

It was Kevin's turn to chuckle. He could be a little on the geeky side, but he and Tara melded together seamlessly. Kevin had become like a big brother to Lori—a logical thinker compared to her sister's hit-the-ground-running impetuous nature. He was a sweet man who loved her sister with all his heart, which only made Lori love him more.

"That's not the way a man's mind works, Lori. He'd hire you because you're single and pretty before he'd hire you out of any sense of obligation."

"Is he married?" Tara piped in.

Lori shrugged, hoping it came off as casual. "I don't think so. He wasn't wearing a wedding ring."

"You looked for a ring?" Tara said with another laugh.

"He looked at my hand, too." She felt her cheeks heat at her defensive tone, and the fact that she'd noticed when Matt noticed her bare ring finger.

"I'm sure the man hired you for your qualifications and skills as a writer," Kevin said.

"Yeah, Lori, he hired you for your skills," Tara added. "I bet he remembers your skills really well."

"Why do I tell you anything?" Lori said, shaking her head. "You'd think I'd learn over the years. Or that you'd mature."

"Hey, I'm mature."

"Right." *Mature as a fourteen-year-old, boy-crazy girl.*

"When are you going to tell Martha and Henry?" Kevin asked.

"I don't know. I'm afraid Mom will show up at Matt's

office with homemade baked goods and an invitation to dinner. You know how she is."

Her parents were disappointed when she brought Jim home the first time. Her dad said he didn't know a crescent wrench from vise-grip pliers, and he didn't tell her mom she looked radiant like Matt did when he visited. Until the moment she walked down the aisle, Lori knew they'd secretly hoped she and Matt would get back together.

"Tell Kevin about your first date."

Lori shifted in her chair. She still considered the story Matt-style romantic. "Matt and I met in an English class. Every time I saw him on campus, he was surrounded by a crowd—walled in by girls. I'd try to slip by unnoticed, but he usually broke away from the group to say hi and ask me out. I didn't want to be included among the throng of Matt Kelley worshippers, so I turned him down. He didn't give up."

Lori hadn't thought about that night in years. She was supposed to meet friends at the Husky building, known to students as the Hub. They wanted her to join them for an old Elvis Presley movie so badly they bought her a ticket and begged her to come. In her opinion, the paper she had to write for general psych class sounded more exciting.

When she arrived, she was surprised by the size of the crowd filling the dimly lit theatre. Scanning the room, she spotted her friends waving.

Making her way down the aisle, she stopped at their row. Great. She only had to climb over five people to get to the only empty seat.

"Excuse me," she said to the guy on the aisle, then did a double-take when Matt Kelley grinned up at her.

"Hi, Lori." He lowered his knee so she could step over his outside leg.

All four football players between Matt and her friends got up and moved down a seat. She glanced at her friends, who suddenly wouldn't make eye contact. That's when she realized she'd been set up.

She tried to step back into the aisle, but Matt raised his knee. She shot a glare at her friends who finally dared sneak a peek. Matt lowered his inside leg and she stepped over and dropped into the vacant chair beside him.

"I didn't know you liked Elvis movies," he said smoothly.

"I don't."

He chuckled.

She turned to him. "You planned this?"

He raised a shoulder. "Would you be mad if I did?"

"Not mad, just wondering why you'd go to this much trouble."

"Why?" One eyebrow raised with his question. "Every time I ask you out, you say no."

"Not used to a girl declining your invitations?"

"Nope," he stated.

"Did it ever occur to you that I have a reason for turning you down?"

"I know you're not dating anyone else."

It was her turn to raise a brow. "How do you know?"

"I've asked around."

"You've asked my friends if I'm dating anyone?"

"I didn't want to set this up if you're already with some guy. I'd have to figure out a way to get rid of him first."

"Unbelievable." She fell back against her chair. "Did you have to buy all eight tickets to set this up?"

"Yes."

She fought a threatening smile. "You're persistent."

"If it's something I want, I go after it."

The lights dimmed and the movie started while she tried to decide if she was insulted or flattered. Maybe a little of both. Insulted that he'd referred to her as an *it*, and flattered that he'd gone to this much trouble. Did he do this kind of thing for all the girls he dated? And yes, she knew he had quite a reputation, because she'd asked around too. "I hate to burst your bubble, but you don't always get what you want."

"I do."

She felt his arm on the back of her chair but kept her eyes on the screen as the Las Vegas Strip filled it.

He leaned close enough that she felt his warm breath on her neck. Goose bumps popped up along her arms. "Would you like some popcorn?"

"No, thank you," she whispered back, still looking ahead.

"You need popcorn for a good movie."

She turned to find his face just inches away. "I'm not sure this is a good movie."

His eyes held hers for a long moment before his devilish grin appeared. "Want to watch a good sunset instead?"

This time she couldn't hide her smile. "Do you know where to catch a good one?"

"Yes." He stood and pulled her to her feet. "Thanks, guys. Enjoy the movie."

Outside, he led her to a beat-up truck with bench seats. Instead of opening the passenger door, he steered her to the driver's side. She scooted under the steering wheel and he jumped in and grabbed her hand to keep her close. When he got on I-5 South, she knew they were headed for Kerry Park. When they arrived, he grabbed a blanket and her hand and led her to a spot among other sunset watchers.

She couldn't help but wonder how many times he'd been to this particular spot, and with how many others.

Minutes later, leaning back on their elbows, they watched the sun go down in a brilliant glow of blues and oranges that slowly faded to feathers of pink and lavender. Watching a sunset together sealed their bond as a couple.

She told a generic version to Kevin, leaving out the hand-holding, goose-bump details.

"Think he's still as persistent?" he asked when she finished.

Lori nodded. She couldn't imagine Matt had changed much in twenty-four years, at least in that respect.

~

*L*ori repeated her mantra for the night—*The newspaper's Christmas party will be a great way to meet my new coworkers.*

Walking into a room full of strangers was not one of her favorite pastimes. She felt like she was back in college, walking into Professor Hill's class, hoping to see one familiar face.

The Uber driver pulled to the curb. "The door is just around that corner."

"Thank you, Conrad."

She climbed out of the car, grateful the weather had held. She'd taken an Uber because she wasn't sure of parking and didn't want to walk blocks in heels.

She stopped just outside the door to take a couple of deep breaths. Time for the truth. Walking into a room full of strangers wasn't the only reason her stomach was performing flip-flops.

She'd see Matt tonight. Like a silly schoolgirl, she spent more time in front of the mirror than usual. And for what? She'd never look eighteen again. After another deep breath, she stepped inside and checked her coat at the door.

The overhead lights were dimmed, but thousands of tiny white Christmas lights lit the room. As her eyes adjusted, a tall man came toward her and swept her up into a bear hug. "Hey, woman, I heard you were coming."

"Phil." Lori laughed, happy to see an old-neighborhood friend. His brown hair was just as unruly as ever, and tonight it stuck up every which way. Dark eyes sparkled with their familiar hint of mischief. He'd been the instigator of all kinds of trouble in their youth.

"How are you, besides gorgeous?" he asked setting her on her feet.

"I'm fine. How are you?"

"Great." He looked her up and down, making her blush. "You look beautiful."

"Thank you. You look pretty great yourself." She reached up and smoothed a hand over his whiskered cheek. "I like the facial hair thing you have going on. It's a new look for you."

"I grow this thing every winter to keep my face warm. Makes me look dashing, don't you think?" He gave her a profile view.

Lori laughed. "I think you haven't changed a bit. Aren't you supposed to have some wrinkles and a potbelly by now?" She looked him up and down like he'd done with her. He was still as skinny as a beanpole, and his height only made him look skinnier.

"You're not exactly a hag yourself. It's a good thing none of the high school crowd are around. They'd run us out of town for looking so great at forty-three."

"Excuse me, but I'm still forty-two and I plan to stay that way until the absolute anniversary moment of my birth in June."

"Oh, that's right, you were the baby of the class."

"I was afraid I wouldn't know a soul here to— Wait. Why are *you* here? Do you work for the paper?"

"Do I work for the paper? I'm the best reporter they have. There wouldn't be a paper if it weren't for me."

"I see you're still as humble as ever," Lori said with a laugh. Easygoing Phil would make the night much easier to get through. She kept her attention riveted on him so she wouldn't glance around for Matt. "I don't remember you mentioning you were a reporter."

"I started working for the *Star* right out of college."

"How did I not know that?"

Phil shrugged. "I'm sure I told you. You know I love to talk about myself."

"So, you know Matt—"

"I couldn't believe it when he said you were coming to work for the paper, and doubly shocked to learn you two dated in college."

Lori was surprised Matt had mentioned that to anyone.

"When did you move back?"

"Three weeks ago."

"Where are you living?"

"Fifty-second Street."

"In the thick of things."

"Not too far from it."

He took her hand and rubbed her ring finger while looking her in the eye. "What happened?"

She swallowed, still feeling the sting of failure. "Divorce."

"How long?"

"Almost three years," she replied, as he placed her hand on his chest.

"Sorry. Why didn't you bring a date to tonight's shindig?"

"I just moved, Phil. I don't know anyone."

"So, you're not dating anyone? You didn't move here to be with someone special?"

"Nope. I moved home to be closer to family." Lori slipped her hand from his. "Enough about me. Tell me how you are. Is your wife here?"

As soon as she asked, a petite blonde with a big smile joined them. Lori recognized her immediately.

"So, this is the woman you and Matt have been talking about."

Phil slipped his arm around Lori's waist. "Lori, this is my lovely wife, Faith."

"Hi, Faith. We met at our"—Lori motioned between her and Phil— "high school reunion. It's nice to see you again," she said while wondering what Matt said about her to Phil's wife.

Faith glared up at her husband, who loomed over her by a foot and a half. "Phil has been reminiscing about you a lot— down to a blue and white polka-dot bikini."

"Phil!" Lori elbowed him in the side.

"Oh, come on, Legs. I bet you remember my blue Speedo."

Faith pointed at Lori's elbow. "Nice move. I see you know how to handle yourself around my husband."

"Years of practice."

"I bet." Faith laughed. "Ignore Phil. He says he's known you since you were both five. As you can see, he hasn't matured a bit."

"Hey, I'm standing right here," Phil exclaimed, holding both arms out like they could overlook his tall, skinny frame.

"I didn't realize the last time we met that you write fabulous women's fiction," Faith said, taking Lori's arm. "You have to promise to speak at my book club. We've read all your Bainbridge series. In fact, you should join the group. It would be fun to have an author's perspective."

Lori gave Phil a wave as Faith led her away.

"Let's get you a drink, then I'll introduce you to some of the other crazies who work for the paper."

$\sim$

*M*att had been watching the door since before the party's actual start time. Denise said Lori responded that she would attend, but she hadn't shown up yet. He felt like a kid waiting for Christmas morning.

Making idle chit-chat, he circled the room with Madelyn, stopping to speak with the *Star's* cub, Carrie Eubanks, and her husband, Steve. Carrie commented on his date's dress. While she and Madelyn discussed stores and clothes and shoes, Matt glanced toward the door.

Since her interview, he'd thought of Lori more times than was healthy. He wondered where she was, what she was doing, had she gotten settled, had she visited her parents? Were her kids living with her? He'd considered driving past her house, but how would he explain if she saw him?

He might be a grown man, but since his meeting with Lori, he was thinking like a sixteen-year-old boy.

Dave and his wife, Mary, joined their group and Matt went through introductions again for Madelyn.

As they chatted, the atmosphere in the room shifted, and the hair on the back of his neck stood on end. Lori was here. He glanced toward the door to confirm and spotted her in Phil's arms. A stab of jealousy hit so hard he wanted to laugh aloud. He hadn't experienced that emotion since college. Since Lori.

Matt felt like he'd swallowed a golf ball, and tried to clear his throat, which didn't help.

Dave tapped Matt's arm with the back of his hand. "Our new columnist is here."

He nodded as he watched Lori run her fingers over Phil's cheek and the green-eyed monster inside him bellowed.

Dave's wife gasped. "She's the author you hired, isn't she? You have to introduce me."

"I will, but let's give her time to visit with Phil," Dave replied. "I hear they went to high school together."

Matt nodded without taking his eyes off Lori. He wanted to interrupt her and Phil's way-too-intimate conversation. Phil took Lori's hand and she looked down as he rubbed her ring finger, then placed her hand on his chest. *Come on, Phil.*

When Faith walked up to them, Phil put his arm around Lori's waist. Madelyn squeezed his arm, but Matt couldn't pull his eyes away, completely caught up in the anticipation he felt to have Lori so close again after all these years.

Faith pinned Matt with a look when she took Lori's arm and led her toward the bar. He'd been ducking her invitations to dinner since Lori's interview because Faith had a way of worming information out of him that he'd rather keep to himself.

"Would you like another drink?" Matt asked Madelyn.

"Yes." She grabbed his hand when he took a step toward the bar. "I'll come with you."

"Sure."

"What's up with you tonight?" she asked, once they were out of earshot. "You're acting weird. Uptight."

"I'm not uptight."

Faith looked over her shoulder as they approached. "Hi there, handsome."

"Hey, beautiful." He bent and they exchanged kisses on the cheek.

Lori flushed pink when he kissed her cheek. "I'm glad you could make it, Lori."

"Thank you for the invitation."

Faith nodded toward his date. "Aren't you going to introduce us?"

"Yes. Sorry." He glanced down at Madelyn, who waited with narrow-eyed irritation at his slight. "Faith, Lori, this is Madelyn Keys. Faith is married to Phil Cates, the tall, crazy man you met earlier. And Lori is the *Star's* new columnist."

"It's nice to meet you," Lori said.

Faith smiled. "Hi, Madelyn."

Lori turned slightly in the light, and the purple of her dress sparkled under the lights. She'd pulled up her hair, leaving a few tendrils falling around her face. She looked beautiful.

The bartender set two drinks on the bar. Faith picked them up and handed one to Lori. "I'm going to introduce Lori around."

Faith didn't get far before Phil and Kirk Parkman, one of the *Star's* sports writers, waylaid them. Kirk, immersed in an animated description, gestured wildly while Lori smiled at whatever he was saying. About the time Matt decided to join the conversation, a man with the catering company stepped up on the small stage and asked everyone to take a seat so their dinner could be served.

He felt another stab of jealousy when Kirk put his hand on the small of Lori's back and escorted her to a table, followed by Phil and Faith. Without thinking, he led Madelyn in that direction.

Lori glanced up when they took their seats on the other side of the round table. He couldn't read the expression that passed over her face, but it wasn't *happy to see you.*

Dave and Mary also joined their table.

Over dinner, Lori laughed several times at something Phil or Kirk said. She still had a quick smile and an easy laugh. Her embarrassment shined through with a blush when Mary mentioned her books.

"So how long have you two known each other?" Dave motioned between Phil and Lori.

"Lori has had a crush on me since kindergarten," Phil said. "We've known each other so long I can tell you the first boy she kissed."

Lori turned toward Phil, her green eyes blazing, and Matt's breath caught like he'd been kicked in the gut. He'd missed her green eyes, her pink blush, her curly strawberry-blonde hair. He'd missed everything about her, but like an idiot, he hadn't realized just how much until this moment.

Phil laughed. "Your looks don't scare me, McGuire."

While Phil told a story about Lori in the seventh grade, Lori sat back in her chair. She glanced up and met his gaze. Matt winked discreetly, then grinned when the corners of her mouth turned up ever so slightly.

CHAPTER 4

*A*fter dinner, Matt climbed the stairs to the stage, where he gave a you're-all-doing-a-great-job, thank-you-for-your-hard-work speech and handed out some awards. Then he introduced Lori as the paper's newest employee and asked her to stand. To her embarrassment, Phil jumped to his feet and gave her a round of applause and whistles. She resigned herself to blushing a lot whenever Phil was around.

Next Phil got up and roasted the departing columnist, embarrassing Lori again by saying he'd enjoy smelling her rather than Tom. She wasn't sure what he meant by that until Tom pulled a chair between her and Kirk—which was way too close—and held out his hand. "So, you'll be taking my place. Have you had much experience?"

She smiled while trying not to breathe in his noxious cologne. "A little."

He told her what Leland had expected compared to Matt, but she let the information go in one ear and out the other since Leland wasn't the editor anymore.

From her periphery, she noticed Matt's date pull him to

the dance floor. She was glad to see them go. With all the tables in this room to choose from, Matt led Madelyn straight to this one. During dinner, she had a hard time keeping her eyes on everyone around the table but them. Only once had she allowed her gaze to drift to Matt with his dazzling grin and shining eyes. Once there, she had a hard time turning away.

". . . and you've got to watch out for the office politics," Tom said. "Things can get real dicey at times."

"Okay." She waited for him to elaborate. He didn't.

"Lots of favoritism goes on and that can make life dicey, too."

Again, he didn't elaborate. She could navigate the office politics, but wondered about the favoritism part.

While Tom droned on about things that wouldn't involve her, she glanced around the room, trying to remember the names of people she'd met so far. A mistake because she spotted Matt dancing with the gorgeous brunette. Madelyn was exactly the sort of woman Lori had imagined Matt with when she allowed herself to think of him at all.

"Excuse us, Tom," Kirk said, taking her arm. "It's time for a dance."

When it came to Tom versus Kirk, Lori wasn't sure if she should be grateful for the interruption or not. Kirk was nice in a I'm-so-great kind of way, but unlike Phil, Lori didn't think he was joking.

As she and Kirk danced, she tried to focus on their conversation, but she was so busy *not* looking at Matt, she had a hard time paying attention. Kirk turned them and her gaze locked with Matt's. She glanced away.

As an employee, she needed to maintain a professional working relationship with an ex-boyfriend. The perfect time to get that set in her mind was right now. She could do this. Matt was with Madelyn.

Promising not to be affected, she looked up just in time to see Madelyn fingering the hair at the nape of Matt's neck. He leaned toward her when she whispered something in his ear.

Not affected. At all. That silly twinge in her stomach was just the chicken she ate for dinner. Or possibly Tom's cologne, which might have singed her nostrils.

~

*M*att sat at a table far from the dance floor watching Lori and Kirk. He felt a hand on his arm, different from Madelyn's possessive touch, and knew Faith was poised to pounce. Actually, he was surprised she'd taken so long. He could tell by her reactions, sometimes as little as a look, if she liked or disliked his date—usually the latter. He'd already noticed her many raised-eyebrow glances tonight.

"Where's Barbie?"

"Madelyn is in the restroom."

Faith picked up Madelyn's glass and sniffed. "Is she old enough to be drinking?"

He flashed a glare. "She's thirty-five."

"Really? Only nine years younger this time." Faith sat in the chair next to him. "You're getting closer to your age. Maybe this one will last longer than three months."

Doubtful. Kirk's hand moved lower down Lori's back. "What makes you think I want a relationship that lasts longer than three months?"

"Aren't you tired of playing this dating game after all these years? Maybe it's time to find a wonderful woman. Someone you can go home to after a long day at work, someone you can share a romantic dinner—"

"I can do that now and still go home to my bed when

we're done . . . sharing." He regretted his comment as soon as he saw Faith's look of disappointment.

"You live an empty life that you mistakenly assume is fulfilling."

"Go away, Faith."

Instead, she sat forward. "When was the last time you were truly happy?"

"I'll be truly happy right now if you'll—"

"Leave you alone? Not going to happen." She pointed to the dance floor. "Why didn't you ask the woman you've been staring at all night to come with you?"

"I'm not staring," he mumbled.

"Oh, well then, it's probably better that you didn't invite Lori."

"Faith, I'm really not in the mood."

"What do you think Kirk is whispering in her ear?"

He didn't know, but he didn't like it.

"At first, I thought she hurt you, but it was the other way around, wasn't it?"

Matt sat back in defeat. Faith wouldn't budge until she'd scraped off as much hide as possible. "Yes. I was full of myself in college and I screwed up big time."

"Just so you know, you're not the only single guy here who can't keep his eyes off her." She paused long enough to reload both barrels. "Kirk will have to move fast or someone else will snap her up."

"Would you like a sharper knife? I still have a couple of places on my back that aren't bleeding yet."

"Would a sharper knife make a difference? You know I can dig deep and not feel a bit of guilt."

"Yep. You've done a really good job so far. Thanks."

Faith flashed a sweet smile. "Anytime, handsome. Not sure you deserve it, but here's the scoop via Phil. She moved here to be close to family. She's been divorced for almost three years, and she's not dating anyone."

He nodded.

"You know, I do love you, even if you are awful. Now go ask Lori to dance while I head off your cheerleader."

~

After three dances with Kirk and one with Phil, Lori decided it was time to escape. She started toward Dave's table to thank him when a hand caught her arm. "You're not leaving already, are you?"

She turned and found herself looking into Matt's incredibly blue eyes. "It's getting late."

"One more dance. Maybe two."

He didn't give her a chance to protest. On the dance floor, he took her into his arms. They'd danced together in college, and though it was years ago, matching his steps came easily. His hand cradled hers gently as he moved her through the crowd.

Jim didn't dance. At her ex's company parties, she would sit on the sidelines and watch the other couples dance while Jim talked business with his fellow workaholics.

"Tara," he said on an exhale. "Your sister's name is Tara. I've been trying to remember since your interview."

Lori was impressed that he remembered and surprised that he'd been trying.

"How is she?"

"She's doing well." Lori felt herself relax. This was good. To be comfortable around your boss was good. "How are your siblings?"

Matt smiled down at her, and her heart thumped hard. Several times. Okay, so she might not be completely at ease yet.

"My siblings?"

"Sorry. Like you, I'm not sure I'll remember their names." She saw the challenge in his eyes. "But I'll give it a try. If I remember even one, I'll be doing as well as you," she teased. "You have two sisters and a brother."

He nodded.

"All their names start with M. One sister, I think your oldest, is Melissa. Your brother's name is . . . Mike and your younger sister is— Oh, wait, your oldest sister is Melinda." She tipped her head waiting for confirmation.

He nodded. "It is Melinda, and you have one more to go to prove you have a better memory, *for some things*, than I have."

"What do you mean, *for some things*?"

"Well, seeing you after all these years, I've suddenly got all these crazy memories tumbling through my mind. I'm sure, if you have the same memories, there would be discrepancies. In fact, if you *are* remembering, I'm surprised you agreed to dance with me."

She narrowed her eyes. "You didn't exactly give me a choice."

Matt chuckled. "I guess I didn't, did I?" He pulled her a step closer. "If I had given you a choice, would you have danced with me?"

"Your youngest sister is Maggie," she said, hoping he'd forget the question. If he'd given her a choice, her head would have screamed no, but her heart would have answered for her.

"Very good," he replied, grinning down at her.

The music faded and the band went right into the next song. Matt didn't miss a beat. When the tempo changed, so did his steps, taking her right along with him.

"I can't believe you remembered all their names, especially since you've never met them."

"I guess that means my memories are more accurate than yours, because I got three names in a matter of minutes, and it took you a week and a half to remember one."

"Maybe your memory is better *for some things*, but I'm not willing to concede yet. And you didn't answer my question."

Some questions are better left unanswered. "Thank you for including me tonight. I've enjoyed meeting some of the staff."

"You're welcome. You look really beautiful tonight."

She looked down. "Don't say things like that, Matt. You'll make me blush, and we have an audience." She'd noticed several people, including Madelyn, watching them. They danced in silence for a moment before she dared look up. "Tom filled me in on how you like things turned in. He said he left a list of topics you'd like to see included in the column."

"Oh, he did, did he?" Matt replied, lifting a brow.

That slight action clutched Lori's heart. He used to raise one eyebrow right before he teased her or his wicked grin appeared. It was pure Matt, so much a part of everything she used to know about him.

"We'll have to go over the things he told you. Tom usually did it his way and sometimes his way would have lost us readers. Leland usually had to step in and make corrections."

"I'll disregard everything he told me. I'm good at following directions."

Matt added his wicked grin to the raised brow and a slow burn worked its way across her cheeks.

"You still look pretty in pink."

"Matt, people are still watching."

Matt stared at her, unfazed by her comment. "I'm glad you came tonight. I didn't think you were going to make it."

Had he been watching for her? No. She wouldn't read invisible script between the lines. As they danced, he'd inched her closer, so the instant the music ended, Lori stepped away. "Thank you, but I really should go."

"I'll walk you to your car."

"I didn't drive."

"Do you need a ride?"

"I'll call Uber. Good night, Matt."

She said goodbye to the people she'd met and texted for a car on the way to get her coat. She didn't dare look around in case Matt was watching.

~

*L*ori climbed off the ladder and pushed the speaker button on her phone with her pinky. "Hello?"

"Lori?"

She recognized Matt's voice immediately, and her heart kicked erratically. She pressed the heel of her left hand against her chest. "Hi, Matt. Can you hold on for just a minute?"

"Sure."

Lori set her brush on the edge of the paint can and grabbed a rag to wipe her hands before taking the phone off speaker. "Sorry."

"I'm the one who's sorry if I caught you at a bad time."

"I'm not the neatest painter in the world."

"What are you painting?"

"The walls in my office."

"Didn't you just move in?"

"Yes. I'm just making a few changes."

"Do you get more paint on you than on the wall?"

Lori glanced down at her paint-splattered sweatshirt and jeans. "I think you could say that."

"Color?"

"Gold."

"Gold?"

She smiled at the shocked doubt that replaced the smile in his tone. "It's a soft gold, not garish."

"Soft gold," he replied skeptically.

"You'll just have to"—Lori managed to stop herself before saying *see it*— "use your imagination."

"How was your Christmas?"

A common question asked among friends. *Friends.* She and Matt were friends. Of sorts. Employees could be friends with their employers. She'd been good friends with her previous editor. "My kids were in town. We all went to my parents' house, so it was nice. How about yours?"

"Quiet. Dave and I split the holidays. I worked Christmas since I got to spend Thanksgiving in Astoria with my family."

"Sorry." The image of Madelyn and Matt curled up by a fire popped into her mind. She left it there to remind her that not only was Matt with Madelyn, he was also her boss.

"Don't be. I'll be off for New Year's Eve."

Yay for you and Madelyn.

"You're busy, so I won't keep you. I know you don't officially start work until next Monday, but I'd like to start the New Year with your column. How quickly can you crank out a couple?"

"Pretty quickly." She'd already *cranked out* three just in case they asked.

Matt chuckled. "Were you anticipating this call?"

"No. I just like to be prepared. I can email them to you in about ten minutes."

"Actually, I was hoping you could come by the office to fill out some paperwork before you start. We can assign a laptop and a company email address while you're here. You can email them from that address."

"Would tomorrow be okay?" She had lunch plans with a

high school friend and could swing by the *Star's* office right after.

"Tomorrow would be great," he replied.

"Is there a specific time I should come by?"

"How does two o'clock work for you?"

Perfect. "I'll be there at two. Is there a specific person I should ask for?"

"I'll meet you in the lobby."

"Oh. Uh . . . okay." *Isn't there an administrative person or someone in HR who takes care of these things?*

"I'll see you tomorrow, Lori."

After Matt disconnected the call, Lori finally removed her hand from her chest, feeling even more discombobulated than she felt the night of the Christmas party. Taking this job was going to be a problem if simply talking to Matt over the phone or seeing him in the office sent her into cardiac arrest.

~

*L*ori walked into her parents' house the next morning. She'd been trying to stop by every other day, but that would have to taper off once she went back to work. Her parents lived forty-five minutes in the opposite direction of the paper and another thirty-five minutes back to Seattle.

Her mom and dad were at the kitchen table, each reading a different section of the paper.

"Lori," her mom said in surprise. "I still haven't gotten used to you living here."

Lori didn't know how to interpret that, so she just hugged them both from behind instead.

Her dad stood. "Did you eat?"

Henry McGuire loved to feed people. Anyone who stopped by got asked if they wanted something to eat.

Lori pulled out a chair and sat on the opposite side of the table. "I ate breakfast and I'm meeting Cyndi for lunch."

"Oh, how nice," her mom said. "How is Cyndi?"

"I'll find out today and let you know."

"Want some orange juice?"

"No thanks, Dad."

"Did the kids get off okay?" he asked, pouring her a glass anyway.

Christmas had been fun. Her kids and Tara's were home for the holidays—the first time they'd all been together in years, and she loved having Megan and Taylor home for a whole week. They shopped and saw a couple of movies and visited her parents.

Now both were in Chicago spending the rest of their Christmas break with their dad and visiting with friends who were also home for the holidays, leaving her anxious for spring break and their next visit.

"They left early yesterday morning. Both said to tell you thank you again for Christmas. We had a wonderful time."

"We did too. Didn't we, Henry?" Her mom smiled. "It's been ages since we could all be together."

"Your mom is making beef stew for dinner. Why don't you stop by again later?" her dad said.

"I'd love to, but I have to go to the *Star* to fill out some paperwork. Matt wants—" She wanted to bite her tongue off as soon as she said his name. She still hadn't told them Matt was the editor, and her boss.

Her mom latched on immediately. "Matt?"

"Matt Kelley. You remember him, don't you?" she asked, trying to sound casual. "Turns out he's the editor of the newspaper. Crazy coincidence, huh? Anyway, he asked if I could come in today to get a company email address and probably fill out some paperwork. They want to start my column on January first. I'm not sure how long I'll be there."

"You didn't mention Matt was the editor." Martha adjusted her glasses, her short red hair softly framing her face.

"I just found out. Shortly after my first interview the former editor resigned and Matt was promoted."

"Why didn't you tell us?"

Suddenly thirsty, Lori took a gulp of orange juice. "I wasn't sure you'd even remember him, Mom. We dated a long time ago."

"Of course we remember him. You remember him, don't you, Henry?"

"He was the football player from Oregon."

"Is he married?" Martha asked.

Not how is he, but is he married. As if she needed to be reminded of why she hadn't mentioned his name. "No, but I met his girlfriend at the newspaper's Christmas party."

Frustrated that she'd mentioned Matt, Lori was relieved at the same time. She hadn't planned to keep the truth from her parents for long, but she'd hoped to at least get her feet on solid ground before revealing she worked for Matt.

She finally escaped for her lunch date with Cyndi, which turned out great. They'd been friends since Cyndi moved into the school district when they were in seventh grade, and hadn't lost touch over the years, although they were only able to get together when Lori visited Seattle. Cyndi married her college sweetheart, Scott Gaddis, who had played football with Matt. The four of them double-dated several times before Lori transferred to North-western.

During lunch Cyndi mentioned that they ran into Matt occasionally.

"Every time we see him, he's with a different woman. He has a *type*." She made quotation marks with her fingers. "Long legs, brunette, with plenty of curves."

A perfect description of Madelyn, so the information didn't surprise Lori.

"Is it going to be hard working for him?"

"I don't think so," though it might have been if she didn't know he was with someone. "Did you know Phil is a reporter for the paper?" she asked, hoping to change the subject.

Cyndi laughed. "Yes. His articles are hilarious."

"I don't remember him ever telling me. I was stunned when he greeted me with a bear hug at the *Star's* Christmas party."

"Did Matt bring a date to the party?"

And we're back to discussing Matt. "Yes. Madelyn . . . I can't remember her last name. She's gorgeous."

"They always are. Except for Tammie Bennett. Remember her?"

Lori glanced up from her salad. "You're kidding, right? Do you think I could ever forget Tammie Bennett?" She speared a cucumber. "And Tammie was pretty."

"And a boyfriend thief."

"Tammie couldn't steal Matt or anyone else against their will. People blamed her, but Matt was a big boy and capable of making his own choices, just like every other boyfriend who strayed."

Cyndi dredged a fry through a puddle of ketchup on her plate. "Does the fact that he cheated bother you?"

Lori shook her head. "It happened a long time ago. We were kids."

"I wouldn't be so forgiving if it had been Scott. I'd probably punch Tammie in the nose if I ran into her."

Lori let all that go a long time ago.

Cyndi leaned forward, resting her elbows on the table. "He still asks about you when we run into him."

Information that surprised her. "Well, he and Madelyn looked very happy together."

"Isn't it funny how things work out? Everyone thought you and Matt would get married, have lots of babies, and live a fairy-tale life together. No one thought Scott and I would end up together, and we've been married for twenty-two years."

Life did have a witty and sometimes heartless sense of humor. "No one deserves more happiness than you and Scott."

"Thanks. That's sweet of you to say."

"Not sweet. True." She popped a cucumber into her mouth. "In all the times we talked, why didn't you ever tell me Matt still lives in Seattle?"

Cyndi shrugged. "It never came up in conversation. Why didn't you ever tell me you'd gone through a divorce?"

Lori mimicked Cyndi's shrug. "It never came up in conversation."

"What happened?" Cyndi asked, with a prompting roll of her hand.

"Work always came first for Jim. We had very different views about family life. His dad was a workaholic too, so Jim didn't know how to be different—didn't want to be different. We lived separate lives for so long, I could barely remember what it was like to be together. He was a great provider, but not much of a husband or father."

"You're over him."

This subject always made Lori sad. Despite giving everything to her marriage until she had nothing left to give, she failed to keep them together. "I'm not sure it's something you ever get over. Life just moved us in opposite directions."

CHAPTER 5

*L*ori pulled into the paper's parking lot and found a spot. Flipping down the rearview mirror, she touched up her lipstick. *Ridiculous.* She grabbed a tissue from her purse and wiped off the fresh coat, aggravated with herself.

She climbed out of the car and rounded the building. When she reached the door, the young security guard who helped her the first day pushed it open. Matt stood behind him in the reception area.

"Ken, this is our new columnist, Lori Maguire. Lori, Kenneth Baker is the building's daytime security guard."

"Hi," he said.

His shy smile told Lori they were kindred souls and he'd be a friend. "It's nice to meet you, Kenneth or do you prefer Ken?"

"Either is fine."

She'd call him Kenneth.

Matt waved her toward the elevators. "I thought you might like to see the lay of the land before you start Monday."

"That would be nice." But couldn't he have assigned someone else to show her around? Surely he had more important things to do than play host to her. "I don't want to take you away from your work, though."

"You're not taking me away from anything," he said after they stepped into the elevator. "How's the painting going?"

"My office is finished." She caught a waft of his cologne when the doors closed. Panic settled in. Just the two of them, in an enclosed space.

"Gold."

"You seem to have an aversion to gold," she said glancing up at him.

He grinned. "Maybe I'll have to stop by some time so you can convince me otherwise."

Instead of answering, she breathed a sigh of relief when the elevator doors opened.

He pushed one of the glass doors of the newspaper's offices open and they stopped at the receptionist's desk. "Amy Hill, this is Lori Maguire."

"Hi, Amy."

"I didn't realize when you came in a couple of weeks ago that you're the author Lori Maguire. My dad said he used to live next door to you."

"What?" Suddenly the resemblance was uncanny. "You're Professor Hill's daughter?"

"I am. My dad said he introduced you to Matt."

"He did," Lori said with a laugh. "Please, tell him I said hello. I don't get updates from my parents since your grandparents moved out of the neighborhood."

"I'll tell him. He's out of the country right now, but he wanted me to ask if you'd sign the book you dedicated to him." Amy pulled the third book in Lori's series out of a desk drawer.

Lori's throat tightened at the request. "Has your dad read it?"

"He's read all your books. Mom and I read them too."

She'd signed a lot of books in the past couple of years, but this one had sentimental significance in more than one way.

After adding a personal note and her signature, she straightened and handed Amy her pen.

Amy closed the book without reading the message. "Thank you. He'll love this."

"Nice meeting you, Amy." Lori gave a little wave as Matt led her around the desk and down a hall.

He stopped at several office doors, reintroducing Lori to the two managing editors and chief human resources officer. She remembered their faces from the party. Now she could add positions and names to those faces.

Dave looked up when they stopped at his office door. "Is Matt showing you around?"

"Yes. It'll be nice when it's not new anymore."

"It won't take you long to settle in."

True. She'd lived in Chicago since she was nineteen, but after four short weeks, Seattle already felt like home again.

They followed the hall around to a large room with cubicles.

"We call this the sports wing," Matt said. "The department has a sports editor, two copy editors, and six reporters."

He touched her elbow as they walked through the department, which set her heart banging like a jackhammer against her ribs.

Matt is with Madelyn and he is my boss. Matt is with Madelyn and he is my boss.

Kirk grinned and held up a hand. Thank goodness he was busy on the phone. He'd been a little too hands-on at the Christmas party.

Just past the sports department another room held more

cubicles. "Marketing, IT, and news copy are also on the second floor. Stairs or elevator to the third floor?" he asked.

"Stairs." She'd much rather climb a flight of stairs than be enclosed in an elevator with Matt again.

The third floor housed the life and entertainment reporters. Graphics, photography, design, and video also had cubicles there.

They climbed the stairs again, and he opened the door to the fourth floor. Aisles of cubicles filled the room, and offices ran along two of the four walls.

"The *Star* has twenty-nine reporters." He gestured toward the left. "The conference room and breakroom are on that side, and my office is around this corner," he added, pointing to the right.

She knew each reporter specialized in a different interest or region. Matt led her through the cubicles, reintroducing her. He paused at the end of an aisle. "I'm sure you remember this guy."

Phil jumped up from behind his desk and hugged her. "Welcome to the office. I didn't know you were coming in today."

"Just getting a tour and filling out some paperwork."

Matt waved to an office in the corner of the big room. "And here's your office."

Stunned she turned to Matt. "I have a private office?"

"Right across the aisle from me." Phil squeezed her shoulders from behind.

"I don't mind being in a cubicle with the other reporters."

"The other columnists have offices on the second and third floor."

She scanned the room before stepping over the threshold, and glanced down at the desk and over at the file cabinet while her feet continued to the windows. "Thank you. This is more than I expected."

"The laptop is new, and my assistant ordered another chair." Matt leaned against the doorframe. "Tom decided to take some vacation time, so you can move in whenever you're ready. He did leave some files. Feel free to keep whatever you want. I'll get the rest out of your way."

Lori was used to being in a big room with all the other reporters, short, temporary walls, and no privacy. With her own office, she had enough room for a couple of pictures and a plant, and enough natural light that it would actually grow. This was perfect. "I met Cyndi for lunch today. She said to tell you both hi."

"How's she doing?" Phil asked.

"Good. Scott is doing well, too," Lori said to Matt.

Matt nodded. "I run into them occasionally."

"Did you get the invitation Faith sent out for our New Year's Eve party?" Phil asked.

"I did. I called and left a message with Faith that I already have plans."

"With who?" Phil asked, glancing at Matt.

"I'm going to a couple of parties with Tara."

"My party will be better. Bring Tara with you."

"Hi, Lori." Theresa Carpenter pushed past Phil. "I saw you come in. How do you like your office?"

Lori smiled at a reporter she remembered meeting at the Christmas party. She hadn't come up with an excuse to miss Phil's party, where she was bound to see Matt and Madelyn bring in the New Year, so Theresa was a welcome interruption.

Looking bohemian chic, Theresa wore a patchwork dress and suede boots. She was tall, with flawless olive skin taut over defined cheekbones, and ebony hair pulled back in a ponytail.

"Uh, we were having a conversation here, Theresa," Phil said.

"Why don't you go shave your face?" Theresa turned from him to Lori. "My husband's out of town for a few days. If you're not busy, why don't we meet for dinner tonight?"

Since moving back, Lori had spent a lot of time alone or with family. Other than lunch with Cyndi, she hadn't been out much. The idea of dinner with the possibility of a new friendship sounded perfect. "I'd like that, Theresa. Thanks."

"Hey! I was going to invite her to dinner at my house," Phil said, frowning at Theresa.

"I guess you should have asked her sooner," Theresa replied. "You like Chinese, Lori?"

"I love Chinese."

~

Knowing Lori was on the other side of the fourth floor filling out employment forms made work impossible for Matt. He was acutely aware of her unease around him earlier, but other than giving her time, he had no idea how to change that.

He'd flirted with the idea of inviting her to dinner, but Theresa beat both him and Phil to the punch. If Phil had asked her first, Matt would have been included. And she was more likely to have accepted Phil's invitation than his.

Matt had Frank from IT come up to assign Lori a work email address. She sent three columns to him as soon as she sat down at her desk.

He read the first paragraph of the first file and laughed aloud. This one would run January first, perfect for people setting New Year's resolutions. She grabbed his attention with her very first line and held it throughout the article.

The paper's regular readers were going to love her column. He'd get Sid from marketing to drop a couple of promo ads. Lori could generate new readers with her refreshing point of view and unique sense of humor, which she didn't display in public.

Her second column might capture a younger generation of readers. He'd text a note to Sid to work on promo for that too.

Matt combed fingers through his hair and smiled. Lori Maguire was home.

~

*L*ori could hear the music at Phil and Faith's New Year's Eve party from the parking lot. People packed the barn-turned events center almost to the rafters.

"We should have come here first," Tara yelled in Lori's direction. "This place is rocking."

Her sister shrieked in surprise when someone picked her up from behind.

"Tara Maguire, you look great," Phil shouted.

"Aw, you were always a sweetheart." Tara smooshed Phil's cheeks in when he set her on her feet. "Kevin, this is Phil Cates. His parents live by mine."

"Nice to meet you." Phil shook Kevin's hand, then pulled Lori back against his chest and wrapped his long arms around her. "How were your other parties?"

"I just told Lori we should have come here first. Thanks for letting me and Kevin tag along with my little sis."

"Glad you could make it. *Siéntanse como en casa.*"

Lori tilted her head straight up to look at Phil. "Which means?"

"Make yourselves at home. Well, as much as you can in a barn."

Faith joined them. "Hi, Lori. I see my husband is manhandling you again."

Phil bent close to his wife's ear, taking Lori with him. "Babe, this is Lori's sister, Tara, and Kevin."

"Welcome," Faith said.

The music stopped but Lori's ears continued to buzz from noise overload.

"Phil, show Tara and Kevin where the bar is. I'm going to steal Lori from you." Faith took her arm. "Would you mind helping me in the kitchen for a few minutes?"

"Not at all," Lori said honestly. The clock was ticking down closer to midnight with each breath. If she could hide in the kitchen until after the partygoers brought in the New Year, she'd go home a happy woman.

She waved to Theresa and her husband John and acknowledged another woman she recognized from the paper, but couldn't remember her name. Mainly she kept her eyes on Faith's back or the floor to keep from seeing Matt and Madelyn.

Faith pushed through the swinging kitchen door. "Is Kevin with you?"

"No, he and Tara have been together for years." Lori glanced around the large industrial kitchen, which was a bit jarring after the rustic charm of the main room. "This place is perfect."

"We used to hold this party at our house, but it just got too big. We decided to go in with a couple of neighbors and rent this space every year." Faith picked up a bag of lemons and another of limes. "Would you mind cutting these into wedges for me? A couple of the hosts had to run out for more food and ice, and I should help Phil watch the door for party crashers."

"I don't mind at all."

"How much alcohol have you had? I don't want you slicing a finger."

"I don't drink, so I'm safe with a knife."

"Thanks, Lori. This is such a help." Faith swung out of the kitchen.

Lori should be thanking Faith. She'd had enough partying for one night. Kevin introduced her to one of his single friends at the first party they attended, and Tara pushed her at a single friend of hers at the second party. Lori would gladly slice citrus until the two of them were ready to leave.

~

Matt knew his New Year would start right the minute Lori walked through the door. He recognized Tara and hoped the man was with Tara and not Lori. After another bout of jealousy over Phil and Lori's close friendship, he watched Faith lead Lori into the kitchen.

He made it to the door just as Faith came out alone.

"Okay, Prince, Kelley I got Lori in the kitchen. You have until midnight before you turn back into a little green toad, so you'd better get moving."

"Who's the guy?"

"Kevin. He's with Lori's sister," Faith said over her shoulder as she walked away.

Matt pushed through the door and grinned.

Lori stood at the counter with her back to the door. Moving her hips to the music made her iridescent purple blouse shimmer under the harsh kitchen lights. When she reached for another lime, she spotted him and stopped. Pink rushed up her neck and over her cheeks.

"I didn't know you were there."

"I didn't want to interrupt." He walked to her side and handed her a lime.

"Did you need something?"

"No. Faith told me she left you in here all alone, so I came to see if I can help."

"This won't take long, but thanks for the offer." She sliced the lime he handed her.

He watched her every move, tempted to reach out and touch her hair. He'd always loved her reddish-gold curls and how she wasn't preoccupied with keeping it tied back.

He leaned a hip against the counter. "I enjoyed the columns you turned in. I even laughed out loud a few times."

She tipped her face up to him and smiled. "Good. I've heard it's helpful to get on the boss's good side."

Matt raised a brow. "Oh, really?"

"That's not what I meant."

"What did you mean?" Unable to resist her hair any longer, he lifted a tendril and let it curl around his index finger.

Lori turned toward him and the curl slipped away. "Isn't Madelyn looking for you by now?"

When she moved, he caught a whisper of her perfume. "Madelyn?"

She frowned. "Isn't that her name? The woman you brought to the Christmas party."

Matt reached for another strand of hair, but Lori took a step back. He let his hand drop. "I don't think Madelyn's here."

"You don't know if she's here or not?"

"She doesn't know any of the people hosting the party."

Turning away, Lori went to the sink. "My invitation said I could bring a date."

"And yet you didn't."

She washed and dried the knife and cutting board. When she came back, she left extra space between them. Her eyes traveled to a bag of lemons near his hip. "I just thought if you came, you'd bring your girlfriend."

"Madelyn isn't my girlfriend."

The surprise on her face was almost comical. "She's not?"

"No. We only dated for a few weeks."

Her eyebrows puckered. "You broke up with her?"

This conversation didn't seem to be headed in a good direction. "It was a mutual decision."

"You two seemed pretty cozy at the party." She reached for the lemons, but he put his hand on the bag.

"You were watching?"

"Kind of hard not to with the two of you sitting across the table."

She seemed to be flustered about something, but he had no idea what. He slid the bag toward her and took a step closer. After washing the lemons, she started slicing them with swift, sharp strokes.

"You're going to slice your finger off." Moving her with his hip, he appropriated the knife and took over the job. "Did I say something to make you mad?"

Turning toward him, she opened her mouth and inhaled a shaky breath, then shook her head. "No."

He decided not to push. "Have you acclimated to Seattle after being away for so long?"

"I came to visit often enough that it's not completely unfamiliar."

"How often?" As he sliced the lemons, her perfume mixed with the fresh citrus scent.

She picked up the slices and put them in a bowl. "At least once a year, sometimes more."

When he finished, Lori went back to the sink and scrubbed the knife and cutting board again. He dried them with the towel she'd used earlier. They each picked up a bowl.

"Thank you for helping."

"You're welcome," he replied, following her into the party.

"I recognize that handsome face," Tara said when they reached the bar.

He returned her hug. "How are you, Tara?"

"We've been hearing all about you."

"Really?" Matt glanced at Lori, whose cheeks flushed crimson.

"Tara," Lori said in a warning tone.

"What?" Tara asked, innocently. "We were talking about him right after you took the job at the paper. Remember? You were asking if we thought—"

A man wrapped his arm around Tara's neck and placed a hand over her mouth. He extended his other hand. "I'm Kevin Diaz."

Funny, Lori's name had come up during a dinner with his family, too. "Matt Kelley," he said, shaking Kevin's hand.

Kevin looked at Tara. "Are you going to leave your sister alone?"

Tara nodded and he removed his hand. Tara immediately took Matt's arm and turned them away from Kevin and Lori. "So Matt, are you married?"

He chuckled. "No, I'm not."

"Imagine that—you're single and Lori's single."

"Imagine that."

"Are you dating anyone seriously?"

Kevin took Tara's hand. "If you'll excuse us, I believe it's time for a dance."

Dancing sounded like a good idea. Matt turned to Lori only to see her being hauled to the dance floor by Kirk.

"Oh, my gosh, Matt," Faith suddenly appeared next to him. "I handed Lori to you on a silver platter."

The music slowed down and Kirk tucked Lori close. "I turned away for a split second to talk to her sister and Kirk stepped through the crack."

"Seriously, how did you ever get her to go out with you in college?"

"I bought eight movie tickets." He turned his glare from

Kirk to Faith. "You know, you could help instead of standing there laughing."

"How, exactly? I got her in the kitchen by herself. You turned around and gave her to Kirk."

His glare turned back to Kirk, who said something close to Lori's ear. She smiled.

"You're turning green behind the ears, Kermit. It's almost midnight and Kirk will be kissing the beautiful princess while you turn back into a toad."

Matt took Faith by the shoulders and steered her across the room. "I'll have her on the dance floor by midnight." When they reached Phil, Matt pointed at Lori. "Lori would love to dance with you."

His friend moved in like a rhinoceros during mating season, whisking Lori away before Kirk had a chance to react.

Matt smiled down at Faith. "Want to dance, beautiful?"

"I thought you'd never ask."

CHAPTER 6

*P*hil could make Lori laugh with a look. At the moment he was reminding her of the time he, along with a group of friends, put her car in neutral and high-centered it on a hill of dirt left in the high school parking lot after a construction job.

"So not funny. Bobby Haines pointed out the window during history class and said, 'Hey, isn't that your car?' Sure enough, my car is teetering precariously on top of a pile of dirt."

"I'm sorry I missed that part. I would have loved to see your face."

She caught sight of Kirk at a table near the dance floor. "Thanks for saving me."

He put a finger under her chin and lifted her face. "You didn't look like you were enjoying your time with him."

"I didn't want to be with him when midnight strikes." She pointed at his chest. "You need to find Faith so you can bring in the New Year together."

"What about you?"

"If you can sneak me into the kitchen, I'll hide out until either Kirk gives up or Tara and Kevin are ready to go home."

"Aw, my beautiful bride is here to ruin our fun," Phil said, looking past her. "As much as I'd love to kiss your delectable lips, my wife is an extremely jealous woman."

Lori glanced over her shoulder, and her heart jumped when she saw who was dancing with Faith.

"Don't believe a thing Phil says, Lori. He's the jealous one. He doesn't want me to kiss Matt because he knows I'd never come back."

Phil placed Lori's hand in Matt's as he took Faith's and they danced away.

Matt smiled and tugged her closer. "Relax, Lori. I don't bite. Well,"—he raised an eyebrow—"I guess I did bite occasionally, didn't I?"

She sucked air into her lungs and smiled. He had bitten her neck or nibbled her earlobe many times. "Occasionally."

"We used to have fun dancing."

She nodded. They did have fun on the few occasions when they got to dance together.

"Phil had you laughing pretty hard a minute ago. What were the two of you talking about?"

Lori knew Matt's questions were a ploy to distract her, since he must have felt her tense up the minute he took her in his arms. The crowded dance floor pushed them even closer together. "He was reminding me how irritating he could be as a kid."

"It's not hard to imagine Phil as a kid."

"That's because he hasn't changed much. He's still annoying."

"Is that a bad thing?"

"No." She huffed out a laugh. "Phil wouldn't be Phil if he changed. I can't imagine him any other way. Have you known him long?"

"Phil started at the paper two years after I did, so yes."

"You seem just as close to Faith as you do with Phil."

"Phil married Faith about a year after I met him. We've vacationed, skied, and attended concerts and conferences together." He smiled down at her. "Faith is like a sister—gives me more grief than they do."

"What does she give you grief about?"

Matt pressed his lips together like he might not answer, which only made her more curious.

"She doesn't approve of my dating habits."

Not the answer she'd been expecting. "Do you have bad dating habits?"

He actually shrugged his eyebrows. "Faith thinks so."

Lori was a little surprised Matt wasn't married with a basketball team-sized family by now. He used to be great around kids and talked about wanting them. "Sorry."

"For what?"

"I shouldn't have asked a personal question."

"You can ask me anything."

Midnight was growing near. She and Matt would be in the middle of the crowd when the clock struck twelve. She'd been alone for the past three New Year's, and she'd planned to spend this year alone too, but Tara bugged her until she surrendered. At this moment she wavered between being glad she'd come and wishing she hadn't.

The music stopped and the DJ started the countdown. "Ten. Nine."

Matt joined in and her stomach flipped.

"Eight. Seven."

Everyone around them counted. Lori grew breathless.

"Six."

Lori took a step back.

"Five."

"Kirk's behind you," Matt said.

"Four."

She stepped into Matt's arms while trying to swallow her panic.

"Three. Two."

Matt cupped her cheek. "We used to have a lot of fun doing this, too."

"One!"

"Happy New Year, Lori." Matt tilted his head and his lips touched hers . . . and she fell headlong into a long-forgotten roller-coaster ride Matt used to take her on every time he kissed her. It wasn't a fun-loving Happy New Year kiss, but a lingering, hauntingly gentle kiss that left her completely breathless and wanting more. When he lifted his head, she got lost in his blue eyes.

Before she could collect her senses, Phil and Kevin kissed her. Tara, Theresa, and Faith hugged her, then Kirk kissed her. He pulled her close and started swaying to "Auld Lang Syne." Shouldn't she be dancing with an old acquaintance for this one? Like Matt?

She closed her eyes because she didn't want to see him kissing another woman the way he just kissed her.

~

*M*onday morning, Lori stepped off the elevator carrying a box of personal items. She noticed a light in Matt's office but was careful not to look that direction. Their kiss on New Year's had plagued her all weekend. That silly kiss, a simple wish for a new year filled with new beginnings and happiness. She'd been trying to convince herself of that ever since it happened.

About a third of the reporters were at their desks. To her relief, Phil wasn't in his cubicle. If anyone brought up the kiss between her and Matt, it would be Phil.

In her office, she set the box down on the corner of her desk and smiled. A vase with half a dozen yellow roses sat on the corner. She pulled the card free. **Welcome home.**

She knew the roses were from Matt without even looking at the card, amazed that he remembered yellow roses were her favorite after all these years. Not only did they smell yummy, but they added a touch of sunshine on a dreary winter day. She slipped the card in her purse.

Putting the box and vase of roses on the floor, she maneuvered the desk around until it sat at an angle in the room. Then she rolled her chair into the corner, situated the other two chairs in front of her desk, and returned the roses to her desktop.

Satisfied that the office now looked more like a woman's than a man's, she unpacked her box. A framed photo of her kids went on the corner of her desk near the vase. She set a small plant and another picture of her with the kids on top of the file cabinet.

Making a second trip to her car, she carried in three boxes of homemade cinnamon rolls, leaving one in the breakroom on each floor.

Denise, Matt's assistant, was away from her desk when Lori passed by again, so she turned that way. Might as well get the uncomfortable moment out of the way.

She paused at the door of the big corner office. The gold plaque to the left of the door said **MATTHEW J. KELLEY – EDITOR** in black letters. Inside Matt's office, to the immediate right, was an overstuffed leather sofa and two armchairs. Situated straight ahead, Matt sat at a large mahogany desk thumbing through a stack of papers. Two leather chairs faced his desk. A large conference table and twelve chairs dominated the left side of the room. Beyond Matt, the floor to ceiling windows provided a spectacular view of the city.

"Good morning."

He looked up and grinned. "Lori, come in."

Nope. She felt safer where she was. "Someone left beautiful yellow roses on my desk. If I knew who, I'd tell them thank you."

"Yellow roses, huh?" He stood and rounded his desk, walking toward her. "They used to be your favorite, didn't they?"

"They still are."

Her already pounding heartbeat accelerated as he advanced. She fought the urge to run. "I didn't mean to interrupt you."

"I have an open-door policy, and you're not interrupting." He took her arm and pulled her over the threshold. "How was your weekend?"

"Good. How was yours?"

"Long."

Arms encircled her waist and a body propelled her forward, almost pushing her into Matt. She put up her hands which landed flat against Matt's muscular chest. Heat flashed over her cheeks and she dropped her hands to the arms around her.

"Hi, gorgeous. Someone said you were responsible for the cinnamon rolls in the breakroom."

Lori looked up at Phil licking frosting from the corner of his mouth. "Looks like they turned out pretty good."

"There are cinnamon rolls?" Matt asked.

"Delicious, homemade cinnamon rolls." Phil tightened his hold. "When did you learn to cook?"

"I've had years of practice since seventh grade home economics, Phil."

Phil chuckled. "Lori and I were in the same class. Our first assignment was cinnamon rolls. Who accidentally used salt instead of sugar?"

Lori laughed at the memory. "Tommy Richardson, but I don't think it was an accident."

"Remember our go-kart ride?" Phil asked.

Lori held up her hand and pointed to her palm. "You scarred me for life with that ride."

Phil chuckled.

Matt took her hand and ran the pad of his thumb along the white line on her palm. "What happened?"

"Lori and her friends claimed they found *my* go-kart abandoned in some bushes near her parents' house, which is where I'd stored it for safekeeping."

"You'd better let me tell the story if you're going to lie."

Phil held up his hand. "I'll tell the entire, unvarnished truth. I hid the go-kart and Lori found it."

Matt laughed when Lori rolled her eyes.

"To get it back, Lori challenged me to a race. I agreed, but only if I made the rules. We each had to drive with the other one on the cart so the weight would be the same. Since the go-kart didn't have an engine, and Lori weighed *way* more than I did, I knew she'd go farther. The problem was my long legs. When it was my turn to drive, Lori had to ride in the front, so she became my handicap because I couldn't see over her head."

"Since she's so tall and you probably had a hard time getting your arms around her, because she weighed so much," Matt said, helping Phil out.

"Hey!" she said. Based on his grin, Matt was having as much fun listening as Phil was telling.

"You can see my dilemma," Phil said. "Anyway, we crashed —because of my handicap—and Lori got a piece of glass in her hand, which she'll never let me forget, as is evident this morning."

"The only part of the story Phil got right was that he sat behind me both times. When we crashed, my *big, fat body* broke his fall." She slipped out of Phil's arms and backed toward the door. "He came out of it without a scratch. I scraped both my knees, both hands, and the side of my face."

"You did get pretty scraped up. I felt bad."

"Yeah, you felt so bad you stole the go-kart."

"You can't steal what's already yours. Hey, who sent you flowers?"

Of course Phil would notice. "An anonymous giver."

"Are they from Kirk?" he was quick to ask.

She thumbed over her shoulder. "I'm going to my office to begin my first day at the *Star*."

~

*M*att and Phil watched Lori until she turned the corner just past Denise's desk.

"Thanks. She smells so much better than Tom," Phil said.

"Yeah, she does."

"I didn't get flowers when I started. Are you going to play favorites?"

"Absolutely."

Phil glanced at him. "You got a game plan?"

"Not yet, but I'm working on it."

"You know you could just drive over and ask to see her house."

"That's a little obvious."

Phil barked out a laugh and turned to Matt. "Since when do you have a problem with obvious?"

"True."

"On a serious note,"—Phil's expression turned somber—"if you hurt her, I'm going to have to break something—your arm or toe or something."

"Duly noted," Matt said with a chuckle. "I'm going to the

breakroom to get one of those cinnamon rolls before they're gone."

"Good call."

Matt noticed Lori had relaxed considerably when Phil stepped into his office. He wanted her to feel comfortable around him but hadn't come up with an idea of how to get there. Lori was and always had been so different from any of the other women he dated.

He'd used the holiday as an excuse to kiss her, but what they shared had been more than a simple good wish for the New Year. He knew she felt it too as soon as he looked into her green eyes.

Everyone in the breakroom was moaning in cinnamon roll ecstasy. He took a bite and had to agree. The cinnamon roll melted in his mouth.

"Who made these?" Theresa asked.

"Lori."

"They're the best I've ever eaten."

Matt took a second bite. Better than his mom's, and hers won blue ribbons at the county fair.

After finishing his cinnamon roll, Matt conducted his usual Monday morning meeting with department heads. When they left his office, he called Lori's extension.

"*Seattle Star*, Lori Maguire."

"Can you come to my office?"

"Sure."

"You're not going to ask who this is?"

"I recognize the authority in the boss's voice."

When Lori walked into his office minutes later, Matt stood. "Thanks for coming. Hope I didn't interrupt your work."

"No." She pointed at a framed photo on a file cabinet behind his desk. "That's a nice picture of your parents."

"Thanks. I took it last year on their anniversary." Matt

glanced at the photo. "I told my mom you started at the paper. She said to tell you hello." He loved the smile that lit Lori's face.

"Tell her I said hello back."

He indicated one of the chairs in front of his desk and she sat.

"You have great parents," she said.

"I got lucky. How's your first day going?"

"Great. Everyone has been very helpful."

"Good." He sat down. "I'd like to go over a few things."

He explained the new edge he and Dave had been looking for. "The columns you've turned in so far are right on target."

A pretty, irresistible pink rushed over her cheeks.

"I want to do some advertising because I think your columns will not only keep our established readers interested, but you have the skills and viewpoint that may attract a whole new generation."

"What kind of advertising?" Lori asked cautiously.

"Don't worry. I won't ask you to pose for a billboard, but I would like to talk to a PR firm." He could tell by the look on her face that she hated the idea. "I promise it will be tasteful. I assume you've done this sort of thing with your books."

She responded by chewing on her lip.

He looked up at a tap on the door.

"Brock Stones is on line one," Denise said.

"Tell him I'll call him back, Denise. Will you shut my door, please?"

Denise looked from him to Lori, then closed the door.

Matt leaned forward, elbows on his desk. "I read your first two books."

"You did?" The surprise on her face was unexpected.

"My sister bought my mom the whole series, so I read through the first two, then thumbed through the first few pages of all the other books."

The dedication in the fourth book said **To Matt, who believed in me before I believed in myself.** He was just vain enough to think she meant him. In college, he'd encouraged her to write, and when she did, he encouraged her to trust her gift with words. He'd never understood why she was so self-conscious about putting her work in front of others.

Matt got up and circled his desk to sit in the chair next to her. She blinked several times and pushed her hair back over her shoulder. She'd worn it down today, all that curly, strawberry-blonde hair that he used to get his fingers tangled in. He resisted the urge to reach for a strand. "They're good."

"Thank you."

"My mom devoured them, then passed them off to my sisters, so you have new fans."

Since she didn't say anything about the dedication, maybe he wasn't that Matt. Faith teased him all the time about being full of himself. Had there been another Matt? That would be a question for another day. "Back to the advertising. I want to spread the news that we have a new columnist in town."

"I don't want to be on a bus bench, either."

Matt laughed. "I promise no benches. Phil will write a story about a childhood friend who is now a columnist at the paper."

He held up a hand when she started to protest. "The story is at the request of the mayor, whose wife also loves your books. I was in a meeting with him last week, and he thought it would be good for the city to know we have a famous author working at the *Star*, and I agree. I told him you'd hate the attention, but he insisted I try to get you to agree. You can read over the article before we run it."

"You're making me sorry I didn't write under a pseudonym."

"You should be proud of your accomplishments, Lori."

Glancing down, she shook her head.

"Will you let me take you to dinner tonight?"

She looked up, wide-eyed. "No."

"Why? We haven't seen each other in more than twenty years. Dinner will give us a chance to catch up."

Lori bit her lower lip. "People will talk."

"About what? Two old friends going to dinner?" He took her hand. She immediately pulled it out of his grasp and glanced at the door.

Matt chuckled. She'd gone into survival mode. Like a scared rabbit, she skittered away, looking for a place to hide. "It would be an innocent dinner in a public place, Lori."

"You're my boss." Before he could protest, she stood up. "Are we finished? I really should get back to work."

Matt huffed out a resigned breath. "Yes. I'll let Phil know about the story."

He walked around his desk after she rushed out of his office. She'd put up a wall, but he'd scaled her walls before. It took him a while, but he got over them. And she'd been worth it.

Then he ruined everything.

CHAPTER 7

*L*ater that afternoon, Matt spotted Phil standing at the open door of Lori's office, so he headed that way. Before he reached Phil, he heard another voice. Kirk. He could tell by Phil's grin that he was running interference and enjoying every second.

Phil turned sideways so Matt could enter Lori's office. "What's going on?"

"Kirk and I are just visiting with the *Star's* newest staffer. In the process, she isn't getting a column written."

Kirk stood up. The poor guy had to know he wouldn't get any further with Lori today. "I'll let you get to work. I just wanted to say thanks for the cinnamon rolls. They were great. Maybe we could grab lunch one day."

Lori smiled. "Thanks for stopping by, Kirk. Have a nice afternoon."

"You really shouldn't encourage him," Phil said once Kirk was out of earshot.

She threw a wad of paper at him.

Phil laughed. "Now that I know you're safe from Kirk's clutches, I'll leave you to Matt's."

"Thanks, buddy," Matt said, pushing Phil out. He turned to Lori, who looked panicked again.

"You make this place look much better than Tom ever did." He stopped in front of her desk and picked up a framed picture. "Your kids?"

"Yes."

Matt swallowed against the unexpected emotions. He and Lori had talked about having children one day, but he'd allowed pride to ruin their plans. He didn't like living his life with regrets, but losing Lori would always be one that haunted him. "Names?"

"Taylor and Megan. They're twins. They turned twenty-one in October."

"They favor their mother."

"You've never seen their father."

You're wrong. He saw her engagement picture in the paper, but he kept that information to himself. He set the framed photo back in its place. "I like what you've done here. The angle of the desk, the picture. It looks welcoming."

"I hope it was okay to hang something on the wall. I used the original nail hole."

"It's fine. Where are your kids?"

"Taylor is at Cornell studying veterinary medicine and Megan is at Vanderbilt. She hasn't quite decided on a major yet, but she's leaning toward law like her dad. Maybe polit-ical science."

"Juniors?"

She tucked a few strands of reddish-gold behind her ear. "Yes."

Since her terrified bunny expression had fallen away, he'd keep asking questions. "If they're both on the other side of the country, what made you settle so far away?"

"I don't want to crowd my kids. They've been joined at the hip since birth, and both were ready to spread their wings. Once they graduate, who knows where they'll end up?"

"And you wanted to be close to your parents and your sister," he finished for her as he circled her desk and sat on the corner, close enough that he could smell her perfume. "Does it worry you that your kids are spreading their wings?"

"No. I'm really lucky in that sense. They don't require a hovering mother, and both know where to find me."

She smiled while she talked about them, a sweetly gentle upturning at the corners of her mouth. "How often do you see your kids?"

"They were here over Christmas."

He stood, knowing she wouldn't agree to dinner tonight. "One day I'd like to hear about where you get the ideas for your books." He walked to the door. "And about how you choose your dedications."

He waited just long enough to watch the blush rush over her cheeks before leaving.

~

Over the next couple of days Lori steered clear of Matt. At first, she was embarrassed because he found the dedication to him in book four of her series. That feeling changed overnight. She'd dedicated each book to a specific person for a specific reason, which was nothing to be embarrassed about.

She settled comfortably into her work environment, becoming fast friends with Theresa right off the bat. The woman's quick wit and snarky attitude reminded Lori of Tara, and she envied the reporter's ease of style.

Carrie Eubanks, another coworker, often joined them when they went out for lunch. Carrie was Theresa's complete opposite. She was tall, model-thin, and blonde, with expressive brown eyes. She carried herself with such poise and sophistication, she seemed more like royalty that reporter.

According to Theresa, Carrie's husband, Steve, worked as the Seattle mayor's chief of staff, and Carrie often used him to get inside stories. And since she was still considered a cub reporter, with only a year under her belt, senior reporters were assigned to support and proof most of her articles, which Carrie hated.

Carrie also hated that Lori was single. In one short week, she tried to set Lori up twice.

On Friday, Lori had joined Theresa and James Hernandez, a legal affairs reporter, in the breakroom. They were discussing a story Phil wrote about the misuse of election contributions when Matt walked in.

"Good morning," he said.

Theresa and James greeted him in unison, along with several other people occupying surrounding tables. Lori fisted her hands in her lap, digging her nails into her palms, trying to calm her suddenly fluttering heartbeat.

He went to the vending machines and bought a soft drink. Then, out of all the seats at all of the tables in the room, he took the only chair left at their table, which happened to be next to her, hemming her against the wall.

"Am I interrupting?"

"Not at all," Theresa responded, her glance bouncing from Matt to Lori. "We'll just have to be more selective about conversation topics with the boss at our table."

"Since when has my being at your table stopped you from talking about anything?"

"Never," James said with a laugh.

"Theresa, I just read over your article about the changes at the city council meeting and made one small correction." He held up his hand when Theresa's mouth opened. "I only made the change because the mayor gave me some new information this morning."

Lori had learned quickly that Theresa was extremely meticulous about the details of her stories and got offended when anyone questioned the facts, because she'd already checked and rechecked them.

"What do you think about that article Phil did on the election contributions?" James asked Matt. "Pretty gutsy reporting."

Matt leaned back in his chair, totally at ease, and let his knee touch Lori's thigh. "I think Phil likes to go out on a limb as far as he can until he hears the faint cracking of the branch —then he goes just a little farther, somehow managing to stop before the resounding snap."

"He's not the only one," Lori said, glancing at Matt before shifting her leg away.

Carrie breezed in. "There you are, Lori. I've been looking everywhere for you."

"What's up?" she asked, tearing her gaze from Matt's grin.

"I went to a cocktail party last night with Steve and met the nicest man. I told him all about you, and he wants me to hook you two up. He doesn't even care that you're a few years older. He's a successful attorney . . ."

Matt's knee touched her leg again.

". . . said he's available tomorrow night."

Every eye in the breakroom turned from Carrie to her, because Carrie's voice carried like a megaphone, announcing to the world that she'd found a date for pathetic Lori. "I appreciate your attempt to *hook me up*, Carrie, but I'm capable of finding my own dates."

"You said you weren't dating anyone," Carrie replied. "When was the last time you went out with a man?"

"Saturday."

Theresa turned her attention from Carrie to her. "You went out on a date and didn't tell me?"

"We just met, Theresa," Lori said.

"Who did you go out with?" Carrie's tone dripped skepticism.

"I'm not discussing my personal life with everyone in the breakroom."

James laughed. "Don't you know yet? Your personal life is office fodder. Word is Kirk has a thing for you."

"You went out with Kirk?" Carrie asked.

"No."

"What do you know about this guy if you just met him last night, Carrie?" James asked.

Carrie crossed her arms and glared at him. "I know a lot about him. He's extremely handsome and successful. And he's nice. Steve said he has an expensive home in—"

Theresa waved Carrie's description away. "I want to hear about your date, Lori."

Everyone in the breakroom seemed to lean their way, waiting.

Okay, she'd tell them. "It was interesting. My sister introduced me to a guy she works with on New Year's Eve. She said he was extremely handsome and successful. Over a two-hour dinner, he told me about how his ex-wife didn't shave her legs, so he'd run a bath, get her drunk, and shave them for her. He told me all about the dog and boat he lost in the divorce settlement because he shaved her legs while she was passed out. Then, just as dessert was served, he told me I had very enticing breasts."

She didn't look at Matt, but James and Theresa's jaws dropped.

"He did not," Theresa said.

Lori nodded.

"Why did he wait until dessert?" Matt asked.

James laughed.

"You are *not* serious," Theresa said.

"I promise. He said it right before he asked me if I wanted to go back to his place or mine."

"Whose place did you choose?" Matt asked, right before his knee touched her thigh again.

"Or did you just tell him thank you?" James asked.

"No, I told him it was amazing he could tell, since I was wearing such a heavy sweater."

"I don't want to tell this guy you're not interested yet," Carrie said. "I'll tell him you're dating someone else."

"You can tell him I'm not interested." Lori turned in Matt's direction. "If you'll excuse me, I need to get back to work."

~

att stood up so Lori could pass. He knew she wasn't comfortable having her private life discussed in front of everyone. He also knew he'd been pushing his luck when he kept touching her with his knee. Her blazing green eyes and her tongue would have cut him in two if they'd been alone.

After James and Carrie left, Theresa leaned forward, resting her forearms on the table. "You need to work on your poker face around Lori if you don't want anyone else to notice how you feel."

Truly, he didn't care who noticed, but Lori would. "Am I that obvious?"

"Only to someone watching." She studied him for a moment. "I like Lori. I don't think I've ever made a friend so fast, so if you do something to make her quit, I'll have to break your leg."

The second threat to break one of his limbs from one of

Lori's friends. "I won't do anything to make her quit. I do have a question, though. How often does Carrie set Lori up with dates?"

"She's tried a couple of times, but she's not having much luck. Lori is pretty private. She did tell me you two dated in college, but only because I overheard a conversation between Phil and Lori's sister at the New Year's party and asked her. She wouldn't have offered the information on her own."

"No, she wouldn't."

"What happened?"

Matt took a swallow of his soft drink to give himself a moment. "What did Lori tell you?"

"She didn't elaborate, just said she transferred to North-western after her freshman year. My guess, Lori's too nice to say that you did something only a schmuck would do."

"There's no beating around the bush where you and Faith are concerned. Just point that knife and jab." He swirled the soft drink around in the can. "Yes, Lori is too nice." Matt stood.

"Why don't you just ask her out?"

"I did. She said no."

~

*L*ori looked up from her computer when Carrie walked into her office later that afternoon. "Can I talk to you?"

"I haven't changed my mind," Lori said, looking back at her computer screen.

"I didn't come about that," Carrie said, taking one of the chairs in front of her desk. "Are you any good at cracking passwords?"

"I'm horrible at cracking my own passwords, so I'm going to say no. Why?"

She held up a USB flash drive. "I can't get into this. Do you think you could try?"

"Where did it come from?"

"Oh, uh . . . I found it in my desk, but I can't remember the password."

Lori didn't want to stick a corrupt flash drive in her new computer. "Are you sure it's yours?"

"Of course."

"I'm no hacker. Why don't you take it down to the IT guy? Maybe he can help."

Carrie stood. "I don't want to get him involved. Maybe I'll remember the password."

"Sorry I couldn't help."

After Carrie left, she got caught up on research for a column and lost all track of time. When her stomach growled, she looked at her watch. No wonder she was hungry. It was past six.

Outside, fat, fluffy flakes of snow floated through the air, illuminated by the lights in the parking lot. She'd just reached her car when a truck pulled up next to her.

Matt climbed out, sending the butterflies that had taken a break since this morning into a frenzy. A week hadn't changed the fact that just seeing Matt still affected her.

"You're here late," he said.

"So are you."

"I got halfway home and remembered a file I need for a meeting Monday morning. Have you eaten?"

"No," she answered hesitantly.

"Good. Neither have I. Let me grab this file and we can get something together."

She scoffed. "Not after the dating discussion in the break-room this morning. I don't want us to be in the middle of that."

He stepped close and wiped a snowflake off her nose. "You're already in the middle of that."

"But the conversation just involved me. If someone sees us, the conversation will involve you, too."

"I don't care about office gossip. Come to dinner with me, and I promise not to say a word about your enticing breasts, at least not on the first date."

Lori couldn't suppress her smile. She ducked her head. "I shouldn't have told that story. It was inappropriate."

He lifted her face with an index finger. "But true."

"Sadly, yes." She studied him for a long moment. "If I say yes to dinner, it won't be a date."

"Right. That's what I meant to say."

She could be home in ten minutes, but she hadn't planned anything for dinner. Since the kids went back to college, she ate alone a lot. Why not go to dinner with Matt? She could keep it friendly. "Just two old friends catching up."

Matt lifted a brow. "Is that a yes?"

She looked at the snowflakes dancing in the light. "Yes," she said on an exhale.

He took her arm, walked her around his truck, and opened the passenger door.

"I thought you had to pick up a file," she said before climbing aboard.

"I'll get it later. I'm not giving you a chance to change your mind." He closed the door and went around the front of his truck.

In college, Matt's truck had been an old Ford with a bench seat and a rough ride. This one was sleek, steel gray with a dual-cab and leather seats.

"I won't change my mind," she said when he slid behind the wheel.

"Still not taking any chances," he said with a laugh.

She liked his laugh. She always had. "I can't stay late. I'm flying to LA in the morning and I haven't packed."

"LA?"

"Book signing."

He started the engine. "I imagine you hate every minute of book signings."

"I don't hate book signings. I just don't love the attention. It's fun meeting my readers, though."

"I can imagine you there." He pulled out of the parking lot. "Vietnamese, Mexican, or Italian?"

"Oh, tough choice. Let's go with Vietnamese."

"I know a great place."

He touched the phone icon on his dashboard and she settled into the seat, enjoying the heat swirling around her legs. The cab of the truck held his scent. Fresh, woodsy, with just a hint of sweet.

The radio played country music. Matt had turned her on to country, and she'd never left. Jim hated it. He was a 70s rock fan.

"Hey, Quyen, it's Matt Kelley. Got anything in about ten minutes?"

A woman's sultry voice came over the speaker. "We can make it work. Table for two?"

"Yes. Thank you."

Lori imagined Matt could call in favors all over town. Being a people person, he probably had many connections.

It didn't take long before they were in the Capitol Hill area of the city. Matt pulled into a parking lot and found a spot. "Wait."

She had to smile. Independent by nature, she always used to climb out before he could get around to her door. He said if his mother saw it happen, she'd box his ears for not being fast enough to help a lady out of the car.

Tonight she waited, and even savored the moment. Once

the kids reached double digits in age, she and Jim were rarely in a car together. It felt nice for someone else to be in charge, even if only for a couple of hours.

Matt helped her out, and she could feel the pressure of his hand on the small of her back as they went inside a small place by the name of Quang. The little restaurant was packed on a Friday night and smelled so tantalizing her stomach made all kinds of complaints. Luckily, the noise level in the restaurant was louder.

They were immediately greeted by a gorgeous woman with midnight black hair almost to her waist. She exchanged cheek kisses with Matt. They were both very discreet, but Lori suspected money changed hands before she led them to a table in a corner.

A waiter appeared immediately with glasses of water. "Welcome, Matt."

"Hi, Chi."

"Would you want the regular for starts?"

"That would be perfect. Thank you."

"You must come here often," Lori said when the waiter walked away.

"Phil and I eat lunch here a couple of times a month." Matt picked up the menu. "Mind if I order for us?"

"Not at all."

The waiter came back with a combination of appetizers and a salad.

Matt ordered drunken chicken, spicy green beans, and crab fried rice for two. Lori looked from the huge appetizer plate that held spare ribs, grilled asparagus, a bowl of noodles, and two egg rolls. "Is there someone else joining us?"

"No."

She laughed. "Matt, you ordered enough food for a party of six."

"I ordered the same things Phil and I get." He passed her a small plate and gestured toward the appetizers.

She put one of each of the choices on her plate. While she spread a napkin over her lap, Matt did the same.

"Finally, I have you all to myself. Tell me more about your kids."

Easy topic. "I might be a little biased, but they're the best kids in the whole wide world. They're smart and funny and kind—I hope they're kind."

Matt leaned forward, his blue eyes intent.

"Based on the majors they chose, they must be good students."

"Yes. I'm lucky to have two kids who like school and learning."

"What were your kids like when they were little?" Matt asked before taking a bite from a spare rib.

"Taylor was big-hearted with people and animals. He always had a smile on his face. Still does. Though he has a lot of friends, he's more of a homebody than Megan. Loved sports. Still does. Baseball is his favorite. He could entertain himself for hours with cars or puzzles or action figures. Megan was the opposite. She wanted your undivided attention at all times. She was a girly-girl who wore pink, lived pink, breathed pink. That's changed a little over the years. Megan also has lots of friends, is outgoing, and would rather do anything than stay home. Her sport of choice is soccer."

Matt's smile grew as she talked.

"This dressing is so good," she said, after taking a bite of salad. Heavy on the garlic, but she didn't have to worry about any kissing on this non-date.

"What was it like having twins?"

They'd talked about having kids and even twins when they dated. His dad was a twin, and her mom had twin sisters, so they ran in both families. Matt thought it would be great. She thought it would be busy. She'd proven them both right, and she loved every second of being a mom, from the moment she took a pregnancy test to present. "Pretty perfect."

When their dinner arrived, the dishes covered almost every inch of their table. Everything smelled so wonderful, Lori couldn't decide where to start.

"Dig in," Matt said.

"I'm afraid to. I'm so hungry, I might forget to chew."

"I won't tell anyone."

He grinned and her stomach dipped. No fair that he was still so magnificently handsome.

Two bites in, she decided to ask a question of her own. "Why didn't you ever marry and have children, Matt?"

He chuckled. "You don't want to hear the answer so early in our relationship."

She narrowed her eyes. "You mean our friendship."

"Yeah, that's what I meant." He winked and her stomach sank even further.

They ate in companionable silence for a few minutes. Lori tried to taste a little bit of everything.

"Where do you live?" she asked, realizing she didn't know.

He took a moment to chew and swallow. "I bought a fixer-upper in Woodinville. I've been working on it for six years."

"I didn't know you were a handyman."

Matt laughed. "I grew up on a farm. My dad had me wielding a hammer before I could walk."

She wiped her mouth with her napkin and took a sip of water. "Tell me about it."

"Come and see it."

She pressed her lips together and set her water glass down. "Maybe I will . . . one day," she said, without making eye contact.

CHAPTER 8

*L*ori kept their dinner conversation on safe ground. She asked about the house and he mentioned a few details. He'd enjoyed the physical labor, and it kept him busy on the weekends he didn't have to come into the city for work. He originally intended to sell the place when he finished, but now he wasn't so sure. The house and property had tripled in price thanks to the renovation.

After dinner, he drove her to the newspaper office to get her car, noting it was a crossover, so it should have 4-wheel drive, which she might need with the snowfall. Seattle might surpass their yearly average of 5.9 inches with this storm.

"Stay inside," he said, once he pulled up next to her vehicle. He grabbed his long-handled window scraper from the back seat and jumped out.

Of course she followed him, because Lori, still as independent as she'd been in college, would insist on helping. She even insisted on paying for half their dinner tonight. In her mind, that solidified their *non-date*.

She pulled up the hood on her coat, started her car with the remote, then reached into the back for another scraper.

"I'm not going to sit in your warm truck while you're out here cleaning my windows," she said when he sent her a stern look.

He didn't argue, since it would have been a waste of time. They worked around both ends of her car and ended up next to each other on the passenger side.

She looked up and met his gaze before brushing his shoulders off with one hand. "Don't forget your file."

"Thanks for the reminder."

"Thank you for the dinner invitation."

"I'll admit, I was surprised when you accepted."

She smiled. "Me too."

"I'm glad you did." He wiped a snowflake off her cheek. "Be careful on your drive. The roads are getting slick."

"I only live ten minutes away, but I'll drive like a grandma."

He snorted a laugh. That was something she used to say to him in college when he told her to drive carefully. He brushed a snowflake off her other cheek before his gaze dropped to her lips.

She pressed them together and held up a hand. "Don't you dare."

"You should know by now that I dare."

"We have to keep our relationship professional." She glanced nervously toward the office.

"Okay." He took a step back and ran his teeth over his bottom lip. *I'll give you a little more time before we make it personal.*

~

*M*onday morning dawned cold and bleak. Lori longed for spring, when she could work in the yard with the sun warming her face. Her yard in Chicago had been a labor of love from the beginning, and deeply satisfying—as well as beautiful.

This house had been remodeled a year earlier, but the owner stopped at the front yard, leaving the back for the new owner, and she couldn't wait to get started.

She fixed a cup of tea, slipped her coat on, and walked out onto her elevated deck.

"Good morning."

The greeting startled her so much she sloshed her tea.

"Sorry," said a man on the deck of the house next door. "I didn't mean to scare you."

"I didn't know anyone lived next door."

"I moved in yesterday. I came by to introduce myself last night, but you weren't home."

"I'm Lori Maguire."

He held up his hand. "Gage Farr."

"It's nice to meet you, Gage," she said, repeating his name so she'd remember. He had dark, curly hair, a slim nose, and a neatly trimmed mustache and goatee.

"You, too." He motioned between their houses. "We don't have much privacy."

"I don't mind if you don't." She shrugged. "Unless you have a problem with sacrifices under the solstice moon."

When his eyebrows raised, she smiled.

"Oh, you're kidding."

"Yes." She thumbed over her shoulder. "I have to get to work. Have a nice day."

"You, too." He waved as he headed inside himself.

As soon as she stepped inside her house phone rang. She smiled when she saw her daughter's name on caller ID. "Good morning, sweetheart."

"Hi, Mom. I just called to check in."

Lori loved the smile she heard in Megan's voice. "I'm glad you did. How was the first week of school?"

"Great. I only have one professor I can't stand."

Lori laughed at her dramatic kid. "What class?"

"Public speaking."

That might be brutal. "Sorry, honey. Other than that, everything is good?"

"I met someone," Megan said, after a pregnant pause.

Lori's breath caught. She loved watching her kids grow up and branch out as they got older. She loved that they were independent thinkers with goals. And she'd been waiting for the phrase, *I met someone.* So why did it make her short of breath? *First step toward not needing me anymore.*

"Tell me about him, honey."

"His name is Michael Chapman. He's a journalist major. I think he's the one."

Eek! Lori remembered that instant connection with Matt, something she'd never felt with any guy she'd dated before or since. "Wow. That's . . . wonderful."

Megan laughed. "I know that tone. I just freaked you out."

"Just a little. Only because you just met him. You've only been back on campus a week."

"How long did it take for you to know Dad was the one?"

"Longer than a week." *A lot longer.*

"Don't worry, Mom. We aren't running off to get married. We've only been out twice. I just feel so happy and wanted to share."

Lori took a deep breath. "If you're happy, I'm happy, sweetie."

"I've got to go. I just got to class. I love and miss you."

"Love and miss you too."

She stood at the kitchen sink for a long time, imagining her beautiful girl in a wedding gown. Her ex-husband would spend an exorbitant amount of money to assuage the guilt he felt for being an absent father. Every time he missed a game or school function, he opened his wallet, never understanding that the kids didn't want his money. They longed for his time, something the workaholic in him wasn't able to give.

*a*n hour later, Theresa entered Lori's office wearing wide-legged pumpkin-colored pants cinched at the ankles, and an open-crocheted, long-sleeve sweater with an ocean blue shirt underneath. Lori wished she could pull off that look with Theresa's natural ease. Instead, she'd come out looking like a bohemian wannabe.

"Morning," she said, taking one of the chairs in front of Lori's desk.

"Have I ever told you how much I love your style?" Lori asked.

"Once or twice, but you can tell me again. How did your book signing go?"

"How did you know about that?"

Theresa fingered one of two chokers around her neck. "A little birdie told me."

Besides her family, Matt was the only person she told. "What little birdie?"

"A different birdie than the one who saw you getting out of Matt's truck in the parking lot Friday night."

She'd been afraid someone would see them from the office windows.

Theresa eyed her. "You have a semi-guilty look on your face."

"I don't have a guilty look, semi or otherwise."

Theresa narrowed her eyes and studied Lori. "Yeah, you definitely have a guilty look. What's going on?"

"Matt and I went to dinner together. That's all. Two old friends catching up," she said, repeating Matt's phrase. She pointed at Theresa. "It's not what you think."

"How do you know what I think?"

"I can see it in your eyes."

Theresa crossed one leg over the other and picked up the picture of Lori's kids. "Who paid?"

"We both did."

"Is there going to be a next time?"

Lori shrugged. She had a nice time with Matt, but he'd been front and center in her thoughts ever since. Shrugging seemed safer than voicing her thoughts. "Who's the birdie?"

Theresa replaced the picture and stood. "I want details later."

"Details about what?" Phil asked from her doorway.

"Snitch for details," Lori countered with Theresa.

"Ah, I can't give up my stoolie."

Lori waved as Theresa disappeared.

"What are you two negotiating? Who snitched about what?"

She mimed turning a key near her lips and throwing it away. *Saved by the bell* popped into her head when her phone rang.

"*The Star*, Lori Maguire speaking."

"Lori, it's Denise. Can you come to Matt's office?"

"Give me five minutes." She wanted to finish the thought Theresa interrupted before she forgot.

Ten minutes later, when she turned the corner at Denise's desk, Matt was leaning against the door frame of his office, arms crossed, casually waiting. Just seeing him made her nervous. She waved to Denise as she passed her desk and stopped in front of him. "You wanted to see me?"

"That took longer than five minutes."

She glanced at her watch. "I was in the middle of a thought."

"Come in," he said, indicating with his head.

She entered his office and he followed, closing the door

behind them. One thing she'd learned since starting at the paper, Matt's door was rarely closed. Her turn to cross her arms. "Why did you do that?"

"Do what?"

"Close the door."

"So you'll relax and talk to me." He took her arm and led her to one of the chairs in front of his desk. He took the other.

"You shutting the door isn't going to make me relax. It's only going to make Denise curious." She crossed one leg over the other and Matt glanced at her bare knee. She pulled the hem of her dress down. "Matt."

"What?" he asked innocently.

"What do you need to see me about?"

"Your interview. Phil and Dale will be here in a few minutes."

"I could have used some warning." She didn't enjoy talking about herself, and Phil was guaranteed to make the interview as uncomfortable as possible—just for fun. She smoothed a hand down her green knit dress. Good thing she'd worn a color she felt comfortable in.

"Sorry. I leave tomorrow for a conference all week. Then I'll be in Astoria for a few days while my dad has surgery."

"Is he okay?"

"Yeah, it's nothing serious, but Mom will need help moving him around."

"I hope his surgery goes well." She might as well get another topic in the open. "Someone saw us on Friday."

Matt captured her hand and held on when she tried to pull away. He rested his elbows on his knees and looked into her eyes. "Lori, there is nothing wrong with two friends having dinner together."

"Except for two things. I don't want to be part of the

office rumor mill, and I don't want anyone thinking I'm getting preferential treatment because we're *old friends*."

He started drawing circles on her palm with the pad of his thumb. She looked from his eyes to their joined hands.

"Office gossip won't hurt either of us."

"You say that because you're numb to it."

"Ouch," he said with a frown.

She was immediately sorry she'd said that aloud, yet, she'd also heard the rumors. Plus, she had firsthand experience.

"You're going to draw blood if you chew on your bottom lip much harder."

Lori stopped chewing and tried to tug her hand free.

His gaze dropped from her eyes to her mouth and he leaned forward.

Tap, tap, tap. "Matt, Phil and Dale are here," Denise said.

Lori jerked her hand away and jumped to her feet.

~

*M*att dropped his head and growled under his breath.

"Are we interrupting?" Phil said, bursting through the door.

"Nope." Matt pushed to his feet, frustration leaking out of him.

"Nuts." Phil glanced from Lori's red cheeks to Matt, then turned to the *Star's* chief photographer, who carried in a camera and a stool. "I don't know, Dale. I think if Denise hadn't announced us, we might have interrupted something."

"You're not interrupting, Phil," Lori said.

Dale held out his hand. "I haven't met you yet, Lori. I'm Dale Benlow."

"Hi, Dale."

He set the stool near the window and beckoned Lori over. "I like the light in this room."

Lori perched on the stool and let Dale turn her slightly to the right.

"Be sure and get some leg in the shot, Dale." Phil grinned when Lori flashed her green eyes. He pulled a chair close and flipped open a notebook. "So, Lori, who was your first love?"

Matt had to smile at the shot Dale took when Lori's mouth dropped open.

"Come on, Lori, the public wants to know. You know it was me, and I know it was me, but our readers are in the dark. And you don't have to worry about Faith. She understands I'm irresistible."

Dale pointed a finger between them. "You two used to date."

"No," she stated.

"But she's carried a torch for me since kindergarten." Phil looked from Dale to her. "I promise I won't slant the *whole* story toward me."

Matt chuckled.

If looks could kill, Lori would have reduced Phil to a pile of cinders. "Ask me a real question or I'm going back to work."

Dale lifted her chin with a finger and took a shot.

Lori glanced at him. "I have headshots I can give you."

Matt shook his head. "Let Dale get something new."

After a few more shots, Matt held out his hand for the camera. "Let me see what you've gotten so far."

Dale was lead photographer for a reason. He'd captured the essence of the Lori Matt remembered from college in several shots. In one, Dale caught her leaning forward with a sweet smile.

"Let's use this one." He held the camera out for Lori to

see. After glancing at the picture, she met his gaze and nodded.

"This is the one. Thank you, Dale." He handed the camera back. "Phil, you're up. You have thirty minutes before lunch. Time to get serious."

"I am serious."

"Phil."

Huffing out an exaggerated breath, Phil hunched in his chair and lifted his pencil. "What made you want to be a writer, Ms. Maguire?" he asked in a monotone.

~

*L*ori went from Matt's office to the breakroom to get her salad out of the fridge.

After Phil's questions frazzled her nerves, she needed some quiet time in her office. Matt sat through the entire interview with zero expression while she kept fantasizing what might have happened if Phil and Dale hadn't arrived when they did. If he'd tried to kiss her, would she have let him? She'd like to think she was smarter than that, but wasn't sure.

Carrie sat at a table facing the door, looking forlorn, so Lori detoured over and pulled out a chair. "Why so gloomy?"

Carrie held up a flash drive.

"Is that the same one you showed me last week?"

"Yes. I still can't get in."

"Did you ask Frank down in IT?"

"Yes. He said getting in would be almost impossible and he didn't have the time."

"You found the flash drive in your desk and you have no idea what's on it?"

Carrie nodded.

Lori held out her hand, and Carrie furnished a standard

USB with a red slide. No brand name or marking. "I get the feeling you're not telling me everything."

"Ah, just the two I was looking for," Theresa said, breezing in. "Want to go out to lunch? I didn't bring anything."

Carrie took the USB from Lori and slipped it into her pocket. "Sure. Where are we going?"

"Did I hear someone say we're going out to lunch?" Phil asked, slipping into the chair next to Lori.

"I'm positive no one invited you," Carrie said.

"Matt, we're going to lunch with the ladies," Phil said when Matt walked in.

"Great." He glanced at Lori. "The dean of UW's fine arts department just called. The university has a visiting artist here for winter semester. The dean asked if the paper would interview the guy. Your column coincides with the art world so I think you should talk to him."

"I've never conducted an interview."

Matt shrugged. "Then don't interview him. Do what you do for your column."

Lori bit her lip. Something new and different to try. "Okay."

"Would this afternoon be convenient if the guy's available?"

"This afternoon is fine. Does *the* guy have a name?"

Matt rubbed a finger under his lower lip. "Uh, Grant or Grange. Something like that."

"I need to get my purse before we go," Carrie said, standing.

Phil hopped up from his chair. "We'll meet back here in ten."

Once he moved, Lori was able to scoot out. She glanced at Theresa. "Thanks for the invite, but I brought my lunch."

"You're not going?" Matt asked.

Lori wasn't about to spend another overcharged hour with Matt and Phil. She pulled her salad out of the fridge. "Not today."

"You have to come with us," Theresa said.

Nope. I don't. "Have fun."

In the office, she ate her salad standing at the window. From there she could see the parking lot, and she watched Theresa, Carrie, Matt, and Phil head out under a sky overcast with heavy-bottomed clouds.

Just as they were climbing into Phil's SUV, Matt looked up. He and his healthy ego would think she was watching for him. *Admit it, Lori. That's exactly what you were doing.* Instead of turning away, she saluted by holding up her salad. So many windows on this side of the building faced the parking lot. Who'd seen them come back here after dinner and told Theresa?

Matt slid into the passenger seat and closed the door.

Two hours later, she was pondering what she should ask a visiting artist when Matt stepped through her door. A dark-haired man stopped at the threshold.

"Lori, this is—"

"My new neighbor," she said standing.

"Lori," Gage said, relief showing on his face. "It's nice to see a familiar face."

She came around her desk and shook his extended hand. "What a crazy coincidence."

"You already know each other?" Matt asked.

"We met this morning via our back decks," Lori said.

"Huh. That is a coincidence. Gage is the visiting artist I told you about earlier."

"Oh, really?"

"That's me," Gage said, flashing a smile.

Lori waved to one of the chairs in front of her desk. "Have a seat and we'll get started."

~

"Mind if I stay for a minute?" Matt didn't like the interest he saw in Gage's eyes or the fact that he and Lori were neighbors.

"I don't mind," Lori said. "Do you, Gage?"

"Not at all." He took a seat as Lori went around her desk. Matt sat in the other chair.

"Start by telling me a little about yourself."

Gage said he was from North Carolina, owned a gallery, and his parents were both artists. His mom painted with any medium available. His dad worked with clay and junk.

"Junk," Lori said with a laugh.

Matt stopped listening after that. He watched her animated expressions while she and Gage talked. Though she jotted a few things down on a piece of paper, he could tell she was taking more mental notes than physical ones.

The combination of Lori and Gage's comfortable rapport and them living next to each other made Matt nervous.

CHAPTER 9

Matt wasn't sure how his call would be received, but he scrolled to Lori's cell number anyway.

He hadn't seen her for almost three weeks. After the editors' conference in Vegas, he'd gone to Astoria to help his mom following his dad's hernia surgery and ended up staying an extra week when his dad got an infection.

"Son, do you want another piece of pie?" his mom asked, coming out of the kitchen.

"No, I can barely move as it is, Mom."

She sat next to him on the sofa. "I bet you're anxious to get back to the paper, especially now Lori's there."

Though he hadn't told his mom much—because there wasn't much to tell—she brought up Lori's name every chance she got. "Are you sure you'll be okay if I head back to Seattle tomorrow?"

"I have your brother and both sisters close by if I need help. You didn't need to stay this long."

"I don't mind, Mom. And I can stay longer if you need me. It's been a while since I was able to help." He only lived a little over three hours away, but didn't get home as often as he should.

"Well, I appreciate you being here, and so does your dad." She stuffed a pillow behind her back. "Now, tell me about Lori."

"Haven't we already covered this?"

"We haven't covered anything yet. I want all the details. I looked up her website, so I know she's still as pretty as she was in college. Is it hard working around her?"

"No. And yes."

"I also read that she's divorced."

He smiled. No deflecting his mom tonight. "For about three years. She has two kids in college. She bought a small house in Seattle. As you know, she writes books that appear to be very successful. She seems happy. Everyone at work likes her. She's pleasant to be around. Her laugh is as easy as it was in college. Phil grew up around the corner from her, and they have a cozy friendship that I envy. We've been to dinner together once, but she insisted on paying half so she could say it wasn't a date."

"She's going to make you work for it this time."

He chuckled. "She made me work for it the first time. I asked her out for two weeks before I finally tricked her into a date. She wouldn't be Lori if she made things easy."

"You *tricked* her into a date?"

Matt set his phone aside and settled in to tell his mom the story about buying eight movie tickets.

~

*L*ori walked into her office, but stopped short when she spotted another small bouquet sitting on her desk. The card simply read **Happy Valentine's Day**. She bent to smell one of the pink lilies that were interspersed with white roses. The card was unsigned, but she knew the flowers were from Matt. She'd only seen him in passing since he'd been back, but he'd called her three times over the past four weeks. Their conversations were fun and flirty and left her anticipating the next one.

Lori glanced at her watch. Denise always went to the breakroom around nine-thirty, so Lori worked on her column, checking the time on her computer repeatedly as the minutes ticked by. At nine-thirty, she made the trek to Matt's office. Denise wasn't at her desk and she found Matt sitting with his back to the door, looking out the window. Lori could see clouds shifting in the distance.

"Good morning, Matt."

He turned his chair and stood with a grin. "I was hoping you'd stop by. Come in."

She shook her head. "Thank you for the beautiful flowers, but you have to stop."

"Someone gave you flowers again?" Matt strolled to where she stood, took her hand, and pulled her into his office, shutting the door behind her.

"You have to stop doing that, too." She reached for the handle, but he stopped her.

"Absolutely not."

She didn't put up a fight as he led her to the sofa. "Matt, it doesn't look right for a boss to give an employee flowers. And if Denise comes back and sees your door closed with me inside for the third time, she'll get suspicious—if she isn't already."

He tugged her down on a leather cushion next to him, ignoring the point she was trying to make.

"I don't want to be the topic of gossip around the office."

"Why are you so sure anyone would care enough to gossip?" He stretched his arm along the back of the sofa, inviting her closer with his eyes.

She shook her head and stayed perched on the edge of her seat. "It's human nature."

Matt took her hand. "What gossip have you heard about me?"

"Are you sure you want to know?"

"I wouldn't have asked if I didn't."

"I've heard that you aren't a lonely bachelor. You seem to travel from woman to woman every three or four months."

Matt frowned.

"As soon as a woman starts to get serious, you move on. You've dated every *single* woman from the Canadian border to Oregon. You usually go for leggy, well-endowed women" —a blush burned her cheeks—"and brunettes are the popular choice, but—"

"Okay, I get the idea." Matt's frown turned to a scowl. "No wonder you're scared to go out with me."

"I'm not scared. I don't want to be counted among Matt Kelley's harem. You were always surrounded by girls in college. Sounds like that hasn't changed."

"This is for you, Lori." His scowl disappeared and he lifted her hand to his lips and kissed the sensitive skin on the inside of her wrist. "I've never kissed another woman here."

Her heartbeat fluttered like a flock of birds were trying to burst free.

"Let me take you to dinner for Valentine's Day."

She tugged her hand free, and walked to the door on unsteady legs. "No more flowers, Matt," she said before leaving his office, grateful to see Denise's desk still empty.

Once she got to her office, she struggled to keep her mind on work. Luckily, she managed to get a couple of columns ahead while Matt was out of town. Eventually he would tire of asking her out. He was a ladies' man and wouldn't be alone for long.

Theresa walked into her office. "Hey."

"Hey, yourself."

"You got flowers."

"So did you. I saw the bouquet John sent you. It's gorgeous."

"Who sent these?" Theresa bent to smell a white rose. "Let me guess. An old friend?"

Lori wondered how much Theresa knew. Had Matt talked to her? "Good guess."

"Want to have dinner with me and John tonight?"

"No!" Lori exclaimed with a laugh. "My friend and her husband pity me, so much they invite me to join them for Valentine's Day dinner." Lori grabbed a sticky note and started scribbling. "I can get a column out of this. Names will be changed to protect the pathetic."

"Who's pathetic?" Phil asked, sticking his head around the corner.

"Lori."

"I don't think you're pathetic. Are you sad because you don't have a Valentine?" He slipped into the chair next to Theresa. "You can come over to our house and have dinner with me and Faith."

"I don't want to have dinner with either of you," Lori replied, laughing.

Theresa stood. "I've got to get back to work."

"I, on the other hand, have all afternoon to talk about your pathetic life, so you have plenty of time to tell me who sent the flowers." Phil leaned back in his chair and stretched out his long legs.

Theresa stopped at the door and glanced back at Lori. "Are you sure about dinner?"

"I'm positive, but thanks for thinking of me."

She glanced at Phil. "I hope you did something extra special for Faith. She deserves a medal for putting up with you."

"As a matter of fact, I have a very special evening planned for my beautiful bride. She gets to spend the whole night with me. We'll be watching a very important basketball game on TV." He flashed a grin when she laughed. "I've already ordered my favorite pizza, and I bought a candle, so we can turn the lights low. Nobody can say I don't know how to romance my woman."

Lori wiped the laugh-tears from the corners of her eyes. "The saddest part is, I believe your every word."

Carrie stopped at the door. "What's so funny? I could hear you laughing from my desk."

"I'd like to know, too," Phil replied, trying to look hurt. "Faith's in for a treat. I plan on wearing my sexiest red boxer briefs."

The picture of Phil lounging on the sofa in red, his skinny legs white as the winter snow was more than Lori could handle. She covered her face with her hands, trying to get control of her giggles. How cute little Faith put up with this tall, lanky goofball was beyond her. Probably because he was too loveable to stay mad at. She hoped he was kidding, but she could easily imagine him doing exactly what he said. She peeked through her fingers. Phil was grinning from ear to ear.

"You're awful." She jerked a tissue out of the box on her desk and wiped her eyes.

"What did you do to her, Phil? She can't catch her breath." Carrie pulled out another tissue and handed it to Lori.

"I told her about the special Valentine's evening I have planned for Faith. I'm not sure what she finds so amusing. Me in my sexiest briefs, basketball on the TV, and the finest pizza in town."

The tissue Lori ran under her eyes came away black with mascara. "Faith is in for a special treat tonight. I have a comfortable bed in my guest room, ready and waiting for when she kicks you out."

"Pizza and basketball, Phil?" Carrie asked.

"You betcha. All my favorite things." Phil waggled his eyebrows. "I'm gettin' lucky tonight."

"Shouldn't Valentine's Day be about some of *her* favorite things?" Carrie asked.

"*I'm* her favorite thing."

Lori had to cover her face as another bout of giggles bubbled up.

"Well, I did my good deed for the day. I came in here to cheer Lori up. She doesn't have a date for Valentine's Day." When Lori composed herself enough to glare at him, he winked.

Confusion crossed Carrie's brow. "Then who sent you flowers?"

"I sent the flowers to cheer her up. I also invited her to join me and Faith for dinner tonight, but she declined." Phil looked at Lori. "Red briefs"—he waved a hand down his body—"that's all I'm saying."

"As hard as it is to turn that offer down, I'll leave you and your Valentine's briefs for Faith." Lori threw a cork coaster at him. "Now get out of here."

He stood up and Carrie followed him to the door. "If any of you happen to talk to Faith, don't tell her. I want tonight to be a big surprise."

"Oh, I'm sure she'll be surprised," Carrie said sarcastically.

Lori dabbed at her eyes after they left, trying to remember the last time she and Jim spent Valentine's Day together. She usually fixed a nice dinner that she shared with the kids. Jim would walk in late and hand her a box with an expensive piece of jewelry that his secretary probably picked out or he ordered last minute online. She might get a kiss on the cheek and a "I got stuck at the office." But she knew *stuck at the office* was his choice.

Hours later, Lori walked into her house through the kitchen door and immediately kicked off her heels. She carried them to her bedroom closet and traded work clothes for a pair of comfy pants, a soft pink sweater, and thick socks. In the bathroom she brushed, then braided her hair. She went into her office and opened her laptop to check email messages. Scrolling through them, she decided there was nothing that couldn't wait until after dinner.

Before she could pull out salad fixings, someone knocked on her front door. No one she knew said they were stopping by tonight. As soon as she turned toward the living room, she spotted the top of Matt's head through the panes of glass on her door.

She opened it about twelve inches and peered up at him. "What are you doing here?"

"Is that any way to greet a guest?" He looked her up and down, then grinned. "Camouflage cargo is an article of clothing I never thought I'd see Lori Maguire wearing. You even look sexy in camouflage."

"What are you doing here?" she repeated.

"I didn't think you should be alone on Valentine's Day. I bring a peace offering," he replied, holding out a handled bag.

She looked from him to the bag.

"Are you going to invite me in, or make me stand on the porch to eat? It's a little cold out here."

She opened the door wider and caught a whiff of whatever he'd brought as a peace offering. Her stomach growled. "You can come in, but only because I'm starving and whatever you brought smells amazing."

She took the bag while he shrugged out of his coat and toed off his boots.

He opened the door of the entry closet and hung up his

coat. That simple gesture made the butterflies in her stomach take flight. Matt was the kind of guy who'd make himself at home whether she liked it or not. A small, insignificant act, but so Matt.

"I have a friend who owns an Italian restaurant. He set me up with a dinner he said would make even an obstinate woman smile. By the way, I love the front porch swing."

"Thanks. It came with the house. And I'm not obstinate."

"Uh-huh." He glanced around the living room. "Your home is nice, Lori. There's been a lot of renovating going on in this part of town."

"I got lucky the previous owners renovated last year."

"Can I have a tour before dinner?"

"As you can see," she said, waving a hand. "This is the living room." She pointed to an arched opening behind her. "The dining room is through there. And this is the kitchen." She set the bag on the countertop.

Matt followed along. He'd changed into jeans and a blue sweater that enhanced the color of his eyes.

She led him down a short hall and flipped on a light. "Guest bedroom, bathroom, and master bedroom."

Last, Lori showed him her office. She could tell he liked the gold by his expression.

"It looks good."

"Thank you."

"Where did you find the desk?"

She was still proud of her secondhand find. Jim hated the desk because it was used. "I bought it at an auction in a downtown Chicago law office."

"It's in great condition. How old is it?"

"Around 1890," she said when Matt ran his hand over the top.

"Your whole place is very nice."

Lori shrugged. She wasn't sure why his approval meant so

much to her, but it did. Maybe because a lifetime ago they talked about features they'd want in *their* home. This little bungalow had none of the huge family spaces or the over-the-bed, stargazing skylight they discussed. "It's small, but it suits me. I don't need much."

"Both the kitchen and your office have doors leading outside?"

"To a deck." She opened the office door and he stepped outside.

He pointed. "Is that where Gage lives?"

"Yes."

He shut and locked the door while she closed her laptop, sure she wouldn't get to any emails tonight.

Last she led him down to the finished basement.

He looked around the large room filled with pool table, workout equipment, and an oversized sofa. "Nice pool table," he said running his hand over the elegant wood.

"It came with the divorce."

Matt glanced down at her, his expression softening. "Do you play?"

She nodded.

Matt lifted an eyebrow. "Are you any good?"

"I can hold my own."

He smiled at her answer. "When did you start playing pool?"

"My kids invited their friends over to play quite often."

"We'll have to play someday."

"Anytime."

"That sounds like a challenge, and you know how I love a challenge." Matt pulled on her braid and offered one of his wicked grins.

"There's another bathroom on that side of the room," she said pointing to a door.

He nodded and turned toward another opening. "A kitchen?"

"I think the previous owners must have rented the basement out. This is a bedroom," she said, flipping a light on around a corner. "The laundry room is through the kitchen."

"This is very nice, Lori."

"Thank you." She could tell he liked her space by his expression. "Are you ready to eat?"

"Yes. I'm starved, too."

"Plates or pasta bowls?" she asked when they returned to the kitchen upstairs.

"I'm not sure," Matt replied. "Let's see what we've got here."

The bag held mushroom ravioli and penne with lobster sauce, warm breadsticks, and two fresh salads with Italian dressing.

"This looks wonderful."

Matt dished up the pasta while Lori put the salads in two bowls, which she carried to the dining room table. She lit two candles and went back into the kitchen to get the breadsticks, napkins, and two glasses of water. Matt turned out the light she'd flipped on earlier.

"What are you doing?"

"It's Valentine's Day. It's supposed to be romantic." He held her chair, then sat across the table from her.

She smiled. "Thank you, Matt. This is really sweet of you."

"You're welcome."

"Can I ask you a question?" she asked, spreading a napkin over her lap.

"You can ask me anything."

"Why are you doing this?"

"Doing what?"

"This," she gestured with her hand. "All of this. Why are you asking me out and bringing me dinner?"

He looked down at his salad for long enough that Lori thought he might not answer, then he set his fork aside and met her gaze. "You asked me the same question a few weeks ago, and I told you it was too early in our relationship for you to hear the answer. Are you ready to hear it now?"

Was she? Just hearing him say *our relationship* again left her a little breathless. She nodded.

"I've never met another woman who affects me the way you do. You make my heart pound and my palms sweat. You make me tongue-tied. Why do you think that is?"

Lori bit her bottom lip while her own heartbeat thumped against her ribs. She didn't know what to do with the information. Despite what happened in college, Matt had never given her a reason to doubt his word. "You've never been tongue-tied a day in your life."

"Oh no? I've never been more tongue-tied than I was the day I interviewed you."

She picked up her fork and speared a strip of carrot. "You didn't seem tongue-tied to me."

"Even Dave asked what my problem was while I stood at the window watching you walk up the street."

"You watched?"

"Of course I watched," he said with a chuckle. "I wanted to follow."

He pulled his pasta bowl close.

So did she.

"I never thought I'd see you again. When I walked into Dave's office, I couldn't believe my eyes. Lori Maguire standing in front of me. And then I noticed you were using your maiden name and not wearing a wedding ring. Did you see me look?"

"Yes."

"You looked too."

She felt the color on her cheeks bloom as his devilish smile appeared.

"If you hadn't applied at the paper, I wouldn't have known you'd moved back."

"Would that be such a bad thing?" she asked, tearing a breadstick in two and holding half out for him.

"It would be for me." He took the breadstick from her. "I like to think I'll eventually knock down the barricades you've built."

She bit into the fresh, yeasty bread. "Can I ask you another question?"

"Anything."

"Why didn't you ever marry?"

"I just told you, there's never been another woman who affects me the way you do." He picked up his fork and speared a ravioli. "Now I get to ask a question."

Lori forked a piece of penne. "You can ask, but I don't promise to answer."

"It's more of a request. Tell me about your divorce."

"Jim and I grew apart over the years."

"You divorced because you grew apart."

She picked up her glass of water and held it between both hands. "Jim is a workaholic, married to his job, and I ended up a single parent for most of our marriage. Once the kids were in high school, we didn't have much left to say to each other."

She took a sip but held the glass to keep her hands occupied. "I think we started to grow apart as soon as the kids were born. Jim was a wonderful provider, and I know he loved us in his way, but he didn't know how to be a father. His parents are stiff and stuffy and proper, and I don't think Jim knew any other way. He never played with the kids, and very seldom interacted with them other than to ask about their classes and grades."

"How did it end?"

"The first day of the kids' senior year, Jim came home from the office early. I remember being so shocked. I could count on one hand the number of times he came home early. I was in the kitchen, wondering what to cook for dinner." A chill had run up her spine. She thought maybe he was sick or had some awful news about his parents. "He stopped next to the island and announced that he'd met someone. I laughed because he said it so matter-of-factly, like someone might suggest green beans rather than corn for a side at dinner."

Matt's jaw bulged like he was grinding his teeth.

She reached across the table and touched his hand. "He hadn't been cheating, or he would have told me. If nothing else, Jim is truthful to a fault. He'd just met someone else and was done being married to me."

That day was still so clear in her mind. Sun shining, the kids were with friends. She remembered thinking *I should feel something. Sad or hurt or upset.* But she didn't feel anything except relief that he was the one who finally made the decision they probably should have made years earlier.

"He packed his bags and left." Her attorney settled on a ridiculous amount of money, more than she could spend in a lifetime. Money that she didn't need, but Jim insisted. She imagined it assuaged his feelings of guilt. Money had been Jim's answer to the meaning of life. It meant more to him than his family. So she took her share and bought this modest house, putting the rest in a trust for future grandchildren.

"What about your kids?"

"Jim set up trust funds for them years ago. They have more than they'll ever need.

"The divorce was easy for us. Not so easy for the kids. Luckily, they were older. I think the very saddest part was that Jim had been gone for a week before I cried." She sat silent for a moment, then added, "I didn't cry because Jim left. I cried because I *didn't* cry when Jim left."

"How is the relationship between your kids and their dad?"

"Strained. Like I said, Jim was a great provider. He made sure we had everything money could buy, but he just couldn't give what we needed most. He missed all the important moments. The kids' first steps and words, their games, and school performances. He almost missed their high school graduation because of some important project at work."

"And your relationship with him now?"

"We don't have any reason to communicate at all. I imagine the next time I see or talk to him will be when Megan and Taylor graduate in a year and a half. Or at one of their weddings."

"Why did you marry him?" he asked after several heartbeats.

She felt her smile wobble. Ten different answers ran through her mind. Which one to use? She exhaled a shaky breath. "I fell in love. Jim was very different before we had kids."

"Were you happy?"

She looked him in the eye. "At first, yes."

CHAPTER 10

*D*espite Lori's protests, Matt helped her clean up after dinner. They got the dishes in the dishwasher and the leftovers put in the fridge. He wasn't ready to leave yet, so he took her hand and led her into the dark living room, the two candles flickering on the dining table the only light.

"Where are we going?"

"To relax." Sitting on the middle cushion of the sofa, he tugged her down next to him, but not too close. He initiated a conversation about work, and they discussed some of the people at the office. He told her a story that made her laugh.

He loved the sound, and loved knowing she was comfortable enough to lower her reserve around him. Leaning his head back, he closed his eyes.

"Does it bother you to know what people in the office say about you?"

He reached for her, but she scooted as far away as the arm of the sofa would allow. Without looking, he knew she sat huddled in the corner like a scared rabbit. He let his hand fall to the sofa. "You're going to make this as hard as possible, aren't you?"

"Make what as hard as possible?"

"Me and you."

She shifted. "You didn't answer my question."

He opened his eyes and stared at the shadows made by the candles in the next room. "No, it doesn't bother me to hear what they're saying, because it's true. What bothers me is that you're hearing it. I've never tried to hide the way I've lived my life, so of course people are going to talk." He glanced at her. "And I never felt ashamed of my lifestyle until you moved back to town."

Her brow puckered in a frown, and she brought her knees up to her chest. "Why would me moving to Seattle make you ashamed of the way you're living your life?"

He smiled before he reached out and wrapped a hand around one of her ankles. "There've only been two people in this world who make me want to be a better person—a better man. Only two people's opinions have mattered to me. My mom and you." He slowly pulled her foot across his lap.

She didn't resist as she watched him carefully. "What about your dad?"

"My dad might not approve of my lifestyle, but he'd never castigate me because of it."

"Your lifestyle is none of my business, Matt."

"You say that on the outside while cringing on the inside. I know you, Lori. I know the way you think. Sure, it's been twenty-four years, but you haven't changed in that regard, and I'm glad. That's one of the things I loved most about you. Your old-fashioned ways."

He took a deep breath of his own. "I've never apologized for my stupidity after spring break. What I did was inexcusable, and I'm sorry I hurt you."

"That was a long time ago, Matt."

"I know, but I haven't lived through many days, especially now you're home, that I don't wish—"

"The past is the past. You have nothing to apologize for."

He started to massage her foot. Her knee-jerk reaction was to pull away, but he was ready. "I won't tickle, I promise."

"I can't help it."

Her calf trembled under his touch. "Trust me, Lori."

After thirty seconds of rubbing, the line between her brows disappeared and her calf muscle relaxed under his fingers. Instead of sitting upright, she leaned into the cushions. This was how he'd envisioned his future when they were in college—until he mucked everything up.

He knew if he left her alone, her tension would disappear, but he couldn't. He grasped her other ankle, pleased when she let him pull her foot across his lap.

"A minute ago, you said I was going to make me and you as hard as possible, but I don't fit your female MO." Her gaze drifted from his hands to his face. "Mile-long legs, well-endowed, brunette."

"I never date a woman under five-six. I never date a woman with curly, strawberry-blonde hair. I never date a woman with green eyes, because those things would have reminded me of you and I didn't want to be reminded. When you take away those features, people assume I prefer women with long legs and dark hair. Not sure where the well-endowed comes from."

She gasped when he pulled her close enough that her bottom touched his thigh. He gently unwound the band holding her braid and slipped his fingers through from bottom to top until her hair hung loose.

"What I prefer is a profusion of red-gold curls, shorter legs, and mesmerizing green eyes. I'll ignore that they're flashing dangerously at me right now."

His gaze dropped to her lips, and he pushed his luck by

wrapping a hand around the back of her neck and pulling her close enough to taste. He pressed his lips to hers in a soft, warm kiss.

When she placed her hand on his jaw, he cradled her closer and moved his lips to her neck. He kissed the tender spot behind her earlobe and triggered the throaty moan he'd never forgotten. He returned to her waiting lips, his heart pounding at the speed of a freight train. The hand on his jaw moved into his hair and he pulled at her bottom lip lightly with his teeth.

"Matt," she whispered. "I can't breathe."

"We'll breathe later, darlin'." His lips met hers again. He wanted her more than he'd ever wanted anything in his life. He wanted a second chance. He wanted to prove he was the only man for her, that they were meant to be together.

~

*L*ori leaned away and dragged in a shaky breath, trying to rein in her emotions. Why had she always felt so safe in Matt's arms? And why did this moment feel so right after all these years? He nudged her head against his chest where she could hear and feel his heart pounding as hard as hers.

Could she trust he wouldn't break her in two after three months, or six, or nine? She didn't think she could go through that kind of hurt again.

He released his hold when she pushed away and glanced at his watch.

"My cue to go. I have to drive to Astoria to check on my dad in the morning."

Her heart sank just a little, but she pushed up from the sofa and held out her hand to help him up. He turned what had started out as a lonely Valentine's Day into a pretty spectacular evening. She could still feel the pressure of his lips against hers, still feel the brush of his whiskers on her neck. Memories of tonight would haunt her dreams.

"How is your dad?"

"Better. Going home will give the rest of the tribe a break."

She headed for the kitchen to get the bag of leftovers. "Thank you for dinner. It was delicious."

"You keep that," he said holding up a hand.

"No, it would take me a week to eat all of this." She followed him into the front room and took his coat out of the closet, remembering her thoughts from two and a half hours earlier.

He slipped the soft suede over his shoulders, then swiftly pulled her against him. "I'm going to win you over, Lori Maguire."

She'd always admired his confidence. She smiled up at him, letting him hold her, because no matter how much she fought the idea, it still felt good to be near him, to look into his beautiful eyes and feel his breath across her cheek.

Prove to me you're in this for keeps this time, Matthew Kelley.

He kissed the tip of her nose. "Eventually you'll say yes."

"Please, drive safely."

Dipping his head, he smiled. "So you do care about me."

"You know I do."

She watched until his truck disappeared down the street, then slowly closed the door. After blowing out the candles, she made her way into her office. The house was too quiet. She missed the noise and confusion twins had brought into her and Jim's very ordered life. He hadn't been as thrilled.

Though he loved his kids, Jim didn't like seeing toys strewn around or her leaving dirty dishes in the sink while she rocked a baby to sleep.

Matt would have been a completely different father. He

would have been hands-on. She could picture him washing the dishes while she nursed one baby and then rocking that one to sleep while she nursed the other.

Not Jim. He'd gone into the other room and shut the door to block out the cries.

She opened the bottom drawer of her desk and lifted out a photo album. It had lain forgotten in a box at the top of her closet since college. During her move, she'd come across the album, but instead of opening the pages, she stuck it in the bottom drawer.

Flipping the cover open, she heaved a shaky sigh at the first picture of her and Matt, taken at the University of Washington's homecoming, him in a suit, her in a long dress. The photographer wanted them to pose a certain way, but Matt had turned her face to his just as the picture was snapped. They were smiling, gazing into each other's eyes. She'd already fallen in love by then, something she'd never experienced before.

She'd been terrified and overwhelmed with excitement at the same time. Being with Matt was—she searched for the right description—exhilaratingly terrifying. He was a big man on campus, the football quarterback, and she was a nobody.

The next picture showed Matt sitting on a bale of hay with her on his lap. They'd gone on a haunted hayride with a group of friends. She'd screamed as bats swooped out of trees and werewolves jumped onto the back of the wagon. At one point she grabbed onto him so suddenly, she almost knocked them both off the bale of hay.

He'd laughed. "You can't push me back any farther, baby, or we'll both fall off the wagon."

"Just don't let go of me."

"I won't, darlin'," he'd said close to her ear, right before biting her neck.

When she looked at him, he'd widened innocent eyes. "What? It's Halloween."

She screamed and turned her face into his chest when a zombie grabbed her ankle. He responded by wrapping his strong arms around her and whispering, "Kiss me, Lori."

And she did.

He finally drew away enough to look into her eyes. "I love you, Lori."

She'd been so shocked to learn he felt the same way. "I love you too."

Running a finger over the picture, she let the memories flood her mind and heart and senses. She didn't need a photo album to remind her of that night and their promises of love.

Lori jumped when the phone rang, but knew it was Matt without checking caller ID. "Did you make it home safely?"

"I did."

She smiled. "Thanks again for dinner, Matt. You made Valentine's Day very special."

"Thanks for letting me in. I was afraid you wouldn't."

"That's not true," she said, touching the smile on Matt's face in the picture. "You knew I'd let you in or you wouldn't have come."

"I was pretty sure, but not positive."

She could hear the smile in his voice.

"Did I interrupt you?"

"Not me, just a memory."

"What memory?"

Should she admit she'd kept a photo album of them after all these years? She decided to share the memory only. "The night we went on the hayride."

Matt chuckled. "You mean the night you were clinging onto my neck so tight you cut off all circulation to my brain." He paused a moment. "I haven't thought about that night since . . . last Halloween."

She laughed at his admission. "Me either."

"Are you just saying that?"

Deciding to keep the answer to that question to herself, too, she said, "Good night, Matt," before hanging up the phone.

~

*M*onday morning Lori left her house early and merged onto I-5 headed north to Snohomish. She pulled into her parents' driveway fifty minutes later. Her father waved from the front porch.

"Good morning," Lori called, climbing out of her car.

"Hello, there. Are you off today?" her dad asked, coming toward her.

"Nope. I'm on my way to work right now. Where's Mom?"

"She's in the shower. Want to come in for breakfast?"

"I already ate. I came by to invite you and Mom to a dinner out tonight."

Her dad's bushy eyebrows knit together. "With who?"

"With me."

"Just you?"

"Yes," Lori replied, trying to hide her annoyance. "Just me. I'm still not dating anyone since the last time you asked less than a week ago."

"Your mother is worried about you."

"I know she is, but I'm fine. I'll pick you up at five thirty."

"The restaurants will start to get crowded by then."

"Okay, I'll pick you up at five so we can beat the crowd. I'll even call ahead to let them know we're coming."

"You can do that?"

She smiled at her dad, who refused to carry a cell phone,

didn't have a computer, and obviously had never heard of call ahead. "Yes, I can. I'll see you and Mom at five."

As Lori drove down the street, she watched her dad in the rearview mirror. Henry wasn't happy unless he was worrying about someone or trying to feed them. Her unattractive backyard had him scouring the gardening section of the local bookstore for ideas. Her parents had been married for forty-seven years, and they had two daughters who were both divorced. Being a mom of kids fast approaching marrying age, she understood why her parents worried, but wished they wouldn't.

She took I-405 to Bellevue, then turned onto the floating bridge over Lake Washington.

An hour after leaving her dad, she got out of her car in the paper's parking lot. Before she could reach the door of the *Star*, it opened from the other side. The security guard grinned at her.

"Hi, Kenneth." Lori walked past him and tugged at his tie as had become her habit. "Why so smiley?"

"The sun is shining."

"And it's going to be a beautiful day."

He followed her to the elevator and pushed the UP button. "Warmer weather is on the way."

"I like your optimism. Have a great day, Kenneth."

"You too," he said before the door closed.

Lori got off the elevator, anxious to see Matt, but his office was dark. Maybe he'd been waylaid in Astoria.

Most of the reporters were in and already busy with weekend news. Waving to a few people as she passed, she headed to her office.

"Good morning, Phil," she said, pausing at his cubicle.

"Hey."

"How did Faith enjoy her Valentine's Day surprise?"

"She gave me the same look you're giving me right now. Just so you know, I'm not even fazed by it anymore."

"No, I'm sure you're not. It probably goes back as far as your mother."

He laughed. "Come to think of it, you're right."

Lori waved and walked into her office, surprised to see Carrie sitting at her desk. "Hey. What's up?"

"Sorry. I came in here so I wouldn't miss you. I was watching from your window." Carrie stood up so Lori could get to her desk. "Can we talk?".

"Sure."

"In private?"

"Of course. You can shut the door."

Carrie cast a nervous glance toward the wall separating her from Phil. "Can we go somewhere else?"

There weren't many places more private than her office. "Okay. How about the conference room?"

They walked to the other side of the fourth floor. Once inside, Carrie closed the door.

"What's going on?"

Carrie sat in a chair and swiveled toward the table. "I lied to you about the flash drive. I didn't find it in my desk."

Lori had already suspected Carrie wasn't telling the complete truth. She pulled out a chair on the other side of the table and sat.

"I received the flash drive in the mail, here at the office."

And Carrie had inserted it into her computer. Not smart, but Lori kept that to herself for now. "You don't know who sent it?"

Carrie shook her head. "Right before I left Friday night, a man phoned my desk and said he had some information about a big story. He said he couldn't discuss it over the phone."

"Do you think he sent the flash drive?"

"When I asked, he didn't deny or confirm. He wanted me to meet him at a warehouse in Georgetown. I went, but he never showed."

"Carrie, you can't just meet some man you don't know at a warehouse. Not alone."

"I said he didn't show," Carrie said impatiently. "I waited for over an hour."

Lori could tell there was more to Carrie's story by the way she kept smoothing a hand over the table, so she waited.

"He called again this morning. He said he couldn't come because someone is following him. He confirmed that he sent the flash drive. I told him I couldn't get in without a password. He said he'd give it to me today at the same warehouse."

"I hope you don't plan on going alone."

"No." Carrie glanced past Lori to the window beyond. "I was hoping you'd go with me."

"Me? When I said don't go alone, I meant you should take a man with you."

Carrie finally made eye contact. "All you have to do is wait in the car."

"What is this story about, Carrie? You could be putting yourself in a dangerous situation for nothing."

"I'm not an idiot, but this could be my big chance to prove to Matt that I'm a good reporter."

Lori knew Carrie was frustrated about being the newest staff member besides herself. "The *Star* wouldn't have hired you if you weren't a good reporter. Do you have any idea who this Mr. Anonymous is?"

"Mr. Anonymous, I like that," Carrie replied. "Hopefully I'll find out today. Will you go with me?"

Lori didn't feel good about any of this. "Why don't you take Phil or James or even Dale? Talk to Matt and see what he has to say about going. Or better yet, have Mr. Anonymous come to the *Star* or another public place. Why a warehouse?"

"He's scared."

"All the more reason not to meet him *at the warehouse*."

"If I put him off, he's going to call another reporter. I have to go today. He said he's leaving town soon."

"At least tell Matt—"

"He'll make me take Phil or give the story to him. Phil gets all the good stories. This one's mine. Do you have any idea how huge this could be?" Carrie set her jaw. "If you won't go with me, I'll go alone. I'm not telling another reporter."

She could tell Carrie meant every word. She'd rather risk her safety than lose the story to another reporter.

"Please, come with me. Just be there in case."

"In case of what? What am I going to do if you don't come out of the warehouse?"

"You're being dramatic. What reason would this man have to hurt me? None. He doesn't even know me."

"Exactly. And you know nothing about him. How did he get your name? Why did he call you?"

"So, you're saying I'm not good enough."

"No, I'm saying why pick a woman? Why pick a new reporter? If this is such a big story, why wouldn't he contact a seasoned reporter?"

"Never mind." Carrie stood. "Sorry I asked."

Lori jumped up and grabbed Carrie's arm. "When?"

Carrie threw her arms around Lori's neck. "Thank you, Lori. Thank you, thank you. Dave's birthday celebration is at twelve. I'll meet you at the elevator at twelve fifteen."

Lori worked until twelve while her stomach churned with building unease. She believed in trusting her gut, and it told her going with Carrie was reckless and stupid. At a little after noon, she grabbed her coat and purse and headed to the conference room on the second floor to wish Dave a happy birthday.

Everyone was singing happy birthday when she entered. She automatically looked for Matt since she hadn't seen him all morning. He stood at the other end of the room near the windows with a Lifestyle reporter.

Jennifer Wills was tall, with huge brown eyes and hair that hung in soft waves. She said something to Matt and he bent toward her. She cupped his jaw and whispered something near his ear. The touch and the look in her eye spoke volumes.

Lori was transported back to spring break of her freshman year so fast her head spun. He'd been kissing her two nights ago.

Yep, I'm that stupid.

Matt glanced up and their eyes connected.

Lori turned to Dave and gave him a quick hug. "Happy birthday."

"Thanks, Lori."

She waved away the piece of cake Theresa held out when she saw Carrie at the door pointing to her watch. "I hate to duck out, but I have an errand to run."

∿

*N*o, no, no!

Matt's gut dropped the second his eyes connected with Lori's. He recognized the hurt, but he couldn't get to her before she left the room. By the time he worked his way through the throng of people, she was gone. He ran up the stairs and checked the breakroom, his office, and then hers.

He dropped into the chair behind her desk. He thought it strange when Jennifer came over to stand by him. They'd dated several years ago, but he ended things when she started talking futures together. Now they were cordial. They spoke in passing. Last he heard, she was engaged, so why had she sidled up and touched him like she wasn't? It happened so fast he hadn't reacted in time. As soon as she put her hand on his face, he looked up, his eyes meeting Lori's.

He stood and looked out the window. Her SUV was still parked in the same space it sat in when he got to the office thirty minutes ago. Then he spotted Lori and Carrie getting into Carrie's car.

Look up here, Lori. Look at me.

She didn't.

He'd wasted enough of his life and wanted to get started on his future. A future with Lori. Their dinner on Valentine's Day had gone so well. She'd let her guard down. She asked questions and he answered truthfully. He wasn't the only one feeling something. She never would have kissed him or let him hold her if she didn't feel the same.

Yet in the space of a heartbeat Jennifer tarnished every step of the progress he made. Lori's walls would be back up and doubly fortified this time.

In truth, he couldn't blame Jennifer. Before Lori moved home, he would have smiled and blatantly flirted in front of everyone in the room. He only had himself to blame. His reckless lifestyle had finally caught up to him, and the consequences would be painful.

He watched Carrie pull out of the parking lot, then went to his office to try and figure out a way to fix his mess.

~

The area Carrie drove into was industrial and run-down, with no foot traffic. She turned down an alley and maneuvered through an open gate that said No

Trespassing without blinking an eye. Enough debris littered the asphalt that Lori was worried they'd get a flat tire and be stranded until they could get it changed.

"This isn't a good idea, Carrie. How much farther?"

Carrie took a left, drove the length of a building, then parked between what was left of two white lines like she might get a ticket for taking up two spaces. They were facing a fence.

"Are you supposed to meet him in the building behind us?" Lori asked, looking over her shoulder.

"Yes." Carrie took a tiny recorder out of her purse and slipped it into her coat pocket.

"I'm nervous about this, Carrie. I wish we'd at least told Theresa where we were going."

"I told you, this is *my* story. If Theresa knew, she'd want to come with us."

Then three of us would be murdered instead of two. "Theresa wouldn't take this away from you. She, like me, would want you to be safe."

"Just keep an eye out," Carrie said, opening her car door.

"Keep an eye out for what? Are armed men going to come blazing in? What if they do? Am I supposed to run in and save you?"

"You're being dramatic again. Just honk the horn." Carrie got out of the car and picked her way through the parking lot toward the building.

Stupid, stupid, stupid. Lori pulled her cell phone out of her purse, ready to dial 911. She turned in her seat and watched out the back window.

Carrie made her way up a narrow cement stairway and opened the door without glancing back at the car. Lori pulled up the camera on her phone and snapped a picture, wishing the zoom was better. She should have asked Dale if she could borrow a camera.

She could see Carrie through the open door after she stepped inside—until someone reached past her and pulled it shut. The door had a small window, so Lori could still see her.

Good girl. Stay in front of the window.

The other person came into view as he peered out the window. Lori could just make out the outline of his face. He had dark hair and an unforgettable, long, beak-like nose. Occasionally Carrie stepped out of sight and Lori's heart slammed into panic mode. How long should she wait before calling for help?

After five minutes that seemed more like five hours, Carrie opened the door. Before she walked out, the man handed her something that she slipped in her pocket. Lori had been holding her phone camera steady on the back of the seat and took several shots of the man and Carrie before he closed the door.

Walking fast, Carrie crossed the parking lot and climbed into the car. Without a word, she started the engine and backed out just enough to drive away.

"Are you all right?"

"I'm not sure," Carrie replied, a tremor in her voice.

"Pull over and let me drive."

Once they were on the street, Carrie pulled her car to the curb and Lori switched seats.

"Do you want to tell me what happened?"

"I've just never been in a situation like that before. It was so scary and one of the most exciting things I've ever done. This is going to be big, Lori." She glanced over with wide eyes. "I should have been working on stories like this all along."

"You got a story?"

"Enough to get started. I have to do some heavy research

when we get back to the office." She touched Lori's arm. "You won't tell anyone about this, will you?"

"No. This is your story, but you need to be safe and smart. Don't get so excited that you let your guard down. And don't think you can trust this guy after a five-minute conversation."

"I'll be careful. Thanks for going with me."

"Did he give you the password to the flash drive?"

"What?"

"I saw Mr. Anonymous hand you something. You put it in your pocket."

"Oh . . . um . . . I set my sunglasses down and he gave them back to me."

Carrie wasn't wearing sunglasses when she entered the building.

When they got back to the newspaper, Carrie went straight to her cubicle and Lori headed for her office. Matt got up from a chair in Phil's cubicle when she passed.

"Can I talk to you?"

She nodded, knowing what was coming before he said anything. She'd hoped he'd feel uneasy enough to stay away, but he was Matt Kelley. Slipping out of her coat, she hung it behind the door, then dropped her purse near her chair. She didn't want to sit down, because he wouldn't be staying long. Leaning against her desk, she crossed her arms, closing herself off. "What can I do for you?"

He closed the door and walked toward her.

With her desk behind her, she had no way to step back, so she held up a hand. "Matt," she said, going for a warning tone.

"I just want to make it clear that nothing is going on between me and Jennifer Wills."

"It's none of my business if there is."

"She and I dated several years ago, but it's been over for a long time."

"It didn't look ov—" she stopped and shook her head. "As I said, it's none of my business, Matt."

"Will you let me take you to dinner tonight?"

"I have plans with my parents."

"Tomorrow night, then," he said, jamming his hands in his pants pockets.

Her determination not to say anything lost its backbone. "Why? So two years from now another woman can watch me flipping my hair and touching your face in a feeble attempt to get you to notice me? I refuse to be the next Jennifer Wills, Matt. I can't do it again."

"Do what again?"

Lori looked down and swallowed so she could get the next sentence out without tears. "Fall in love with you. I can't do it again."

"Lori—"

He started to take a step forward, but she narrowed her eyes.

His expression fell from determined to resigned. He nodded, took a step back, and ran the fingers of one hand through his hair. "I'm sorry. It wouldn't be like that with you."

"I'm sure Jennifer thought the same thing at one time."

His jaw bulged. "I've never led any woman I dated to believe I cared more for her than I did. I've gone into every relationship with my cards on the table, and I've been very careful to never lead a woman to believe otherwise."

"You led me to believe otherwise." As soon as the words were out, she was sorry. The hurt that passed over Matt's face made her feel awful. She wanted to apologize, but for what? He led her to believe they had a future and then crushed her dream. Telling him the truth wasn't a bad thing.

She'd seen the look on both Madelyn and Jennifer's faces. He might have laid his cards on the table, but they'd still fallen in love with him.

"What we had was different, Lori. I loved you."

"When a woman falls in love, she can't help believing the man will too. Maybe it's our nature to want more, to want it all, to want everything from the man we love. You probably have no idea how many broken hearts you've left behind. You absolve yourself by saying you were up-front with them, but that doesn't change the hurt they endure. That doesn't stop them from feeling."

Matt looked like she'd slapped him. He pressed his lips together and his chest rose and fell with his shallow breaths. Finally, he bowed his head. "You're right. I'm sorry. I'll leave you alone."

CHAPTER 11

att stayed away from Lori for the next two weeks. He saw very little of her, and when he did, he kept his distance. They were the longest two weeks of his life. He was restless and ornery and wanted Lori more than he'd ever wanted anything. He needed her more than he'd ever needed anyone.

He walked through the breakroom one morning, and after grabbing an orange juice from the vending machine, he mumbled a good morning to Theresa. She put up a hand to stop him.

"Long time no see. Take a load off. Have a seat. Let's have a chat."

She was the only one in the room, so he dropped into a chair, twisted the top off the bottle, and took a long swallow.

"What's going on with you and Lori?"

"Nothing," he said, screwing the cap in place.

"You never sit by her in the breakroom anymore. If she's at one table, you pick another. You two never talk. You barely make eye contact. Did you have a fight?"

"No."

"What, then?"

He stretched out his legs. "The day of Dave's birthday, Jennifer—"

She held up a hand to stop him a second time. "And Lori saw."

"Yep." He set his orange juice on the table.

"So your past is coming back to bite you on the butt."

He was sick of beating himself up. Might as well let Theresa do the job for a while. "Yep."

"Here's a thought. Why don't you talk to her?"

"I tried. She doesn't want to listen."

"Wow, I bet that's a blow to your ego."

He already felt irritable enough without those kinds of comments, even if her statement was semi-true. Lori had done a number on his ego, in both the positive and the negative senses. "Lori's the only woman who's ever made me think I'd like to be married. Both in college and now."

Theresa's eyebrows just about reached her hairline. "I bet that's the first time you've ever uttered the M-word out loud."

Matt shifted in his chair, but didn't respond because she was right, except for the times he and Lori talked about marriage years ago.

Theresa stood, then rested her palms on the table. "I have two questions. I don't need the answers, but you do. Number one, are you asking Lori out because it's become a personal challenge to get her to say yes? Number two, do you really care about her, or is it your ego you care about?"

"I love her," he blurted out. He met Theresa's astonished gaze. "That's the answer. I've asked her out because I love her."

Theresa dropped back into her chair. "What are you going to do?"

"If you have any ideas, please let me know, because I don't have a clue."

~

On the first day of March, Lori agreed to lunch with Carrie and Theresa at a Chinese buffet, a fifteen-minute drive from the office. While February had been full of gray skies, cold rain, and blustery wind, March came in like a lamb with partly sunny skies and gentle breezes that smelled fresh and lifted Lori's spirits.

When they entered the restaurant, the hostess asked them how many.

"Three," Lori said.

"Five," Theresa countered, holding up a hand with fingers spread. She glanced at Lori. "Matt and Phil are joining us."

Lori had steered clear of Matt as much as possible since their meeting in her office. And he kept his word and stayed away from her. "You left that part out when you invited me."

"It's just two more," Carrie said.

"Get your lunch and I'll hold the table," Lori said, taking their purses.

The hostess showed her to a large booth. This would work. Girls on one side, boys on the other.

When Theresa and Carrie returned with full plates, she went to get her lunch.

She wandered along the three aisles of hot food, looking at the selections.

"Hi, Lori."

Lori glanced over her shoulder and smiled. "Gage. How are you?"

"Great. I'm glad I ran into you. I wanted to say thanks for the column. You filled my art classes."

"Ah, I think your reputation filled your classes." She

hadn't seen Gage at all since she interviewed him, other than to spot a light next door after dark. She glanced around. "Are you alone?"

"Yes. Are you?"

"I'm with friends. Why don't you join us?" She pointed toward the table where Theresa and Carrie sat—staring. Matt and Phil hadn't arrived yet. This would put a crimp in someone's plan. "We have room at our table."

Gage flashed a smile. "Are you sure your friends wouldn't mind?"

"Do they look like they'd mind?" Lori asked with a laugh. "Seriously, join us."

They made their selections and Gage followed her to the table.

"Theresa Carpenter, Carrie Eubanks, this is Gage Farr," Lori said, sliding into the other side of the booth, so they wouldn't look so lopsided.

"It's nice to meet you," Gage said. "Lori invited me to join you. I hope you don't mind?"

"Not at all," Theresa drawled, glancing from him to Lori. "I recognize you from the column Lori wrote. You're in town to teach a few art classes at the university this semester, right?"

"Yes." Gage slid into the booth next to Lori.

"Where are you from?" Carrie asked.

"North Carolina."

Matt and Phil arrived, full plates in hand. Lori and Gage's backs were to the door, so she hadn't seen them enter.

"Gage," Matt nodded.

"Sorry to crash your work party," Gage said.

"It's not a party," Lori was quick to interject. At first she'd been miffed that Theresa and Carrie hadn't told her Matt would join them before they left the office, but she changed her mind. She had to get used to being around Matt. They worked in the same office, and they'd be running into each other all the time.

"Hey, the more the merrier." Phil slid in next to Theresa and flashed his I'm-so-glad-to-be-here-for-this-moment grin.

Matt sat in the only place left, next to Gage.

Lori felt a nudge under the table. "So did your wife come with you, Gage?" Carrie asked.

Unbelievable.

Gage ducked his head as he chewed and swallowed the bite of eggroll he'd just taken. "I'm divorced."

"Lori's divorced, too," Carrie replied, loud enough for the whole restaurant to hear.

Lori closed her eyes when heat flashed over her face. "Carrie."

"What?" Carrie asked. "You are."

Theresa coughed.

"Lunch with friends is so much fun," Phil said with a laugh.

Lori was so glad she couldn't see Matt's face.

"Tell us about your classes," Theresa said.

From the things Gage said, it was evident he was passionate about teaching something he loved. While he talked, Lori focused her attention on her lunch. Carrie tried to pull her into the conversation at every turn, and Matt didn't say anything unless forced with a direct question.

When they finished, they all walked to the parking lot in a group. Gage thanked them again for letting him join them.

"You can join anytime," Carrie piped in.

Gage turned to Lori. "Now the weather's warming, I guess I'll be seeing you out and about."

She smiled and nodded. "I'll be around. If you need anything, let me know."

He gave a wave and headed across the parking lot.

"He's hot, Lori. I loved listening to his deep voice and that southern accent is so sexy." Carrie turned from watching Gage walk away to Lori. "I think you should get to know him."

"He's my neighbor, so I probably will."

"I mean ask him to dinner or take him a pie."

"That's a great idea, Lori," Phil said. "What do you think, Matt? Should Lori take him a pie?"

Lori refused to look at Matt who stood next to her. Instead, she turned to Theresa's car and reached for the door handle, but Matt beat her to it. He opened the door and she slid into the back seat. Before she could say thank you, he pushed her door shut.

"Lori, you should totally pursue this. Gage is a great guy," Carrie said, climbing into the front seat.

"He might be a great guy, but he's only in town for a few months."

"Quit pushing, Carrie." Theresa shut the driver's door. She caught Lori's eye in the rearview mirror and winked. "Lori will date when the right guy comes along."

Leaning back in her seat, she watched the passing scenery while Theresa drove them back to the office. For some reason, a memory of Christmas from her freshman year floated through her mind. Matt had flown to an aunt's house in Minnesota for a big family Christmas, and then his immediate family flew back to Astoria to spend New Year's Eve together.

By that time Lori was crazy in love with him, but felt nervous because after calling her every day for the first week and a half, the calls had stopped until the night before she was supposed to pick him up at the airport.

She stood at the gate watching a stream of passengers emerge from the jetway. Her heart hammered the moment she saw Matt. He walked forward, searching for her. When their eyes met, he halted, then moved more slowly. She tried to read his mood, but his expression didn't reveal anything. He stopped in front of her and took her face in his hands, lightly pressing his lips to hers for a long moment. Her hammering heart stuttered a few times, making her chest hurt.

He grabbed her hand. "Let's go over there. I need to talk to you."

That's when her heart stopped beating altogether. *Please, don't break up with me here, Matt. Not at the airport in front of all these people.* Then she would have to hold it together for the thirty-minute drive to his apartment.

He led her by the hand to a corner a few gates away, then turned around to face her. She tried to keep her expression neutral. Why couldn't he break up with her when she dropped him off?

Don't cry. Don't cry.

"Lori . . ." He looked at the ceiling and his Adam's apple bobbed when he swallowed. She loved to kiss that spot. He squeezed her hand lightly before he made eye contact. "I . . ." he glanced at the floor.

Just say it, Matt.

"Let's sit down. I need to sit down." Matt slipped his arm around her waist, his hand resting on her hip, and led her to the closest chairs.

This hurt even more than she imagined. "Can't this wait until we get to your apartment?" She cleared her throat to calm her shaky voice. "Or at least until we get in the car."

"No. I need to get this out." He sat next to her and blew out a breath. "I don't know how to say this other than to just say it straight out."

Lori wanted to respond, to tell him she already knew, so he could spare them both, but her mouth wouldn't open. Her jaw felt numb.

He bent forward, resting his elbows on his knees, and blew out another breath. "I ran into a girl—an old girlfriend —while I was home. We were both at the same party. She needed a ride home, so we left together. We were just talking about old times and ended up driving to a place we used to park back in high school." He stopped and was silent for the longest thirty seconds of Lori's life.

Was she just supposed to guess what happened next? She had all kinds of things running through her mind. Finally, she jumped up and started walking away. He was heartless to do this to her at the airport.

"Lori, wait!" Matt caught up to her and grabbed her arm. "Please, wait. I have to tell—"

"I don't want to hear."

"Please." He took her hand and led her back to the same chair, coaxing her down by her shoulders. This time when he sat, he turned to face her. "She kissed me. I let her kiss me. Just once. Then I stopped her before anything else happened. All I could think was how much I love you. And I don't want to hurt you."

He leaned back, then sat forward again. Lori could see the muscles in his jaw working.

Eventually, he glanced at her. "I'm sorry, Lori. I can't— I shouldn't—" he stammered.

She let him.

He shook his head. "I shouldn't have left the party with her." Matt jumped out of his chair and ran the fingers of both hands through his hair. He inhaled deeply, turned abruptly, and squatted down in front of her. He took her hands. "I'm sorry, Lori. I'm so sorry. I don't want to lose you over a moment of stupidity. The whole flight here I was sick to my stomach, knowing I had to tell you. I wanted you to know the truth. I love you."

Lori felt moisture on her cheeks before she realized she

was crying. Emotions buffeted her—too many to define. Was she hurt that he'd kissed another girl? Or relieved because he wasn't breaking up with her? Shouldn't she want to break up with him for kissing another girl? He said he loved her, but how much did that mean if he could let an ex-girlfriend kiss him?

"Don't cry, darlin'." He took her face in his hands and brushed the pads of his thumbs over her cheeks. "Please, don't cry. I can't stand to see you hurt. Can you try to forgive me?" he asked with a catch in his voice. "I'm so sorry."

He stood and pulled her to her feet, tucking her body close to his. She heard him swallow before he kissed the top of her head. After a long minute, he leaned away and lifted her face. "Please, please forgive me."

"I love you," Lori whispered.

"After what I told you, you still love me?"

"Yes." Her throat was so tight she could barely speak. "I still love you."

"I had a rotten New Year's Day, I felt so awful."

He'd brought in the New Year with an ex-girlfriend.

"My mother asked me a million times what was wrong. All I could think about was telling you, but not over the phone. I wanted to get back here to be with you." He kissed her. Warm and sweet. "I thought you'd be so mad."

"I didn't say I'm not mad. I said I still love you and I can't turn that off because I'm mad. What you did hurts." She put the heel of her hand to her chest. "Right here."

"I know. I'm sorry. I'd be furious if the tables were turned."

Lori swiped fingers under her eyes. "Maybe you should be furious, then."

He frowned. "Why?"

She turned away and started walking down the concourse.

"Lori? What do you mean by that?"

She heard his sneakers squeaking on the linoleum floor behind her as he hurried to catch up. "You know that New Year's Eve party Brett had?"

"Yes," he said.

She could hear the hesitancy in his voice. Or maybe it was suspicion. "I went alone, but I didn't leave alone."

He stopped. "Who'd you leave with?"

"Let's talk about it in the car."

He took three long strides and caught her arm, turning her toward him. "I want to talk about it now."

"We need to go. The roads were slippery on the way here and now it's dark and snowing." She pointed towards the windows. "I'll tell you about it on the way home."

"I'll drive. Tell me now," he said, his voice low.

She pulled from his grasp and walked away. He could worry for a few minutes. He could think the same things that had skittered through her mind for a little while.

She'd left the party with Mike, but only because he'd given her a ride home when her car wouldn't start. She was considered Matt Kelley's girl—off-limits—even if Matt was out of town. She was also very much in love with Matt and had no desire to be with anyone else.

～

After work, Lori walked into an Italian restaurant and inhaled deeply. The scents of garlic, yeast, and oregano filled the air. She told the hostess she was meeting someone and the young woman pointed toward Tara.

"That's her. Thank you."

When she got to the table, she hugged her sister, then slid into a chair across the table. "Where's Kevin?"

"Idaho, visiting his mom. It's her birthday."

"Why didn't you go?"

"His mom doesn't like me."

"Impossible. Everyone likes you."

"You're biased."

They both perused the menu and ordered.

"So how is it working for McHottie?"

"Tense, uncomfortable, and shivery."

"Shivery?"

"You know that feeling you get before you step into a cold pool, or when you're sure someone's watching you? You don't react because you're cold—at least not yet. You've only got your toe in the water—but your body still reacts. Involuntary. You can't control the reaction."

Tara was staring with raised eyebrows. "Are you saying you can't control your body when Matt's around?"

"No. I'm saying I can't always control my internal reaction around him. I wish I could, but I can't."

"Has he asked you out?"

"Yes." Lori smiled when the waiter set bread in the middle of the table along with a plate of spices and roasted garlic. "Thank you."

"Did you go?"

Lori picked up the bottle of olive oil on the table and poured it over the garlic and spices. "We went to dinner once."

"Why only once?" Tara asked as she tore a piece of bread off the loaf and handed it to Lori.

"I've already been involved with Matt once. I'm not sure I want to go down that road again." Lori dipped her bread in the oil, making sure to get some garlic since she wouldn't be kissing anyone anytime soon. "Can we please talk about something else?"

"Sure. You choose."

A couple walked past and Lori recognized the *she* of the couple. *Jennifer Wills.*

"Do you know them?"

"The woman is one of the lifestyle reporters at the paper." *And she's with another man, who has his arm around her. And she's wearing a diamond ring.*

"Do you want to say hi?"

"I don't know her very well." She turned her attention from Jennifer to Tara. "Tell me about the kids."

They spent dinner catching up on news of their kids. Tara was anxious about Christine's upcoming wedding. She filled Lori in on some of the plans, then listed all the things she still had to do. Lori listened to her sister express frustration with her ex-husband, who refused to help financially.

"You didn't think he would, did you?"

"No, but I hoped, as I always do, that maybe he'd change. It doesn't matter. Kevin treats Cole, Christine, and Caleb like they're his kids. Every time I stress about money, he tells me not to worry. He'll cover Ted's share, but he shouldn't have to."

Lori giggled.

"What?" Tara asked.

"I just realized your kids' names start with C. Matt and his siblings' names start with Ms—not sure why I never put that together before." She waved her hand, dismissing her thoughts circling to Matt yet again. "You're right, Kevin shouldn't have to, but he's a good man who loves your kids. Let him help if he wants to."

Tara didn't speak for a full thirty seconds. "Tara, what is it?"

"Kevin asked me to marry him again, and I think I'll say yes."

Lori laughed with relief. "That's the best news I've heard in a very long time."

"I'm scared."

Lori reached for Tara's hand, hurting for her tough sister in a weak moment. "I know you are, but you know how much Kevin loves you and the kids."

"But what if—"

"Tara, you can say 'what if' for the rest of your life. There will always be 'what ifs.' Kevin thinks you walk on water. You'll never find a more wonderful man."

Tara's eyes filled with tears. "He is wonderful. I don't deserve him."

"Stop. You deserve to be happy, and Kevin makes you extremely happy."

"I just don't want to hurt him. I mean, if we don't work out."

"Why wouldn't you work out? You two have been dating for years. Is there anything you argue about?"

"That's the bad part. We agree on just about everything."

"That's the bad part? Are you crazy? Didn't you get enough fighting in your first marriage?"

"But make-up sex is so great."

Lori looked around, embarrassed by her sister's outburst. "You haven't married Kevin because you don't fight? Are you kidding me?" At Tara's grin, Lori relaxed into her chair. "You are kidding. Please, tell me you're kidding."

Tara laughed.

"You're unbelievable." Lori shook her head. "Marry Kevin and find one thing to fight about."

"Mom and Dad don't know."

"The way they ride me, do you think I'd mention the subject of marriage?" Lori lifted a brow. "Though, if I tell them about you, maybe they'll get off my back."

"Don't you dare."

After they paid the bill, Tara stood and tugged her coat over her shoulders. "You know, the little 'what if' speech you gave me sounds like good advice. Maybe you should follow your own counsel. And I quote: You can say 'what if' for the rest of your life. There will always be 'what ifs.' End of quote."

Maybe Lori should take her own advice. Nothing ventured . . .

"I remember the way Matt looked at you on New Year's Eve. And the kiss you shared wasn't just a friendly Happy New Year."

"Thank you, Sigmund Freud."

CHAPTER 12

"Can you go out with me at lunchtime?"

Lori glanced up from her computer to see Carrie standing just inside her office door. "Where?"

Carrie shifted from one foot to the other. "Mr. Anonymous called again. He wants me to meet him one more time. I told him I couldn't get into the flash drives—"

"Plural? I thought you only had one."

"He gave me another one when we were there."

Ah, so that's what he handed out the door.

"He gave me a couple of passwords to try." She slid into one of the chairs in front of Lori's desk. "I told him they didn't work. He has a couple more."

"Why can't he give them to you over the phone?" Lori swiveled her chair to face Carrie.

"I don't know, but he won't." She leaned forward and clasped her hands in her lap. "Please, Lori."

"I think you going there again is a bad idea."

"He's leaving town in a couple of days and not coming back. He wants me to have all the information I need to expose the details of the story."

"I thought he said he was leaving town the last time you saw him, more than two weeks ago."

"He did, but something came up. Please, Lori. I promise this will be the last time I ask."

"Why don't you take Phil with you?" Lori usually trusted her instincts, and they were screaming right now.

"I'll go alone before I take Phil."

"Talk to Matt, then."

"I don't have anything concrete to tell him. I believe this is going to be a big story, I just don't have enough information yet. Please come with me. I promise I won't ask you again."

Lori bit the inside of her lip as she studied Carrie. As stupid as this was, she knew Carrie would go alone. She considered Lori safe since she wasn't a reporter. "This is the last time, Carrie. I mean it."

Carrie jumped up and gave her a quick hug. "Thank you, Lori. And I promise—last time."

"Hello, ladies."

Faith stood in her doorway. "Hi, Faith."

She pointed toward Phil's cubicle. "I'm looking for my husband."

"I haven't seen him today." Strange since he always stuck his head in to say hi.

"I saw him go into Matt's office earlier," Carrie said, walking past Faith. "I'll meet you at the elevator at noon, Lori."

Faith sat in the chair Carrie had vacated. "Lunch date?"

"No. She asked for help with a story. How are your boys? Phil says same-old, same-old whenever I ask him."

"I don't know how you feel about being an empty nester, but I love it. Don't get me wrong, I love my boys, but after twenty-three years of raising babies . . ."

Lori smiled. If she had still been married, and, if it was a happy marriage, she might feel differently, but she missed having her kids around.

"How are your kids doing with their mom so far away?" Faith asked.

"Enjoying their independence." She talked to Megan almost every day and Taylor—not a phone person—called or texted when he needed a mom moment.

Faith cocked her head to the side. "I'm trying out a new pasta recipe tonight. I know it's short notice, but would you be interested in coming to dinner?"

"Oh, that's so nice. Are you sure it wouldn't be too much trouble?"

"I wouldn't have asked if it was any trouble."

"Can I bring anything?"

"How about a salad?"

"I can do that."

"It won't be anything fancy. Just me and Phil and . . . casual." Faith crossed one leg over the other.

"I love casual. Are you sure I can't bring a loaf of bread?"

"No, I have everything else."

"Is that my lovely bride I hear in Lori's office?" Phil hollered.

Faith shook her head. "Is he always this obnoxious?"

"Always." Lori smiled when Phil walked into her office. Matt followed.

Phil leaned down for a kiss before taking the other chair. "Hi, sweetheart."

Faith offered a loving smile that tweaked Lori's heart. She quickly jotted down a note on a sticky pad—a possible column on watching love.

"Hey, beautiful." Matt leaned over and kissed Faith's cheek.

"Hey yourself, handsome."

He took a seat on the corner of Lori's desk.

"What're you doing here?" Phil asked, reaching for his wife's hand.

"I came to see you, but you weren't home, so I'm bothering Lori who, by the way, is coming to dinner tonight."

"Hey, that's a great idea." Phil glanced at Matt. "What are you doing for dinner, Matt?"

"I'm free."

"Perfect," Faith added. "Matt can be Lori's date. I was just telling her I'm trying out a new recipe."

"I'd love to come as Lori's date," Matt said.

Lori couldn't believe she'd fallen into their trap. She'd been set up so smoothly she never saw it coming.

"I'll bring dessert," Matt said.

"Perfect, but not cheesecake. I'm not sure how Phil always talks you into cheesecake, but I want something different. What do you like, Lori?"

Sweet little Faith swooped in and suddenly she's Matt's date for dinner. She glanced at Phil, who grinned like he'd just won the lottery. She knew better than to look at Matt. Had one or all of them been involved in this blindside? "I'm fine with anything."

"Perfect," Faith repeated. "Is six thirty okay?"

Lori nodded. "I'll see you then."

Faith stood and pulled Phil to his feet. "Walk me to the elevator, sweetie."

After Phil and Faith left her office, Matt stood. "I'll pick you up at six."

"Why?"

"You heard Faith. This is a date."

"From your house to my house and then back to Phil's would be a ninety-minute drive for you."

"I'd like to—"

"Meet me there? That's a great idea." Lori replied in a determined tone.

Matt nodded with a smirk. "See you tonight."

Lori turned her chair to the window after Matt walked out. Wow, she'd been played like a fiddle. They planned that out, and she tripped right into the pit where the big, bad wolf waited. Which one came up with the idea? She put her money on Phil.

Before noon, Lori went to the second floor. She passed Matt, who stood at the door of the sports editor's office. Pausing at Kirk's cubicle, she asked if she could borrow a pair of binoculars. Luckily, he was on a deadline and didn't have time to chit-chat.

Next, she stopped at Dale's desk and asked to use a camera with a telephoto lens and a new memory card. She wanted a clear picture of Mr. Anonymous.

Dale offered to ride along with her, wherever she was going, and take the pictures. "It's been a slow day. I could use something to do," he said.

"It's not my party, Dale. I'm just going along for the ride." She held up the camera. "I could use a few pointers, though."

"Do you know much about cameras?"

"Not a lot."

Dale led Lori to a window. "Are you going to be shooting outside?"

"Sort of."

He frowned. "Long-distance?"

"Yes."

Dale turned her by the shoulders and reached around her to give a quick lesson on how to focus right and how to get the clearest pictures when the light changed. Luckily, Carrie had chosen a cloudless day to meet Mr. Anonymous.

"The distance is about from here to that orange SUV down there. Through a window."

"Through a window? Come on, Lori, take me with you."

"Sorry, Dale."

He reached around her again to fool with the focus. "How's that?"

Lori smiled as the SUV changed from wobbly edges to crystal clear. "Perfect." She lowered the camera to see what he'd changed, then watched him load the memory card. "I appreciate this, Dale."

"What's going on?"

She turned. Matt stood behind them, arms crossed. "Oh, uh . . ." She held up the camera. "Dale's just giving me a few pointers."

"Come on, Lori. Take me with you," Dale said. "I'll buy you lunch."

"Maybe next time," she said. "Thanks for the lesson."

"Are you going somewhere?"

"I have to run out on an errand."

He lifted a brow. "With a camera and binoculars?"

She looked up at him for a long moment, tempted to tell him the truth, but she'd promised Carrie. "It's work-related."

Minutes later, Carrie drove them toward the same warehouse. This time Lori had her park at a slight angle so she could see the door more clearly.

Before Carrie got out, Lori grabbed her arm. "Stay in front of the window where I can see you, Carrie."

"Okay, but I can't act too obvious or he'll know you're out here."

Carrie walked through the parking lot and up the stairs. The door opened as soon as she reached for the handle.

This is not smart.

Carrie stayed within view for five seconds before she disappeared.

"Carrie," she groaned.

Lori slipped the camera out of the bag she brought and

trained the lens on the window, taking her time to focus. A full minute passed before Carrie reappeared. Lori pulled her feet up onto the seat, close to her butt, and tried to hold the camera as steady as possible by resting the lens on the back of the seat.

Breathe.

A head appeared and she snapped several shots, then grabbed the binoculars. She recognized the same man by the shape of his nose.

At the sound of tires, Lori glanced behind her. A car with a single occupant pulled in and backed out just as quickly. Someone making a U-turn. But why would anyone be in this abandoned warehouse area?

Swiveling her attention back to the door, she aimed the camera at the window and adjusted the focus. Carrie was out of sight. Instead, the man stood at the window. Lori snapped three more quick shots. The first pictures had been profiles, but these were straight on.

After what seemed like an eternity, but in truth was only a few minutes, Carrie walked out. Lori stuffed the binoculars and camera in her bag since she hadn't told Carrie she brought them.

Carrie got in the car. "Did you notice the car that pulled into the parking lot?" she asked without looking at Lori.

"Yes."

"What color was it?"

"A black sedan. Why?"

Carrie shrugged, started the car, and backed out. "Just wondering."

Lori turned on her. "You're lying to me. What's going on, Carrie? I agreed to come with you, so the least you can do is tell me what's going on. It's your story. I'm not going to tell anyone."

"You don't have to get mad."

"Oh, girl, you haven't seen mad yet."

"Okay." Carrie set her jaw, a reaction Lori was seeing more and more often. "Mr. Anonymous told me about a drug ring operating out of Seattle."

"A drug ring? Did you know this the first time we came here?"

Carrie ignored Lori's question. "The man inside was working the books—"

"What do you mean working the books?" Lori interrupted. "As in stealing money from drug dealers?"

"He's trying to get out of town, but he's being watched."

Lori put a hand to her roiling stomach. "By who? The man who turned around in the parking lot?"

Carrie shrugged as they drove out of the Georgetown area. "Mr. Anonymous says the police are involved, so he can't talk to them. He doesn't have anyone to trust but me."

"And you *trust* him? He admitted that he stole from drug dealers? And you trust him? You're not being smart."

"This story will be a game-changer for me."

The reporter in Carrie wanted this story so badly she wasn't willing to listen to reason. "Has Mr. Anonymous given you a name?"

"Mike."

"Has Mike told you who's operating this drug ring?"

"A Seattle businessman."

"Who?"

"He just gave me the name today. I want to do some research on this before I say any more."

"Is this businessman running the drugs, or is he just a cog in a much larger wheel?" Lori shook her head. "Do you have any idea the amount of danger Mike could be putting you in?"

"This is going to be a huge story. Can you imagine?" Carrie said, ignoring Lori. "A prominent businessman operating a drug ring here in our town, and I have the inside scoop. Carrie Eubanks will have her name on the front-page story. Above the fold!"

"Did you know this was about drugs before we came today?" Lori asked.

Carrie ignored her a second time. "A Detective Stone called me this morning. He told me they've been investigating this businessman for a couple of years. They've also been watching Mike. They heard from an inside source that guys from the operation are looking for him. They want to put him in protective custody, but he doesn't trust them."

"How did this Detective Stone get your name?"

Carrie didn't answer.

"Why would a detective confide in you, Carrie? Why are you still meeting with Mike if the police want to protect him?"

"Have you been listening? He doesn't know who to trust."

"Too much of this doesn't make sense. How does Mike know he can trust you? Why does he think you can help?"

Carrie lifted a shoulder. "Because of Steve."

"He thinks you can help him because your husband works in the mayor's office? How did he get Steve's name? Or yours, for that matter?"

"I don't know!" Carrie huffed out a breath. "You're asking too many questions. I can't think."

"Well, here's what *I* think—you need to start asking yourself some of these serious questions. You don't sound like you have enough to write a story, and you are *not* going back to that warehouse, or I'll tell Matt myself."

"Mike's leaving town tonight," Carrie said as she turned into the newspaper's parking lot. "I won't be able to talk to him again. I just need to get into those flash drives. Mike gave me a couple more passwords to try."

Once Carrie parked, Lori unbuckled her seat belt and

turned to her. "Have you stopped to think of the danger Mike is putting you in—the danger he may be putting Steve in? If the people operating this drug ring find out he gave you those flash drives with their information they may come after you. Or Steve. Is your family's safety worth a story?" Lori shook her head. "If it is, I don't understand. But I do know you need to talk to Matt."

"I will." Carrie opened her door and climbed out.

"I mean it, Carrie," Lori said once she got out and shut the passenger door.

"Let me try these passwords first and research the businessman. Without that information, I don't have much to tell Matt. Once I get in, I'll have my story. Then I promise I'll talk to Matt."

Fighting the anger exploding behind her eyes, Lori followed Carrie into the elevator. The reporter had used her —possibly put her in danger—for a potential story. Because at this point, Carrie couldn't get into the flash drives. If she didn't, she had nothing but hearsay. Lori didn't believe Matt would run a story coming from some random guy hiding out in a warehouse. She did believe Carrie knew drugs were involved before their first trip to the warehouse, and she also believed Carrie knew more than she was saying.

Lori should never have agreed to go with her. But Carrie, young and hungry for an above-the-fold story, would have gone alone. If something had happened to her, Lori would forever feel responsible.

Later that afternoon, storm clouds darkened Lori's office. She got up to look out the window and spotted Carrie walking through the parking lot. Her first thought was Carrie meant to go back to the warehouse. Instead, she walked to the last row of cars and stopped next to the driver's window of a black sedan.

Lori spun around and grabbed the camera. Dale was out

on an assignment when she got back, so she brought the camera to her office for safekeeping. At the window, she quickly focused and snapped two pictures of the car, but couldn't get a clear shot of the license plate.

The driver's window came down and Lori focused on a heavyset man with thick white hair. Carrie was blocking Lori's sightline enough that she couldn't get a great shot, but at least she had something. She aimed for the license plate when Carrie backed away and the car pulled out of the parking lot. Taking her time to focus, she got one good picture.

Lori met Carrie when she got off the elevator. "That was the same car that turned around in the parking lot, wasn't it?"

Carrie's expression changed from wide-eyed surprise to lock-jawed anger. "You're spying on me?"

"I saw you from the window in my office."

"It was Detective Stone." She slipped out of her jacket. "I think he's following me."

"Why would a detective follow you?"

"The police are looking for Mike. Detective Stone thinks I'm involved in some way."

"You *are* involved," Lori almost shouted. "You said Detective Stone was following Mike. If that's true, he'd know where Mike is. A detective wouldn't confide in you, Carrie."

Matt walked around the corner with James. He stopped and studied them for a split second. "Everything okay, ladies?"

"Everything's fine," Carrie said quickly. "We're just talking about a story I'm working on."

Matt looked from Carrie to Lori, then back to Carrie. "Is it the story we talked about this morning?"

"Yep."

When Carrie turned her way, Lori knew she had just lied.

Before going down the stairs with James, Matt glanced at her again, a question in his expression. She gave a slight shake of her head.

Once the stairwell door closed behind Matt and James, Carrie turned to leave, but Lori grabbed her arm. "You're being reckless. No story is worth the danger you're possibly putting yourself in."

"The danger's over. Detective Stone told me they have the situation under control."

"Why did he come to see you? Why not just call?"

"He said I can have the exclusive story once everything comes to a head."

Some of the tension left Lori's shoulders. "Are the police going to make arrests first?"

Carrie shrugged. "He said he'd be in touch."

So this whole story might be coming to an end for Carrie, and just beginning for others involved. "Did you get into the flash drives?"

"No. The passwords didn't work."

"Don't you think you should give them to the police?"

Carrie offered a tight smile. "Good idea. I'll go past the police station on my way home."

Lori stood for a moment after Carrie walked away, trying to collect herself. She ran her fingers across her forehead where a headache had started to pound. This whole warehouse and police thing with Carrie didn't add up.

CHAPTER 13

"Matt, can you get that?" Faith asked at the sound of the doorbell.

He expected to meet flashing green eyes rather than the smile Lori offered when he opened the door. Staying away from her the last two weeks had been the hardest of his life. She literally took his breath away every time she was near.

"Hello," she said.

"Hi." He held the door wider so she could pass under his arm. She'd changed into jeans with knee-high boots and a green sweater a shade darker than her eyes. "You look pretty, as always."

"Thank you." She blushed. "You look nice too."

"Can I take that bag from you?"

She handed him the burlap bag, shrugged out of her coat, and hung it on a rack near the door. Her movements sent a waft of her perfume past and he inhaled deeply.

"Are Faith and Phil in the kitchen?" She reached for the bag.

"Yes. They gave me door duty." He winced at how stupid that sounded.

Faith smiled when they entered the kitchen. "Hi, Lori. Oh, that salad looks delicious," she said when Lori pulled a glass bowl out of the bag. "Let's put it in the fridge since I'm running a little late with dinner."

Lori slid the bowl onto a shelf in the fridge along with a cruet of what Matt guessed was dressing, and another glass bowl of sliced strawberries. "Things don't always run smoothly when trying a new recipe."

"Hey, Lori," Phil said, coming into the kitchen from the mudroom. He pulled her into an easy hug.

Lori ran her hand over Phil's hairless cheek and Matt experienced the zing of jealousy that had plagued him ever since she came home.

"You shaved."

"I did it just so women would touch my face. Here rub this side, too," he said turning his other cheek. "You dress down well."

"Thanks, I think," she replied.

Phil bent and sniffed her hair. "You smell good, too."

"Would you leave her alone?" Faith said.

Lori pulled away from him with a laugh. "I love your house. Your kitchen's beautiful."

"Thanks," Faith said. "We remodeled after the boys left home. Phil, will you get Lori a drink?"

"Just water," she said to Phil.

Throughout the whole conversation, Matt felt like an interloper while trying not to stare at Lori.

Faith pushed the pasta pan into the oven. "Now we wait."

Phil turned to him. "Want to shoot some pool before dinner?"

Matt chuckled when Faith aimed a glare at her husband. Phil wasn't as good at matchmaking as Faith, so Matt gave her a helping hand. "Lori told me she's a pretty good pool player. Should we challenge her to a game?"

"You play pool?" Phil asked her.

"I didn't say I was good." Lori lifted a shoulder. "But I can hold my own."

Phil grinned and rubbed his hands together. "Let's get this party started."

They all trooped up to the loft where he'd helped Phil set up the pool table years ago.

Lori pulled a pool cue off the rack on the wall. "Which one do you use, Faith?"

"I don't play pool," Faith answered. "That's Phil and the boys' thing."

Phil selected a cue stick. "Try this one."

She held it up, looked down the shaft, and nodded. "This will do. Thank you."

"What are we playing for?" Matt asked.

"We can't just play a friendly game?" Lori smiled as she chalked the cue and his gut clenched.

"Of course not." Matt walked close enough that she had to look up. "What'll it be?"

She studied him a moment. "You seem pretty sure of yourself."

"I can hold my own."

"You want to play for money?"

Matt laughed. "I don't need your money, darlin'."

She took a deep breath as she looked into his eyes. "Okay, a date."

"Now this is getting good," Faith said pulling out a stool.

"If I win, you'll go out with me?"

Lori nodded.

There had to be a catch. "And if you win?"

Her eyes twinkled with mischief. "You quit asking."

"No deal. Come up with something else."

"Why? You were so sure of yourself a minute ago."

"Come up with something else," Matt repeated. He refused to take the slightest chance that she might win and have another excuse not to go out with him.

"Clothes!"

Lori slowly turned to Phil. "I'm *not* playing for clothes."

"Scared?" Matt challenged. He'd call the game before he let Lori strip in front of either him or Phil. They tricked her into this dinner, but he wouldn't let things go that far.

⁓

*L*ori glanced at Matt. She didn't know how good he was, but she certainly wasn't stripping in front of him or Phil. Matt might let it go, but Phil never would. He'd make sure everyone knew she'd lost her clothes to Matt. She had no intention of standing around in nothing but a blush.

"Come on, Lori, you said you could play pool. Let's see what you've got."

"You are not seeing what Lori's got," Faith announced. "If they do this and she gets down to underwear, you're out of here."

"Why? It would be like seeing her in a bikini, and I've seen her like that plenty of times."

"That was a long time ago, Phil," Lori said.

She glanced at Matt, who was watching her with wicked eyes and a grin to match. He put his hand in his pocket and pulled out a quarter. "Call it."

"Tails."

He flipped and the coin hit the table, rolled in a circle, and dropped onto the tails side. "You break. What are we playing for?"

"A date, both ways. You win, I'll buy," she answered.

"A date? Come on, Lori. Are you any good, or am I wasting my time up here? Let's go for naked."

Lori turned to Phil. "How about we play to see if you survive this night for setting this whole thing up?"

Phil and Faith exchanged looks. "You knew?" Phil asked.

"She knew before we left her office," Matt replied, watching her.

"You did?" Faith asked.

Lori nodded, watching Matt as closely as he was watching her.

"What are we playing for?" he asked, his voice coaxing and low. He ran the tip of his index finger from her chin to the hollow at the base of her neck.

Lori narrowed her eyes. She was good, but could she beat Matt? She'd never seen him play. He was pretty sure of himself, acting like this would be an easy win. Well, he might not be smiling quite so big in a few minutes. "Clothes."

"Okay!" Phil clapped Matt on the back before he racked up the balls.

Lori decided to play it cool, see how good he was right from the beginning. It worked, because he chuckled after her break. "Oh, honey. This is going to be a very short game."

"Good." She brushed against his arm. "I get cold easily."

"No, Lori," Phil said, pointing at her. "You stay away from him. And Matt, don't you let her get to you, buddy. Remember our goal. Lori. No clothes."

"I'll get her first layer off fast and then we'll take it real slow." Matt winked at Phil.

Matt quickly sank four solids. With a seductive smile, Lori slid off her boots. Then her socks came off slowly until each red toenail was revealed. The next solid cost Lori her belt, which she slipped off and wrapped around the back of Matt's neck before pulling it down his chest, letting her fingers linger.

Matt sucked in a breath. "You're playing with fire, darlin'."

She feigned a sad smile when he missed his next shot.

"Come on, Matt. That was an easy one. Lori, quit playing dirty," Phil groused.

Lori walked around the table. "I'm here playing strip pool because the three of you played dirty."

"That's . . . just stupid," Phil sputtered.

Faith laughed and put her arm around Phil's waist. "Come on, Lori. It's catch-up time. I've never seen Matt's bare chest."

"And you're not going to," Phil stated.

"Oh, so it's okay for you to see Lori naked, but I can't see Matt naked?"

Phil snorted. "You're not going to see Matt naked, because Matt's not going to get naked."

The table looked good and Lori felt confident. She could do this. She sank her first shot.

Matt smiled as he toed off a shoe. Her next three shots left him barefooted and showing his first inkling of doubt. "You have good form."

"Thank you." She sank another ball and Matt shed his shirt.

"His undershirt next, then we're down to bare chest," Faith said, while Phil glowered.

After Lori sank her next two stripes, Matt pulled off his belt and then his undershirt.

Faith jumped off her stool cheering.

Lori leaned on her cue with a casual smile, though she felt anything but relaxed. She'd only seen Matt's bare chest once, and he still maintained a mighty fine chest, with a six-pack to match. She kept her eyes on his, but his wicked grin made heat rise up her neck and wash across her face. "Ready to call it quits?"

"We don't have you naked yet, darlin'," Matt said. Before Lori could react, he pulled her close and pressed his lips to hers. Back on the stomach-dropping roller coaster, she plummeted toward the bottom of the biggest hill. And she enjoyed every second of the ride. When he released her, she never took her eyes off his.

Phil barked out a laugh. "Now we have a game."

With shaky hands, Lori pocketed the cue ball.

"Scratch!" Phil yelled. "You got the entire table, buddy."

Matt picked the cue ball out of the pocket and placed it behind the head string. "I'll give her the advantage." He pocketed another solid.

"Out, Phil," Faith ordered.

"Why? You didn't leave when Matt bared his chest."

"That's not the same and you know it."

"Maybe you better leave, Phil." Matt's tone made it clear he wasn't making a suggestion.

Gallant, Lori thought.

"Let's call it a game."

"Matt, you can't call the game. Lori will win," Phil exclaimed.

"No. If we call the game, it will be so Lori doesn't have to lose any more clothes," Matt replied. "She'll forfeit. We don't want her to get cold."

"I do," Phil grumbled.

Lori took a deep breath, trying to calm her pounding heart. Matt thought he'd won this game, but she allowed herself to hope that kiss shook him just as badly as it did her.

"It's okay, Faith." Lori pulled her sweater over her head to reveal a black camisole.

Matt had moved forward like he might stop her until he saw she had something on underneath.

"No way. I've been sitting here thinking she'd be down to a lacy black bra and that's what I get? Let's get down to business, Matt."

Faith laughed at her husband.

Matt walked around to the side of the table where she stood, his eyes on her camisole. He was trying to unsettle her, but she could play dirty too. When he bent over the table to take his next shot, Lori ran her fingertips down his bare back.

He dropped his cue and pulled her close. She let out a yelp before he covered her mouth with his. Without thinking, she ran a hand up his back and he growled. Literally. He drew back just enough to look into her eyes, then he slowly lowered his mouth to hers again. All Tara's what-ifs swirled around in her head, making her even dizzier than Matt's kiss.

He drew away and ran the pad of his thumb over her cheekbone.

"Uh . . . are you guys still playing pool?" Phil asked.

"Maybe we should go downstairs so they can be alone," Faith replied, fanning her face with her hand.

"Are you ready to finish this game?" Matt asked.

Lori nodded, not trusting her voice.

He picked up his pool cue and missed his next shot.

Phil groaned. "You cheat, Lori."

Matt took a step toward her, but Lori held up her hand. "You stay right where you are. You've had your turn. Faith, have you got a good view? Matt's about to lose his pants."

"Yes!" Faith pulled her cell phone out of her back pocket.

"I think we need to go check on dinner." Phil tried to put a hand over Faith's eyes, but she ducked out of his reach.

"You go check on dinner. I'm not missing this. Matt Kelley, you have met your match."

"We could call the game. You'd forfeit, but at least you wouldn't get cold," Lori said, throwing Matt's words back at him.

Matt slowly shook his head. "I'm not forfeiting."

"Okay." Lori surveyed the table, called the corner pocket and cleanly sank his number six. She looked away when Matt unzipped his jeans. "And now the eight ball in the middle pocket for his briefs."

Faith cheered when Lori quickly pocketed the eight ball.

Matt had his eyebrow raised as he stood in his blue and white striped boxer briefs. "I think I've been hustled."

Lori walked the long way around the table and grabbed her sweater. "You weren't hustled. I warned you, twice, that I know how to play pool."

"You hustled me on the break."

"And you hustled me here, so we're even." Lori turned to Faith. "I'll check on dinner while Matt strips for you."

Lori slipped her sweater over her head and picked up her belt, socks, and boots before heading down the stairs. She urgently needed to put some distance between her and Matt. She'd never seen Matt without clothes, and she wasn't going to start tonight.

She put a hand to her chest and breathed deeply as soon as she was out of sight, amazed she'd managed those last two shots after Matt's heart-stopping kisses.

~

Matt picked up his shirt while Phil dragged Faith toward the stairs. He yanked his clothes on while using the alone time to pull himself together. He and Lori had kissed several times now. Before their first kiss tonight, he'd been careful to block Phil and Faith's full view so Lori wouldn't be completely embarrassed.

That second kiss, though, that wasn't just him kissing her. Her walls were gone. But what did her kissing him back mean? She'd been so distant since seeing him with Jennifer in the conference room. Was she just trying to unnerve him, or had that kiss meant more? It definitely felt like more.

Faith and Phil filled him in on their plan before Faith went into Lori's office, and Lori had been a good sport by not canceling when she realized he'd be here too.

Before he entered the kitchen, he heard Faith congratulating Lori on her win. She'd played dirty, but so had he. In the end, it was a fair game. Even though Lori was getting the high-fives, he felt like he came out the winner.

He finished buttoning his shirt as he walked into the kitchen. Lori had her back to the door, tossing the salad. Faith gave him a quick thumbs-up before she pulled dinner out of the oven. Phil scowled as he sliced a loaf of bread. Matt stopped behind Lori and put his hands on her waist. He expected her to jerk away, but she didn't.

"You played a good game of pool."

"Thank you. So did you."

"What?" Phil exclaimed. "Matt, your game sucked. I saw more naked in high school."

"I'm glad your game sucked, Matt," Faith said with a grin. "And thanks for the almost-naked, Lori."

Lori turned away from Matt with the salad bowl in her hands and headed for the dining room table.

Phil snorted. "Yeah, that's what I wanted to see. Matt naked. I think there should be a rematch after dinner."

Matt watched Lori walk away, a little astonished. She had kissed him upstairs. She hadn't jerked away just now. Maybe her walls *had* crumbled completely.

He looked at Faith to ask what he could do to help and caught her watching him with misty eyes.

"You're in love, Matt. I never thought I'd see the day."

He didn't confirm or deny. "Thanks for tonight. Your idea was genius."

"I'd say it worked."

"We'll see. I don't want to get ahead of myself—or her."

~

*P*hil appeared next to Lori at the dining room table. "So, that was quite a game."

"What do you want?" Lori asked.

"Are you offering a bribe to keep me quiet?"

"Yes. What'll it take to keep what happened upstairs between us?"

"The game or the kiss?"

"Both."

"No can do."

"Okay, the kiss, Phil. What will it cost me to keep the kiss between us?"

"I love cheesecake."

"Topping?"

"Raspberry."

Lori enjoyed herself during dinner. They kept the conversation casual and laughed a lot. After she helped Faith clean the kitchen, she decided to make her escape.

Matt said his goodbyes at the same time and they walked out together. When they reached her car, he turned her around. "Thanks for not holding it against any of us for getting you here."

"How do you know I don't?"

"Because I know you," he said with narrowed eyes.

"I'll admit, I had a nice time, but I probably wouldn't have come if you'd asked me straight out."

"Why?"

"I'm not sure I know why anymore."

"Does that mean you'll go out with me?"

"You're still my boss."

"I can take care of that with a pink slip."

"Don't you dare," Lori said with a laugh.

Matt grinned, and she could see the happiness in his eyes. They were definitely the windows to his soul. He bent and brushed his lips over hers softly and her knees quivered.

"Drive safely," he said.

"Like a grandma."

CHAPTER 14

ori walked over to her file cabinet, opened the top drawer, then tried to remember what she was looking for. "This is nuts."

"Talking to yourself?" Theresa asked, smiling from the doorway.

"Obviously," Lori said with a laugh. She walked around her desk, sat, then jumped up when she remembered which file she was after. "Maybe going crazy."

Theresa came in and sat in a chair. "Who's driving you crazy? Or should I just guess?"

"You're assuming it's a who?"

Theresa rolled her eyes.

Lori slumped in her chair. "You know who."

Theresa leaned forward and planted her elbows on Lori's desk. "I hear you got a standing ovation when you came in this morning."

"And a present." She opened her top drawer, pulled out an 8-ball, and rolled it across her desk toward Theresa.

Theresa palmed it with a laugh. "You've never struck me as a strip pool kind of person."

"Blame Phil for corrupting me. He's the one who pushed playing for clothes."

"Are you going to tell me what happened?"

"Sounds like you've heard the story."

"I heard *a* story from Phil, but you know I don't trust a thing that fruitcake says."

"As a story goes, this one isn't much. Faith invited me to dinner and I accepted. Immediately after, Matt and Phil walked into my office and Phil invited Matt to be my date. When I got there, dinner was just going into the oven, so Phil suggested a game of pool. And of course, we couldn't just play a friendly game. There had to be a wager. Matt wanted to up the ante from my suggestion of money, and Phil suggested clothes."

Theresa rolled the ball between her hands. "And you agreed?"

She felt a smirk appear. "I couldn't help myself. Matt was so cocky and sure he'd win."

"Did you really get him down to his boxers?"

Lori smiled. "He's a boxer-briefs man, and I got him down to naked, but left before he stripped."

Theresa hooted. "Wish I'd been there."

"Faith took pictures."

"Are you having a problem with the boss thing?" Theresa asked, leaning back in her chair.

Lori tipped her head back and forth. "I feel I'm traveling back in time. I mean . . . I'm experiencing feelings . . . Let's just say—" Lori shook her head as her cheeks burned. "Do you know how silly you look with that grin on your face?"

Theresa laughed. "What is Matt doing that has you so discombobulated? Is he wooing you a little too aggressively?"

"I'm not sure I know what *wooing* entails. The aggressive part is just Matt."

"The second time around should be a cinch."

"The first time was easier. I didn't work for the man." Lori caught the 8-ball Theresa rolled back to her. "The part I haven't told you . . . There was kissing."

Theresa hooted again. "College kisses versus now kisses?"

Lori closed her eyes. "They're the same, yet different. It didn't include that"—she rolled her hand in front of her stomach— "that nervous energy of first love." Her eyes popped open at her silly ramblings. "The answer is yes. I think he's had a little practice since college."

Theresa laughed. "You think?"

"So I've heard. The gossip around here doesn't leave much to the imagination."

"Forget the gossip. You've needed a good kiss."

Theresa picked up a pad of sticky notes and flipped them with her thumb. "You and Matt are like peanut butter and jelly. You go together."

Lori smiled at the analogy.

"Which one of you is peanut butter?" Theresa asked.

"That would have to be Matt," Lori replied. "I can't believe you'd even ask."

"I say go for it."

"The office gossip has Matt with a new woman every three to four months. How long do I last before he moves on? Before I end up like Jennifer, hoping to catch a smile from the man I thought loved me."

"Won't happen," Theresa shook her head. "You're the one who got away, the one he could have been happily married to all these years. You're the one he finally settles down with. Think of what you'll miss if you don't take a chance."

There was that "if" word again coming back to haunt her after her little speech to Tara. A broken heart hadn't destroyed her the first time around. She'd licked her wounds and found love a second time. If she didn't try this time, she'd always wonder.

~

M att looked up when Theresa walked into his office and slid into a chair. "Got a minute?"

"Always. What's up?" he asked, setting aside the article he was proofing.

"I hear you're a boxer-briefs man."

He chuckled. "Haven't heard that a hundred times already today."

"You probably shouldn't have been so sure of yourself."

Sucking in a breath, he blew the air out of his mouth. "You're right. I've been learning about humility the hard way over the past three months."

"How's that going?"

"What? Me learning humility?"

"No. You and Lori."

"Fine."

"Is it?" she asked, looking at him like he was a moron. "I stopped by her office earlier. She said something about you wooing her aggressively."

"Wooing?" He laughed. Lori's reserve was coming down, and that might make him crazier than her avoiding him had.

"Actually, 'wooing' was *my* word choice." She picked up a pencil and rolled it across his desk. "Come to think of it, so is 'aggressively,' but Lori did say you're the peanut butter."

Matt stopped the pencil from hitting the floor. "I'm lost. Lori said I'm peanut butter?"

"I said you guys were like peanut butter and jelly, and then I asked which one of you is the peanut butter. She said you are." Theresa punched his stapler down three times.

He moved the stapler out of her reach.

"Is she going to be another notch in your belt?"

"I don't have notches in my belt. And no."

"Well, she's heard all the rumors, so she's going to be skittish." She pointed a finger at his nose. "Don't give up."

"Yeah? Let's hear some words of encouragement."

"It's simple. Don't hurt her. She's in love with you."

That simple statement stole his breath. "She told you that?"

"No." She went back to looking at him like he was a moron.

"Then how do you know?"

Theresa picked up a pen and tapped it against his desk twice before he took it away. She was worse than a kid.

"Women's intuition. Don't smile at her like that!" She leaned back, pointing at his face. "You look like a crazed maniac. You'll scare her to death."

"Any suggestions?"

Theresa snorted. "Aren't you the expert with women? Do what you did in college."

"I'm pretty sure if you and Carrie invited her to an Elvis movie, she'd be onto me."

Theresa laughed and pushed to her feet. "She told me about that and yes, she'd know."

~

"Hi."

Lori's pulse jumped.

Matt stepped into her office and closed the door, then chuckled. "Don't worry. Almost everyone is gone. I saw your light and decided to come check on you."

Lori saved her work and closed her laptop. "I had a hard time working today, what with all the congratulatory visits."

He smiled and paused at one of the chairs in front of her desk. "Okay if I sit?"

"Of course."

He picked up the chair and carried it around the desk, setting it close to her. "Have you got dinner plans?"

She shook her head.

He sat and leaned forward with his elbows on his knees, then swiveled her chair to face him and took one of her hands.

"What if this doesn't work out, Matt? What if we don't work out?"

Lifting her hand, he kissed the inside of her wrist, then slid his tongue over her pulse point. "We worked before."

Her heartbeat picked up. "If we'd worked before, we would still be together."

"If I hadn't messed things up, I believe we *would* be together."

"We can't recreate what we had in college. Life has changed both of us."

"I'm not trying to recreate anything. This is a fresh start." Matt straightened. "Tell me you didn't feel anything when we kissed at Phil's house, and I'll get up and walk out the door." When she tried to look away, Matt cupped her chin. "Tell me."

If she denied her feelings, she'd be lying. No one had ever made her heart flutter the way Matt did. "I can't."

Matt's grin was sure to the point of arrogance. "Dinner at my house. I'm marinating chicken and I'm a great cook."

"You cook?"

Standing, he pulled her to her feet. "Yes. All these years I've had to fend for myself."

She reached into the bottom drawer of her desk for her purse. From what she'd heard, he hadn't been forced to fend very often, but there was no reason to bring up past history.

"So, my place?"

"Yes." She grabbed her jacket from behind the door and they walked to the elevator.

When they reached the parking lot, a rumble of thunder rolled through the air. "Leave your car. I'll bring you back after dinner."

"Give me your address in case I lose you and I'll meet you there."

He shook his head. "I feel like I've already won a war. I'll let you win this battle."

"Thank you."

She entered his address in her GPS, which turned out to be a good thing since she caught a red light. As she drove, she wondered if she was doing the right thing. Theresa told her to go for it, and Tara would say the same. Her biggest worry was what she'd do if she experienced a replay of college. At the moment, though, her desire to spend time with Matt overshadowed her fears.

He waited next to an open door of his three-car garage and directed her in. She parked and he opened her door. "Did you have any trouble?"

"Nope. My GPS led me straight here."

She stepped out onto the driveway to take a better look at the front. Sitting at an angle to the garage, the house was red brick along the lower level. The second floor was wood, painted navy-blue with white trim. Two quaint dormer windows hung over the garage doors. She turned toward the yard and the gorgeous landscaping.

"I don't want to go in the garage door," she told him. "I want to start at the beginning."

"Okay," he said, flashing a grin.

She followed him up the walk, and he hit a button on his phone that unlocked the door.

"Oh, I like that. You don't have to carry a key."

"Very handy." He opened the door and touched her back to guide her inside.

Straight ahead lay a staircase, with the living room on the left, and a home office on the right. The top halves of both rooms matched the navy blue of the exterior. The bottom halves were white-paneled wainscoting. "Matt. You did this? It's beautiful."

"You like it?"

"I love it."

Past the living room they entered a dining room with the same color scheme. The kitchen had oak cabinets with a navy-blue island. Through the kitchen was a family room with an amazing rock fireplace, and down a short hall were a bathroom, laundry, and mudroom.

"Let me get the oven heating and I'll show you the second floor."

She rested elbows on the island. "Double ovens, great lighting, you thought of everything."

"I tried," he said, turning on one of the ovens and pulling a pan of chicken out of the fridge.

"Your wood floors are beautiful. Were they part of the renovation?"

"Yes. I lived with the ugliest carpet you've ever seen until I installed them."

She glanced over her shoulder toward the family room.

"You have a piano. Do you play?"

"A little."

He took her hand and led her around to the stairs. The master bedroom had an adjoining sitting room and bathroom. He walked straight to the king bed, sat down, and patted the mattress. "See how much room I have?"

"Plenty of room to grow in," she said, walking toward the door.

He put a hand to his heart. "So near and yet so far."

Lori laughed at his attempt at a pathetic expression. It wasn't fair that he was so handsome.

He showed her four more bedrooms, each with its own bathroom.

"You did an amazing job, Matt. I'm very impressed."

He tugged her close, locking her in his azure gaze. "I'm glad you like it."

"The whole house is beautiful," she said, feeling breathless with excitement. Coming here tonight, walking through his house, was a huge step forward for her. For them. *Please don't make me sorry.*

Lifting a hand to her cheek, he ran the tip of his thumb along her bottom lip without taking his eyes from hers. "You're beautiful."

"You're pretty spectacular yourself."

He flashed a quick smile; his mouth hovering inches from hers. She could feel their mingled breath on her lips. He closed the distance in a flash and she careened downhill on the-one-of-a-kind thrill ride provided by Matthew Kelley.

A moment later she leaned away, needing to catch her breath. She'd caught a glimpse of his backyard from one of the upstairs windows. "Show me the yard."

He lifted a brow, and his wicked grin appeared. "I'd rather stay right here and keep doing this."

Exactly why they needed to go back downstairs. She took his hand and headed for the stairs.

In the kitchen, Matt slid the pan of chicken into the heated oven, then unlocked the kitchen door and led her out onto the back deck.

The yard was nice-sized, with a fence along the back. Mature trees hid the neighboring homes, making his seem enclosed in a world alone. Down the stairs and to the right, nestled in a stand of trees, was another raised deck. "That's a nice extra space. Did you build it?"

"I did."

She studied him for a minute, seeing a Matt she never knew. "I'm extremely impressed."

~

Matt appreciated her opinion and her approval. He'd spent a lot of time on this renovation, doing most of the work himself. Getting her to come here felt like a huge accomplishment, because he'd never expected to have Lori Maguire in his home.

Matt slipped his hand around her waist as she scanned his yard. When she looked up at him, he stole another kiss and loved her sigh.

He turned her toward the door at a rumble of thunder followed by fat raindrops. "Would you like something to drink?" he asked once they were back in the kitchen.

"Water, please."

He fixed her a glass of water and pulled a colander of green beans out of the fridge.

"Put me to work."

"Will you snap the ends while I throw a salad together?"

"Absolutely."

They washed their hands at the sink together while he reminded himself not to get his hopes too high. Still, he couldn't help but think how much he'd like to do this every night. When she finished the beans, she peeled and sliced a cucumber for the salad as well.

He put the beans in a pot on the stove and the salad in the fridge. "It's going to be a little while. Let's go have a seat."

"How did I not know you play the piano?" she asked as they walked into the family room.

"I guess because I never told you."

"Will you play something now?"

He'd rather snuggle on the sofa and engage in a more

intimate recreation. Instead, he led her to the piano bench and tugged her down beside him. "What would you like to hear?"

She shrugged. "Surprise me."

Matt placed his fingers on the keys and played something she'd recognize.

From his periphery, he could see her turn her head from the piano to him.

When the last notes of "Dawn" faded away, he glanced over to see her wiping away a tear. "I didn't mean to make you cry."

"That was breathtaking. Please play something else."

"I need to feed you."

She put her hand on his arm. "Please, Matt."

Matt gazed into her beautiful green eyes. How could he say no?

We should have been sitting here like this for years.

When he finished playing "All of Me," she leaned close and kissed him.

"If I'd known I'd get this kind of reaction, I'd have played for you months ago."

"Matt, don't joke. That was so beautiful. You gave me goose bumps."

"It might have been said with a smile, but I'm not joking. And I can think of a hundred things I'd rather do to give you goose bumps than play the piano."

Her "Matt" came out as an affectionate reprimand. "I had no idea you could play. Where did you learn?"

"My mom taught piano lessons for years. She taught all of us how to play."

"Why didn't you ever tell me?"

"I was too busy trying to impress you by being a big football jock."

"Did you think I dated you because you were a football jock?"

Matt chuckled. "No, I think you dated me because I wouldn't let you say no."

Lori smiled. "I'm amazed. You write, you play the piano, you remodeled this beautiful home, and you cook. Do you have any other surprises?"

"Oh, darlin'." He stood and scooped her into his arms. "I've got all kinds of surprises for you."

Her scarlet blush made him laugh as he carried her into the kitchen, depositing her on a stool.

Over dinner, he asked questions about her kids. Like most parents, she enjoyed telling stories, and some were pretty funny. He looked forward to meeting Taylor and Megan one day.

After dinner, she insisted they clean the kitchen together.

"I'd better get home," she said after the last pan was dried.

"We just finished dinner. Please stay a while longer."

"I'm afraid I'll get sleepy after that yummy dinner. You're a very good cook."

He took her hand and led her back to the family room. "Come sit with me for a while. I'll be a gentleman."

He turned both the lights and the music low, then guided Lori to the sofa. Rain had moved over the area as they ate. Heavy drops tapped against the window behind the sofa, adding to the ambiance. Distant flashes of lightning lit the room occasionally, and thunder rumbled overhead.

Matt sat sideways with his back to a sofa arm and pulled Lori to him. He stretched out and she swung her legs up next to his and snuggled into the crook of his shoulder. He was careful not to show his surprise.

"Is this your make out music?"

Matt chuckled. "No, but I'd be happy to change to that if you like."

"No. This is perfect," she said, snuggling closer.

Matt felt as content as a puppy having his tummy rubbed.

~

*L*ori felt fingertips gently stroking the length of her face, her chin being lifted, parted lips moving lazily against her own. Her heartbeat quickened while the sound of rain beat against the window, almost drowning out the music. She hadn't been roused awake in all her married years. The thought made her sad.

"What time is it?" she asked when Matt lifted his head.

"Very early in the morning," he whispered sleepily.

"Seriously?"

He caught her arm before she could crawl over him and squinted at his watch. "It's two twenty."

"Please tell me you're kidding."

Just then the room lit up and a loud clap of thunder made Lori jump.

Matt tightened his hold. "What does it matter?" he asked, tucking a tendril of hair behind her ear.

"I've got to go home. We have work in a few hours."

He sat up, pulling her with him. "Let me drive you home."

"I'll need my car to get to work."

"I'll pick you up on my way in. Better yet, I'll bring a change of clothes and get ready at your place."

She pushed to her feet. "People will think we spent the night together."

Matt ran his fingers through his hair. "We did."

"Not like that, but they'll think we did if you take me to work."

Lori took his hand and tugged him to his feet. In the kitchen, she slipped on shoes she'd kicked off after dinner.

Matt took her coat from a hook near the door and held it for her.

"Thank you. And thanks for dinner. It was delicious." Last night their friendship had taken a turn she wasn't unhappy about, but she wanted to take things slowly. "I'll return the invitation."

"When?"

Lori couldn't help but smile. Matt was persistent, tenacious, and stubborn. They'd taken steps toward a relationship, and he wouldn't be patient as she stumbled along. "Soon."

He drew her close and she relaxed into him. Despite the past, she still felt safe in Matt's arms. "Kiss me, Lori."

So she did.

$\mathcal{M}$att couldn't wait to see Lori again. As soon as he got to the newspaper and checked in with Denise, he headed for her office and was surprised to find Carrie sitting at her desk with the top drawer open.

"Carrie. What are you doing?"

"Oh!" She jumped out of Lori's chair so fast she bumped the desk, jarring it hard enough to knock over the framed photo of Lori's kids. "I was just leaving Lori a note. We've been working on a story together." She held up a small florist-sized envelope. When she reached over to right the picture, she knocked over a cup holding pens and pencils, sending them clattering over the desk.

"What story?"

"The fishing one I told you about on Tuesday."

"Lori's helping you with that?" He walked in and set the picture upright while Carrie gathered the pencils.

"She's been checking my work. I want to send you an error-free copy."

"We have reporters who can help you with that."

"Oh, I know. I just wanted a fresh pair of eyes to help. Lori said she didn't mind."

Something wasn't adding up. When he saw Lori and Carrie near the elevators on Tuesday, Lori had seemed agitated. He meant to ask her about it, but the incident had slipped his mind. "Even so, you shouldn't be in her desk."

"I didn't go through her things," Carrie said, a note of indignation in her tone. She walked around Lori's desk, passing him on the way to the door. "I was just going to leave the note here to surprise her."

She was still holding the note. "You're not going to leave it now?"

"I'll give it to her later."

Matt waited until Carrie left the office before he walked over to Lori's desk and opened the top drawer. Nothing seemed amiss, but he wouldn't be able to tell if Carrie had taken something.

When he came out of Lori's office, Phil was at his desk. "Have you seen Lori this morning?"

"No, I just got in. But I was going to come to see you. The murder suspect in the Wallace case got picked up in Idaho."

"When?"

"About an hour ago."

"See what you can find out."

On the way to his office, Matt stopped at the breakroom door and spotted Lori putting a container in the fridge. He waited until she straightened and glanced his way. Her smile warmed his heart and chased away the twinge of doubt that had teased his mind since she left his house just hours ago.

"Sorry I'm late. I forgot to set my alarm."

He wanted nothing more than to wrap his arms around her and kiss her until they were both breathless, but with several people milling about, she'd kill him. He wasn't about to give her an excuse to unravel his hard work. "We'll find a way for you to make up the time."

She stopped in front of him. "How about I stay an hour later tonight?"

He shook his head. "That won't work. I'm driving to Astoria this afternoon for Dad's birthday."

"How's he doing?"

"All healed. Mom says she can't keep him down." He led her out of the breakroom toward his office.

"Where are we going?"

"I have a column I need to discuss with you," he said, loudly enough for Denise to hear as they passed her desk. He shut the door behind them and pulled her close.

"Everyone in this office is going to be suspicious if you don't stop shutting the door."

"You know I don't care." He kissed her because he couldn't wait any longer. "You can make up your time by coming to Astoria with me this weekend. I want you to meet my family."

"I can't. I've got my parents and Tara coming to dinner on Saturday night."

"You weren't going to invite me?"

She smoothed a hand down his tie. "I think it's a little too soon to tell my mom about you."

He bent and kissed her neck, taking a deep breath of her perfume. "Your mom used to love me."

She shivered under his lips. "I'm sure she still does."

"You can't reschedule your dinner for another weekend?"

"Tara's boyfriend's birthday is Sunday and I've already committed, so no." She took a step back. "Now I need to get to work before my boss gets ornery."

She opened the door, but before she walked out, he stopped her with a hand on her arm. "Carrie was at your desk earlier. She had the top drawer open."

"Why?"

"She said she was leaving you a note about a story you're helping her with."

He watched a look he couldn't read pass over her face.

"Is everything okay between you two?"

"Yep." She gave a little wave and walked away.

~

*L*ori glanced toward Carrie's desk on her way past, but her cubicle was empty. She turned into her own office, hung up her jacket, and after stashing her purse, opened her top drawer.

She didn't keep valuables in her desk, and didn't think Carrie would take anything if she did. But this was the second time Carrie had been at her desk. Lori moved a few pens around and shifted the drawer organizer to the side. Nothing seemed to be missing.

She sat down and thought about Matt and his invitation, which brought back a memory of her and her friend Cyndi on one of the many quilts or blankets circling the campus pond. Scantily-clad students rejoicing at the first warm weather of spring while music blared from the speakers of a truck someone had backed onto the grass. It was the Thursday before spring break and everyone was in a party mood.

"Are they going to play volleyball all afternoon?" Cyndi's irritation sharpened her tone.

Lori shaded her eyes from the glaring sun. Cyndi lay on her stomach, her chin propped on her hands.

"I was hoping to spend some time with Scott before he goes on vacation with his family for a whole week."

Scott and Matt were enmeshed in a cutthroat volleyball

game where good-natured insults were being thrown around like confetti.

Lori reached for her sunglasses. "Why don't you go play volleyball with them?"

"There aren't any girls playing."

Lori smiled. "Sounds fun."

"Matt has looked over here about a hundred times. He probably wants you to come watch."

"You go."

"I don't want to go alone," Cyndi whined. "Come with me."

Lori could feel the skin on her arms and legs tingling. She'd be burned tomorrow.

"Never mind. Matt's on his way over. Why can't Scott take a break, too?"

"Why don't you go offer him a cold drink?"

"Hi, Matt."

"Hey, Cyn."

Lori felt a shadow fall across her face. She opened her eyes and looked straight up at Matt. He winked and stepped over to the cooler. "You ladies want something?"

"Yeah. Scott."

Matt chuckled. "I mean do you want something to drink?"

Cyndi sighed. "Yes, please."

"I don't, thank you," Lori replied, reaching over her head, pulling the quilt down, and bunching it under her neck. She took a deep breath and sighed, feeling too content for words. Two soda cans tops popped. A song ended and another started, the music drifting across the pond. She sensed rather than felt Matt sit next to her.

"Is the game almost over?" Cyndi asked.

Lori felt Matt twist a strand of her hair around his finger. "It is for me."

"Did Scott say how long he'd be?"

"Nope."

As always, Lori's heartbeat jumped when Matt was near. She slid her hand toward him and he covered it with his own, lacing his fingers between hers. She ventured to peek his way, and caught him grinning at her.

"What?" she asked.

"I'm enjoying your bare legs."

"Matt," Lori groaned, suddenly self-conscious.

"If you two are going to start talking bare body parts, I'm going to see if I can pull Scott away from the game," Cyndi said.

Lori smacked Matt's leg after her friend walked away. "I can't believe you did that."

"What did I do? I just said I'm enjoying your bare legs, which I've never seen before."

"You've seen my legs when I wear dresses."

"Not this much of them." He touched her thigh. "You have nice legs."

"Don't do this to me."

"What?" he asked, laughing. "Compliment you? I looked over here and realized I've never seen your legs, so I decided to take a closer look."

Lori grabbed for the side of the quilt Cyndi just vacated to cover up, but Matt reached across her and kissed her nose. "I'll stop."

He grabbed the neck of his T-shirt in back, pulled it over his head, and stretched out next to her. Lori's breath caught. She'd never seen him without a shirt. She averted her eyes before he caught her staring while her face burned—and not from the sun.

Matt was quiet for a long time, and Lori thought he'd fallen asleep until he said her name.

"Hmm?"

"How long do you think people should date before they get married?"

The question caught her off guard. "I don't know. I guess it depends on the couple and the circumstances."

He reached down and took her hand in his, lightly rubbing her knuckles before lifting it and kissing the inside of her wrist. "Come home with me over spring break, Lori. I want you to meet my family."

She turned her head. He lay still, his eyes closed. "I told you last week that I have to babysit for my neighbors. They're going out of town and need someone to watch their kids. I've already told them I would."

"I bet they can find someone else if you tell them something crucial came up." He rolled onto his side, propping himself up on an elbow. "This is important to me, Lori."

"Matt—"

"I'd like to think meeting my family would be important to my girlfriend."

"I've met your parents."

"I want you to meet my whole family."

"I'd love to meet your family, but it can't be over spring break." His question about marriage scared her a little. She'd mulled over the idea a few times, but she was only nineteen, and Matt had just turned twenty-two.

While the thought of being married to him was thrilling, she wanted to get through college. She loved Matt with her whole heart, and she'd never felt like this about anyone before. Imagining a life with him came easily. But was she ready for marriage? Was he?

"I bet your neighbors could find someone to take your place."

She sat up and turned to him. "Two days isn't enough notice. I can't do that to them. I promise I'll meet your family this summer."

Matt stood up. "I'm going to play volleyball."

"Please, don't be mad."

"I'm not. Can you catch a ride home with Cyn? I told Gabe I'd take a look at his car later."

He didn't wait for an answer before striding away.

That was the last day they spent together.

~

*L*ori was relieved when the weekend arrived. She hadn't seen Matt before he left for Astoria, and Carrie seemed to be avoiding her like she had the plague.

Saturday morning, she hung a few crepe paper streamers, ran out to a party store for a few birthday balloons, and prepared the Cornish hens she planned to roast.

Midmorning, she answered a knock on her door, delighted to see her neighbor. "Hi, Gage. Come in."

"Sorry to bother you," he said stepping inside. "I've unpacked every box and can't find my hammer. Do you have one I can borrow?"

"Of course."

He glanced toward her dining room. "Looks like you're having a party."

"Oh, just a small birthday dinner," she said over her shoulder as she headed for her basement. "Hey, why don't you come?"

"No, I can't intrude."

"You wouldn't be. It's just my parents, my sister, and her boyfriend. Please come. It's very casual. You won't be intruding at all."

"Can I bring anything?" he asked.

"Just yourself. Come over about six."

"Thank you."

After he left, hammer in hand, Lori finished decorating Kevin's chocolate-raspberry mousse cake, which turned out perfect, then sliced broccoli florets, carrots, onion, celery, sweet red peppers, and mushrooms for her vegetable medley.

She wasn't surprised when Tara and Kevin arrived early.

"How's Matt?" Tara asked before Lori had time to wish Kevin a happy birthday.

"That's all she talked about on the way here," Kevin said, holding his arms out for his hug and kiss on the cheek.

"Happy birthday," she said to Kevin, then turned to her sister. "Matt's fine."

"And?"

"Tara, give your sister a break."

"I had dinner at Matt's house this week. He has a beautiful home he renovated himself, and he's a great cook."

"And?" Tara said, rolling her hand. She glanced at Kevin. "This is like questioning one of the kids."

"Maybe you shouldn't be so nosy," Kevin said.

"Come on, there's more," Tara coaxed.

"I also had dinner at Phil and Faith's house. Matt was there."

Tara pointed at her. "There it is. Your telltale sign. Something happened, or you wouldn't be blushing."

Lori told the quick version of how she'd been tricked into dinner that left Tara bent over from laughing so hard. She left out the game of strip pool. "Phil and his wife are my new heroes."

Lori pointed at her sister when she saw her parents park at the curb. "No Matt talk in front of Mom and Dad."

She opened the door just as Gage raised his fist to knock. "Ha, perfect timing."

He held out a bouquet. "These are for you. Thank you for letting me crash your party."

She took the mixed bouquet of roses. "You didn't need to

do this. Please, come in. Tara, Kevin, this is my neighbor, Gage Farr."

Her mom and dad followed Gage in and handshaking ensued.

Tara leaned towards her. "He's cute."

"Don't," Lori said in a warning tone.

"And he lives right next door. That's convenient."

"I'm not taking the bait, sister of mine."

"Party pooper."

Lori's guests enjoyed the Cornish hens while their conversations overlapped. Kevin and Gage talked baseball with her dad. Tara and their mom talked about wedding plans for Tara's daughter. Lori just enjoyed the noisy atmosphere and wished Matt were here. He would have loved to be a part of this. Even though she knew he couldn't be here, she should have invited him anyway.

After dinner, the men retired to the basement for a game of pool.

"Are you and Gage dating?" her mom asked as soon as Gage was out of earshot.

"No, he's just my neighbor."

"He's nice. Maybe you should ask him out."

"I'm not interested in dating Gage, Mom." Lori took six forks out of a drawer and set them on the counter. "But I have been spending time with Matt Kelley."

Her mom looked at Tara. "What does *spending time with* mean?" she asked, using air quotes. "Is that the new way of saying *dating* these days?"

"I think it means your youngest daughter might be thinking about a second chance romance," Tara said with a smile.

Her mom gave Lori a wide-eyed look. "I'd be okay with that."

Tara laughed and wrapped their mom in a hug. "I don't think she's asking permission, Mom."

After everyone left, Gage hung back. "I want to say thanks for letting me crash Kevin's party. Your family is great."

"Like most families, we have our moments, but they are pretty great. I'm glad you could come."

"Will you let me repay you with dinner Monday night?"

"That's not necessary, Gage."

"I'd like to. Just dinner."

"I'm . . . starting to date . . . someone."

His smile was kind. "Just as friends, Lori. I didn't mean anything else."

Her cheeks flamed to life and she covered them. "I just thought I should throw that out there."

"So, Monday? I'll pick you up at six?"

"Okay," she said with a nod. "That would be nice."

Lori watched him cross the yard to his house, embarrassed because she'd assumed. She was out of her element when it came to dating.

After being married for twenty-one years and then single for three, she felt like she'd been catapulted back to teenage craziness. Those awkward days of trying to find your way through the hierarchy of social circles without falling flat on your face. Wondering if that smile a guy flashed meant he was interested or that you had something between your front teeth.

Her phone rang. Caller ID told her what she already suspected and put a smile on her face. "Hi, Matt."

"Are your guests gone?"

"Yes. How about your family? Everyone headed home?"

"The party broke up about fifteen minutes ago. I bet your dinner was much quieter than ours."

"I bet you're right." She dropped onto the sofa. "There were only six of us."

"Six?" Matt said after a lengthy pause.

"Gage came over to borrow a hammer this morning, so I invited him back for dinner."

"Your new neighbor, Mr. Farr?" he asked, his voice an octave lower.

And this was how complications slithered between the cracks of a relationship that was too new to even be designated a relationship.

"You've finally agreed to have dinner with me after months of me asking. Gage stops by to borrow a hammer and gets invited to have dinner with your family."

"Matt, it's different."

"How is it different?"

"It was . . . nothing. Inviting him was a neighborly gesture, that's all. He's lived next door for two months and I've never invited him to dinner."

"Neighborly gesture. Have you invited any of your other neighbors over for dinner?"

She took a calming breath. "I understand why you're upset, but I didn't invite him here to meet my family. I invited him out of friendship. It meant nothing."

"I can't believe you're naïve enough to believe the man doesn't own a hammer."

Lori's temper flared. "He didn't say he didn't own one, but that he couldn't find it."

"You inviting him might not mean anything to you, but I guarantee it meant something to him."

"Matt, it's a completely different circumstance."

"How is it different?"

"Gage doesn't mean anything to me," she blurted out.

Matt blew out a breath. "I don't want to fight," he said.

"Good. Neither do I."

"I'll be home too late tomorrow. Will you let me take you to dinner Monday night?"

Oh, barnacles. "I can't go on Monday." *Tell him everything.* "Gage asked me to dinner—to repay me for tonight. It means nothing."

"Men don't ask women out to be friends, darlin'," Matt said, his tone dripping sarcasm.

She should tell him that she'd told Gage she was dating someone. Instead, she pushed off the sofa and walked to the dining room window. A light in a back room of Gage's house was on. The rest of the house was dark. "Don't talk to me like I'm a child."

"Then stop acting like one. Your neighbor is asking you on a date. It may seem like nothing to you, but I bet it means something to him."

You'd lose that bet. "This is going to get too complicated."

"Then uncomplicate it. Tell Mr. Farr you can't go," Matt said flatly.

"I can't."

"Why not? You've told *me* no repeatedly."

"Matt, Gage only asked as a gesture of friendship."

"You can believe that if it makes you feel better."

He was being impossible, as usual. Her cheeks burned with anger. She rested her forehead against the cool glass. "Am I the only woman who's ever told you no?"

"I'm not going to listen to you analyze my feelings, Lori. You're trying to pick a fight."

"Seems you already picked the fight."

"I'll unpick it as soon as you tell Gage you can't go to dinner with him."

"Goodnight, Matt." She disconnected the call.

CHAPTER 16

Lori's Sunday had slogged by. When she woke to her alarm Monday morning, she flirted with the idea of calling in sick. Instead, she walked into her office two hours later with her thoughts on spring break her freshman year.

Saturday afternoon at a backyard party, Lori was cheering on a volleyball game. Tomorrow was the last day of spring break, and Matt would be back in Seattle. He hadn't called her once over the week—obviously still angry because she hadn't gone with him to meet his family. They'd parted on such a bad note, she wasn't sure what to expect when he got back.

She missed him, missed talking to him every day. He'd become her best friend over the past six months.

Cyndi stopped next to her.

"Hey, girl. Where's Scott?" When Cyndi didn't answer, Lori glanced at her. "What's wrong?"

Cyndi raked her bottom teeth across her top lip. "Matt's here."

"He is?" Lori turned toward the patio door. "He's not supposed to be back until tomorrow."

"Lori, wait." Cyndi grabbed her arm. Something in her voice made Lori stop mid-step. She looked at her friend. "He's not alone."

Cyndi wouldn't say that if Matt was with one of his friends. Her heart squeezed in her chest, making her light-headed. "Who's he with?"

"Tammie."

Sandy joined them. "Why is Matt here with Tammie Bennett?"

Lori opened her mouth, but nothing came out.

"She's all over him," Sandy said. "What's going on, Lori?"

"We fought before he left for spring break." Lori tried to swallow around the enormous lump in her throat.

"Did you two break up?" Cyndi asked.

"I didn't think so, but if he's here with Tammie, I guess we did."

"Do you want me to take you home?" Cyndi asked. "Scott will let me borrow his car."

"No, I drove." She felt numb from head to toe, and at the same time every nerve ending was tingling.

"I'll stay with her," Sandy said.

"You don't have to stay with me. I . . . I'm okay." She held up a hand when Sandy started to say something. "I just need a minute."

Lori turned her back to the house, trying to pay attention to the volleyball game. She didn't have the courage to go inside and face Matt with Tammie Bennett there. Besides, Matt's buddies would have told him she was there. He and Tammie would come outside eventually. Then what?

Tammie Bennett, of all people. Her reputation around campus was legendary, and she seemed quite proud of how many football players she'd conquered. Now she could add Matt to her list.

Cyndi appeared at her side again. "They just came outside."

"Are they looking over here?"

"Matt glanced this way, but then stopped to get a drink."

Lori couldn't not look. Tammie had her arms wrapped around Matt's waist. His hand rested on her bare shoulder. Lori glanced toward the gate, wondering how to make a graceful exit.

"Hey, Lori. Hi, Cyn."

"Hi, Mike," they said in unison.

His eyes darted toward Matt and Tammie then back to her. "Are you okay, Lori?"

She was anything but okay. She tried to smile but felt the corners of her mouth wobble. "I will be."

"Sandy asked if I'd make an ice run. She thought you might want to go with me."

"I do."

The only way to get out of the yard was past Matt and Tammie. Matt was joking with a friend, but his smile dropped away when she and Mike walked by. Her throat tightened, along with her chest, when she noticed Matt's hand slip to Tammie's hip.

Lori made the ice run with Mike. He tried to make conversation, but she had a hard time paying attention. She helped Mike carry the four bags of ice as far as the front door.

"I can't go back in, Mike."

"Just leave the ice there. I'll come back and get it. Do you need a ride somewhere?"

"No, my car is down the street."

Mike glanced at the door. "I'm a little nervous to go back in there. Matt didn't look happy when we left together."

"He won't do anything. Just tell him . . . my battery was dead, so you gave me a jump."

"Sorry, Lori."

She shrugged. "Have a good time."

On her drive home, she discovered what a broken heart felt like. She could barely stand to breathe, her chest hurt so bad. Twice she had to pull over to wipe her tears away.

The remainder of the semester seemed to take forever. Luckily, she didn't have any classes with Matt, so she changed her route around campus every few days so she wouldn't run into him. If she happened to see him and Tammie, who seemed to be joined at his hip, she turned the other way.

Northwestern had been her first choice. She got wait-listed, but never received the coveted email, so she went to the University of Washington. When she got accepted to Northwestern for a summer class, she jumped at the chance to leave Seattle. She was able to transfer permanently for fall semester.

"You look deep in thought."

Theresa's voice jarred her back to the present. "More memory than thought," she said beckoning Theresa into her office.

"John's out of town. Want to grab dinner with me tonight?"

"I have plans."

Theresa smiled. "Anyone I know?"

"As a matter of fact, yes. I'm having dinner with Gage."

"Gage?" The surprise on Theresa's face would have been comical if she felt like laughing.

"Just as friends."

"Does he know that?" she asked, leaning a hip against Lori's desk.

"Yes. Why are you so surprised? You and Carrie are the ones who suggested I should get to know him better."

"Carrie made the suggestion, and that was a long time ago."

"It was last Monday, Theresa."

"I'm surprised you took our suggestion. You usually don't when it comes to men and dating."

"This isn't a date."

"What about Matt?"

"He's mad."

"Watching you two is like watching a train wreck."

Lori scoffed. "There's nothing to watch."

Theresa shook her head. "I have to go out on a story and was going to take Carrie with me. Have you seen her?"

"I haven't seen her in days." Carrie had made herself scarce since Matt caught her at Lori's desk.

Theresa pushed off her desk. "If you do see her, tell her to call my cell."

"Will do. Have a good day."

~

Matt spent the day in his office cleaning out his file cabinet. He came in early and would leave late. He didn't make any trips to the breakroom, and he ate lunch at his desk. He was mad at himself for losing his temper last night, and mad about being so sure of himself and self-absorbed.

If Lori wanted to date someone else, he wouldn't try to stop her. The past three months hadn't been wasted, because now he knew he still loved her. So, as impatient as he was, he'd wait. If she decided on Gage or someone else, he'd respect her decision. But he was determined not to make her workspace uncomfortable.

Late that afternoon Phil walked into his office and plopped down in a chair. "You been here all day?"

"Yep. Just been busy."

"Did you eat? Dale and I got a pizza. There's a couple of pieces left in the fridge."

"I ate."

"You want to talk?"

"Phil, I've got a lot to do." He pulled a stack of files off the credenza behind his desk and set them on the floor.

"Is this about Lori?"

Matt opened the top folder and started thumbing through papers. "She's going out with Gage Farr tonight."

"The neighbor? Huh, didn't see that coming." Phil shrugged. "If it's any consolation, she doesn't look very happy about it. In fact, she's seemed pretty miserable all day."

"It's not."

"Maybe she's nervous about dating only one guy because of her divorce."

Matt hadn't thought of that. Maybe she *was* nervous, though she hadn't seemed that way at his house.

"Give her time."

"I gave her time twenty-four years ago and she married someone else." Matt swiveled his chair to the credenza.

"Why'd you give her time then?"

Matt raised his head and looked out the window. Clouds were moving in, covering the sun, making the day match his mood. "Pride, ego—who knows? I did something stupid, and then, instead of apologizing and trying to fix things, I waited until it was too late. Lori had already moved to Chicago."

He dropped another pile of folders on his desk. "I don't want to give her time, Phil, and I don't want her going on a date with Gage."

"Maybe she's still mad about what happened in college."

"Did she act like she was still mad the night we played pool?"

Phil grinned and shook his head. "No, she definitely seemed to be over the college thing that night."

Matt and Phil had been friends for a long time, and he valued Phil's opinion, both in business and as a friend. "What do I do? I've given her more than three months."

Phil shrugged, then flashed his grin. "I can get you another woman's opinion."

Faith would annihilate him, as usual. But she liked Lori, so maybe she'd be willing to offer advice. He picked up the receiver on his desk phone while Phil punched in the numbers. "Hey, beautiful," Matt said when she answered.

"Hi, handsome."

"What's for dinner?"

"Tacos. Six thirty. Bring a dessert. No cheesecake."

"See you then."

Phil pushed out of his chair. "Don't listen to her if she said no cheesecake. And add raspberries."

Matt would take a dessert for Faith and cheesecake with raspberry topping for Phil.

~

Gage knocked on Lori's door at six o'clock sharp. He was a handsome man, with a rugged look that didn't fit her preconceived image of an artist, but Gage pulled it off successfully.

"You'll have to recommend a place for dinner," he said. "I don't know very many restaurants around here."

"What are you hungry for?"

"How about some great seafood? I haven't had any since I've been here."

"I know the perfect place. I'll drive."

"You driving will defeat the purpose of this thank-you dinner."

She walked onto the porch, closed, and locked the door. "I know the way. Plus, if I drive, you'll be able to look around, something you can't always do when driving."

Over Dungeness crab cakes, he showed Lori pictures of his three grown children and four grandchildren.

"You don't look old enough to have four grandchildren."

"Believe me, I'm old enough. This little sweetheart has her grandpa wrapped around her tiny finger."

Lori smiled at the photo on his cell phone. "She's adorable. I can see why you wouldn't be able to resist."

He ordered grilled Chilean sea bass and she decided on scallops. They talked about places they'd traveled. Gage described the art gallery he owned and told her about some of the artists who had showings there. Lori asked questions about art and Gage asked questions about writing and said he enjoyed reading her column.

The evening turned out to be thoroughly enjoyable. Gage was easy to talk to and extremely comfortable to be around. His passion about art made learning details interesting.

"I should have taken one of your classes. I bet your students are enthralled."

"I think enthralled is a little too enthusiastic. I hope they find my classes motivating."

They parted with a wave in her driveway.

Lori went inside and had just locked the door when her cell phone rang. The face on her screen made her smile. "Hello, handsome," she said after she connected the call.

"Hey, Mom. Guess what?"

Her non-phone child was always quick to get to the point. "What?"

"I aced that physics test I was worried about."

"Yay for you, sweetie! Congratulations." She set her purse

on the kitchen countertop. "I'm happy for you. How is your statistics class going?"

"Still hate it. How's your weather?"

"Lots of rain. How's yours?"

"Cold and snowy. I'm so ready for spring."

"Hang in there, it's right around the corner. Are you going to Chicago for spring break?"

"Yeah. It's okay with you, right?"

No, she wanted both kids here for the week so she could spoil them and love on them and cook all their favorite dishes. "Of course, it is, hon."

"Dad said he'd take a couple of days off work."

"Oh, that makes my heart happy."

"Well, I've got to go. I'm meeting a study group in the student hall."

"Have a nice time. I love you."

"Love you, Mom."

And he's gone.

She plugged her phone into the charger on the counter and headed down the hall. Without turning on any lights, she went into the bathroom and turned the water on in the tub. Adding some bubble bath, she dropped her clothes where she stood and pinned her hair on top of her head. On the way home, what was left of her energy seeped out like the slow leak of a tire. Exhaustion had her almost in tears.

Sinking into the water up to her chin, she closed her eyes. When she moved here, she believed the most complicated her life would get would be fighting off her mom and dad's questions about dating.

She stayed in her office all day so she wouldn't run into Matt. Hiding out wasn't the kind of work environment she wanted for herself or him. So tomorrow she'd find a reason to go to his office and try to smooth things over enough that they could work together comfortably.

She wanted to go back to January. Sure, there'd been palpable tension between her and Matt, but that was as far as it would have gone. No, she decided quickly. She'd turn the clock back even farther—to October, before she produced a resume, before she talked to Dave and Leland. If she'd searched the *Star's* reporters, she would have seen Matt among them. If she'd known he worked for the *Star*, she never would have sent her resume. She should have done a little more research.

Just as her muscles started to relax, her cell phone rang. The chime sounded loud in her quiet house before it rolled to voicemail. A female talked for about thirty seconds, then the house was quiet. A minute later the chime echoed again. No message this time.

When her phone rang for the third time, she stood and reached for a towel, suddenly panicked it might be about one of the kids or her parents. She didn't make it to the kitchen before the ringing stopped. Her screen announced three missed calls from Theresa. As soon as she scrolled to recent calls, her phone rang again. She connected the call. "Hey, Theresa. Are you—"

"Carrie's dead."

"What?"

"She ran off the road and hit a tree," Theresa said on a shaky sob. "Phil's there now."

Lori's knees buckled and she slid to the floor. "No."

"He called me as soon as he found out it was Carrie."

Lori felt numb. Not Carrie. She lifted the corner of her towel and wiped her eyes. "I can't believe this. Is he sure?"

"Yes." Another sob escaped. "I just didn't want you to find out by hearing it on the news tonight."

Lori stayed where she was long after Theresa disconnected the call. Poor Steve. Had he been told yet? And

Carrie's family? They lived in California. Did they know? She was heartsick for all of them.

How had Carrie run off the road? It rained earlier, but the streets weren't slick. Had she been on her way home? Going out on a story?

Lori climbed off the floor and went into the bathroom. After releasing the water from the tub, she went into the bedroom and pulled pajama bottoms and a thermal top out of her dresser.

Her thoughts kept bouncing to Matt. Phil would have told him by now. She wished they were on speaking terms. She wished she wasn't alone.

She climbed into bed and pulled the down comforter over her head.

When Lori awoke the next morning, it took her a minute to remember why her eyes burned.

Oh, Carrie's dead.

Her mind argued against the news. Maybe it was a slip-up. It was dark. Phil made a mistake.

She'd get to work, and Carrie would be in her cubicle or the breakroom. Theresa would be apologetic for upsetting her and furious at Phil for getting the facts wrong.

She took a shower, made a cup of tea, and walked outside to her front porch for the paper. Yesterday's clouds were gone, the sky so blue it hurt her eyes. Shouldn't it be a dreary day with pouring rain, lightning, and thunder. When some-one's life was over, especially someone as young as Carrie, the day shouldn't be so completely beautiful.

She sat on the porch swing and opened the paper to the front page. Carrie, in black and white, smiled at her. So it was real. No mistakes.

Phil's story stated that an eyewitness saw Carrie going well above the speed limit before her car left the road and hit a tree. The same witness also saw another car pull off the road close to the accident, as if they might help, then drive away. The witness wasn't close enough to identify the make or model of the second car. The article asked for anyone with information to call Detective Mitch Jamison. Only one call to 911 had been recorded, and it was from the eyewitness calling to report the accident.

Life could change so quickly. Everything taken away in the space of a heartbeat.

Back in the kitchen, she set her teacup in the sink. When she picked up her cell phone to drop in her purse, she noticed the light blinking on the landline answering machine. She pushed the button.

"Lori, this is Carrie."

Lori's breath caught.

"I need to talk to you. I know the general area where you live, so I'm headed in that direction." There was a pause. "It's about eight o'clock. Please call me as soon as you get this."

Staring at the answering machine, Lori started to tremble.

CHAPTER 17

The accident site listed in the paper was on Lori's way to work, and she couldn't pass without pulling over. The tree Carrie hit was in a vacant lot, and her car had already been towed away, revealing the horribly scarred bark on the trunk.

She got out of her car and started toward the tree.

A man in jeans, a dress shirt, and tie stepped in front of her. "You can't be here. This is an accident site."

She nodded but didn't turn back to her car.

"Are you a reporter?"

"No. A friend."

"You knew the victim?" he asked, his tone gentler.

"I worked with Carrie at the paper, but I'm not a reporter."

"I'm sorry." The man held out his hand. "I'm Detective Mitch Jamison."

This time when she looked at him, she took note of his dark hair touched with silver strands. His brown eyes were expressive and kind.

"Lori Maguire," she said, shaking his hand. "I don't know

if this would be helpful information or not, but Carrie left a message on my answering machine last night saying she was on her way to my house. I wasn't home when she called, and I didn't notice the message until this morning."

Detective Jamison pulled a pad of paper from his back jeans pocket and scribbled a note. "Your name is Lori Maguire?"

"Yes."

"Did Carrie come to your house often?"

"She's never been to my house. In her message she said she wasn't sure where I lived, just the general area."

"Did she say why she wanted to come over?"

Lori shook her head as she took a couple of steps closer to the tree.

"Phil Cates was here last night and noticed damage to Carrie's back bumper. Do you know anything about that?"

"Her car was new. Her husband gave it to her for Christmas." She narrowed her eyes. "Could that have caused the accident? Someone hit her from behind?"

"Possibly."

She glanced at the road. "Why would anyone have run into her? There's no light or intersection here."

The detective shook his head. "I don't know, but it would explain the other car the eyewitness saw."

The article Phil wrote said Carrie's car was traveling over the speed limit, and she was thrown from the car on impact. Carrie hated wearing a seat belt, complaining it wrinkled her clothes. *One might have saved your life last night, Carrie.*

"Do you think the other car hit her deliberately?"

"We're looking into it." Mitch pulled a business card out of his shirt pocket and held it out. "Are you going into the *Star's* office?"

"Yes."

"Can you ask Matt to call me? The number on this card is

my direct line. I should be back in the office in about an hour, or he can call my cell."

Lori nodded.

"I'm sorry for your loss."

"Thank you," she said. "And thank you for talking to me."

Minutes later, Lori got off the elevator and headed to Matt's office. Denise looked up from her computer, her eyes red-rimmed.

Lori walked around her desk and hugged her.

"Sorry," Denise sobbed out. "I just can't believe it."

"I know." Lori ran a finger under her own eyes. "I need to drop something off with Matt."

"He's in his office."

Matt was sitting in a conference chair, turned toward the window. He swiveled when he heard her footsteps. She wanted to hug him, but simply held out the business card instead. "Detective Jamison would like you to call him. He should be in his office in about forty-five minutes."

"You talked to Mitch?"

"I stopped at the accident site."

"How did you find out?"

"Theresa called me last night."

He stood up and leaned against the conference table, then reached out and took her hand. "Are you okay?"

She'd held the worst of the tears back all morning, but the look in Matt's eyes was going to make her cry. Nodding, she swallowed them back.

"Are you sure?" he asked, tugging her closer.

"As okay as I can be." She was very aware of the open door. "Have you talked to Steve?"

"Yes. He's a mess." Matt looked down and shifted his weight. "The funeral is Thursday morning."

"Okay."

"I'm sorry I got angry about Gage." He blew out a breath and looked up. "I was so jealous."

"There is nothing to be jealous about, Matt."

"I shouldn't have said—"

"Apology accepted."

He met her gaze and swallowed.

"I need to get to work," she said.

Nodding, he released her hand. "If you see Phil, will you ask him to call me?"

"Yes."

The office was like a tomb. Reporters were at their desks, but no one was joking or hollering across the room to each other.

Lori scanned the room for Theresa but didn't spot her.

She stopped at Phil's cubicle, where he sat with elbows on his desk, head in his hands. She walked in and touched his shoulder. He looked up and pulled her onto his lap.

"Are you okay?" Lori asked, wrapping her arms around him.

"Not really," he replied into her neck. "I've never had a story hit so close to home. I've seen a lot of awful stuff, but I've never felt as sick as I did when I saw Carrie on that gurney last night."

"I'm sorry it was you, Phil."

"I just can't believe we were joking around just a few . . ."

When his voice broke, Lori's eyes pooled with tears.

"I went home and held Faith for the rest of the night, afraid to let her go."

A throat cleared and Lori looked up. Matt stood at the door with a frown.

Lori pulled back from Phil. "Oh, yeah. Matt wants you to call him."

Phil pulled Lori close again. "Sorry, but we're a little busy hugging."

Matt stepped aside when they heard a sob. Theresa stood behind him. Lori held out her arm and Theresa knelt and joined in the hug. Pretty soon, Lori felts Matt's strong arms wrap around all of them.

"Group therapy," Phil mumbled against her neck.

"This is Lori Maguire," Lori said an hour later when her desk phone rang.

"Lori, this is Steve Eubanks."

She put a hand to her chest. "Steve. I am so sorry about Carrie."

"Tha—" He cleared his throat. "Thank you. Um . . . I wonder if you could come by the house sometime today?"

"Me?" popped out before Lori could stop it. "Of course. I can come anytime. When would be convenient for you?"

"Now? Co— could you come now?"

"Absolutely."

She took down the Eubanks address and grabbed her purse.

Twenty minutes later, Lori circled a modern concrete fountain and parked behind six other cars in front of a very contemporary mansion. *Holy smokes.* She had no idea Carrie lived like this.

Steve answered the door. His hug felt awkward since they'd only met once, at the Christmas party when she didn't know anyone.

He looked terrible and Lori's heart broke for him.

"Thank you for coming."

"You're welcome."

He led her straight through the house. She heard hushed voices but didn't see anyone as they walked outside to a patio with a view of Lake Washington. He pulled out a chair at a table. "Can I get you something to drink?"

"No, thank you. I'm fine."

Steve sat down across from her, pulled off his glasses, and rubbed his eyes. His brown hair was neatly trimmed and, despite the circumstances, he was impeccably dressed.

Lori sat quietly, waiting for him to begin.

Lowering his chin to his chest, he ran a hand across his forehead. "I got home about ten thirty last night after an event I had to attend. The police were waiting out front. They took me to identify—" he stopped, swallowed, then rubbed his eyes again. "I had to identify Carrie's body. I got home at about two. After calling Carrie's parents and mine, I fell into bed. I didn't check my answering machine until this morning. Carrie had left a message. I could tell she was upset by the tone of her voice, though she tried to hide it. She said you had invited her to see your house and she'd be home late."

What?

Her expression must have shown her surprise, because his jaw bulged like he was clenching his teeth. "You didn't invite her to your house, did you?"

She shook her head. "Carrie left a message on my answering machine too. Like you, I didn't notice the message until this morning."

"Has she ever been to your house?"

"No."

"Lori, I have to know." Steve's eyes filled with tears. "Was Carrie having an affair? Was she meeting someone at your house?"

Lori straightened in shock. "No. I would never agree to that."

"But you knew she was seeing someone."

"No. If Carrie was seeing someone else, she never said anything to me. And I never suspected."

Steve leaned back in his chair and looked up at the

umbrella overhead, wiping one eye with the back of his hand. "I didn't talk to the police about this." He paused as he sucked in a deep breath. "Carrie has been behaving strangely for a few weeks. She'd come home late and say she'd been out with you or Theresa or some other friend. She'd get home at ten thirty or eleven."

He glanced at Lori. "Would Theresa know? Would you ask her?"

"Of course I'll ask, but you need to tell the police what you suspect. If there *was* someone else, they could have been involved in Carrie's accident."

"Money's missing from our savings account. Enough for her to leave me if that's what she was planning."

Lori sat silent for a few moments as she looked across the lake. "I drove past the accident site on my way to work and met Detective Jamison. He's investigating what happened."

"He came by earlier."

"You should call him. The police should have all the information."

Steve nodded.

"Tell him your concerns about Carrie and the missing money. It might be important."

"I'll call." Steve looked out over the backyard. "I don't want this in the paper. It's pure speculation on my part. I don't have any proof."

"Phil's doing the story. He'd never put anything in the paper without talking to you first."

Steve nodded.

"Can I do anything for you?" Lori asked.

He exhaled a burst of air. "I don't know. I can't even think straight."

"Promise me you won't hesitate to call me if there is something. Anything."

"Actually, would you clean out Carrie's desk? I don't think I can manage that."

"Absolutely."

"There's no rush. I'm going to take some time off after the funeral and stay with my parents in California."

"Matt can store everything until you're ready. Just let me know."

"Thank you." He stood up, signaling their meeting was over.

Minutes later Lori drove away, leaving Steve standing near the front door looking into the distance.

~

Since Lori's windows overlooked the parking lot, Matt had been standing in her office, watching for her to come back. He was curious to know what Steve wanted but, even more important, he wanted to see her.

When he spotted her pulling in, he went to the elevator to wait. The door opened and she emerged with red eyes. "Are you okay? What did he want?"

"Let me get Theresa first. Can we talk in your office?"

More intrigued, Matt nodded. "Since Phil's on the story, should he be here?"

"I hope Steve is wrong, but if he's right, it might be the reason for Carrie's accident."

Matt took Lori's hand and led her past Denise's desk. "Denise, will you call Phil and Theresa and have them come to my office, please?"

"Sure."

"Tell them ASAP. Also, ask Dave to come up if he's not busy."

Matt closed the door once he and Lori stepped over the threshold. He pulled her into his arms. "I want five minutes alone with you. I want to apologize again for my jealousy and my stupid behavior."

"It's forgotten."

He cupped the back of her neck and touched his lips to hers in what he hoped she took as a meaningful "I'm sorry" kiss. He wanted her in his life forever, and he wanted forever to start as soon as possible.

Lori stepped away with a smile when someone knocked.

Matt opened the door.

Theresa walked in, followed by Phil and Dave.

Matt motioned toward the conference table and pulled out a chair for Lori. Theresa, Phil, and Dave sat on one side of the table, with he and Lori on the other. "Lori, the floor is yours."

"Steve called and asked if I could come to his house—"

"Is he okay?" Theresa interrupted, tearing up.

"No. He's exactly how you'd expect him to be. People were at the house, so he's not alone. He's going to stay with his family in California after the funeral."

"What did he want?" Phil asked.

"Carrie left a message on my answering machine last night. I wasn't home when she called, and I didn't check for messages until this morning. She said she was on her way to my house. She sounded upset."

Matt pushed the image of Lori with Gage out of his thoughts.

Lori leaned forward and clasped her hands on the table. Matt wanted to reach over and rub her back but kept his hands to himself.

"Steve also got a message from her," she said. "He wasn't home either, when she called, and when he did get home the police were already there. Like me, he didn't check his messages until this morning. On his, Carrie said I had invited her over. He thinks Carrie was having an affair and I let them meet at my house."

Theresa's mouth fell open and Phil shook his head.

"I told him she wasn't meeting anyone at my house. I promised him I'd ask you if you know anything, Theresa."

"Who was she seeing?" Phil asked, glancing at Theresa.

"I have no idea," Theresa said.

"Do you believe it?" Matt asked looking from Theresa to Lori.

"I don't know," Theresa said at the same time Lori shook her head. "I don't."

"Why would Steve think she was?" Dave asked.

"She'd been getting home late almost every night and telling him she'd been with me or Theresa or some other friend. I haven't been anywhere with Carrie besides lunch. Steve also said money is missing from their savings account, enough for Carrie to leave him if that's what she was planning."

Dave leaned forward, elbows on the table. "Has Steve talked to the police about this?"

"Not yet. I told him to call Detective Jamison, because if there is someone else, they might know something about the accident."

"If she was having an affair and things went south, the guy might have been in the car that rear-ended her," Phil said, his eyes wide.

"Did Steve agree to call?" Matt asked.

"He said he would."

"Theresa, are you sure—"

"Yes, Phil. If Carrie was having an affair, I didn't know anything about it."

Phil glanced at Lori.

She shook her head.

"Phil, you have to be one hundred percent positive before anything gets printed," Dave said.

"I'll check with Mitch again—see if Steve has called in," Phil replied.

"I promised Steve you'd let him look over your story, Phil, but maybe we should give him a few days to mourn," Lori said. "It's horrible enough that his wife just died, but if she's been having an affair . . ."

Phil shrugged. "Until we know whether someone ran Carrie off the road, I don't have much to write about."

"I'll make the call to Mitch," Matt said. "If Steve hasn't already talked to him about this, Mitch can stop by his house."

"Steve also asked if I'd clean out Carrie's desk. I told him I would, but maybe you'd like to go through her files first."

Matt stood. "I'll have Mike from the mailroom bring up a few boxes."

After everyone left his office, Matt wandered outside to take a lap around the block. He ran their conversation over in his mind. He didn't think Carrie was having an affair. She loved that her husband was in the limelight and the life he provided. He'd seen them together too many times to doubt that she and Steve were very much in love.

His thoughts turned to Lori. He had to bridle his jealousy or risk losing her. He knew Lori well enough to know she wouldn't have kissed him the way she did if she had feelings for Gage. She said their night out meant nothing, and he needed to start trusting her. She'd never lied to him.

His mind turned to the pool party at the end of spring break. To this day, he couldn't believe he showed up with Tammie Bennett.

He got home from St. George two days early, still angry that Lori chose to babysit rather than meet his family. His thick skull and jock pride would not allow him to call her.

Then he ran into Tammie at a gas station, one thing led to another, and he did nothing to stop it.

He knew Lori would be at that party. He knew she'd be hurt when he showed up with Tammie. But he hadn't thought of the ramifications past that moment. She left with Mike. When Mike came back alone, he cornered him.

"Relax, Matt. Lori went home."

He went to her house the next day. Her mom told him Lori had gone out and they didn't know where or when she'd be home.

After that he caught only glimpses of her on campus until the end of the semester. Then he went home for the summer. It wasn't until the fall semester started that he found out Lori had transferred to Northwestern.

How many times over the years had he wished he could change that one day of his life? Too many to count.

CHAPTER 18

Theresa followed Lori into her office after they left Matt, Dave, and Phil discussing another article. She shut the door.

"Okay, spill the beans. You said you were going to dinner with Gage last night and today you're playing kissy-face with Matt."

"I told you Gage and I were going to dinner as friends. And how would you know we were playing kissy-face?"

"I thought you were kidding about Gage, and you were blushing when we walked into Matt's office."

"Not kidding," Lori said, her face heating again. She pulled back her chair and sat. "I told Matt the same thing, and he didn't believe me any more than you did."

Theresa slid into a chair. "Please, tell me what happened between you and Matt in college."

Lori leaned forward, rested her elbows on her desk, and told an abbreviated version of Matt bringing Tammie Bennett to Sandy's party.

"What did you do?"

"I spent the next day driving around because I had a feeling Matt might stop by my house and I didn't want to see him." Besides being terribly hurt, she was humiliated by Matt's choice of dates. Out of all the girls he had to choose from, Tammie Bennett had been like a slap across the face. When she finally got home, her mother met her at the door.

"Lori, where have you been? Matt was here—he waited for most of the afternoon. He had to go study for a class, but said he'd be back around seven."

Lori headed to her bedroom. It was five thirty, which gave her an hour and a half to get out of the house again. She opened a drawer and pulled out a sweatshirt Matt lent her on a cold night. She also collected several books he'd given her and two framed photos of them together from her bookshelf. Opening her jewelry box, she picked up a gold bracelet he had their names engraved on. A box in the closet held all the cards and notes he'd given her over the past six months. The last thing she collected was the teddy bear he won for her at a festival. She put all the items in a box she got from the basement. At six forty-five, she grabbed her backpack and said, "Mom, Dad, I'm going out to study. I won't be late."

"Wait, Matt will be here any minute," her mother said, following her through the living room.

"I know. Will you please give him this when he gets here?" Lori set the box near the front door.

Theresa leaned forward. "And that was it?"

"I got home at nine, but Matt's truck was still in my parents' driveway, so I drove past, parked down the street, and waited for him to leave. When he left, he didn't take the box of things."

"What did you do when you saw him on campus?"

"I changed my route so I wouldn't."

That first Monday, she spotted Matt waiting near a place where their paths usually converged. For five seconds she thought he was waiting for her, then Tammie ran up and threw her arms around his neck. He hadn't been waiting for her, but his new girlfriend.

Every time she saw them together, her heart ached all over again.

"So you transferred?"

Lori opened her laptop. "I'd actually got accepted for an accelerated class at Northwestern. They already had my transcripts, so I applied for a transfer and got in."

~

The office was quiet after everyone returned from Carrie's funeral. The whole morning had been heartbreaking. Carrie's parents managed to be strong through the service. Steve had been more stoic than Lori expected.

She called Steve and told him Theresa didn't know anything about an affair, but she wasn't sure he believed her, and that bothered Lori. She didn't want him to think she lied.

That night, after everyone had gone home, Phil and Matt were holed up in Matt's office going through Carrie's files while Lori packed up her desk. She wrapped Carrie's pictures and personal items in paper and packed them carefully into two boxes from the mailroom. When she packed a teddy bear that came with the flowers Steve sent for Valentine's Day, tears stung her eyes.

The sound of the elevator door opening echoed through the quiet office. The security guard stepped out along with a stocky man Lori recognized.

"Hi, Lori."

She walked out of Carrie's cubicle. "You have the late shift again, Kenneth?"

"Yeah, I traded with Derrick. This is Detective Stone. He's

investigating Carrie's death and asked if he could go through her desk. I told him I'd have to check with Matt."

Stone, a tall, stocky man with a shock of white hair, wiped the sweat at his temples with a handkerchief. Lori still had the picture she took of him, along with others, on the memory card in her desk.

The detective glanced down into the boxes Lori had just packed and then slowly let his gaze move around Carrie's almost empty cubicle. "Are you here alone?"

"No. There are other people in one of the offices," she said, folding the flaps over the top of the box. "I met the detective investigating Carrie's death. Did he pass the case on to you?"

His eyes narrowed. "Something like that."

"What exactly are you looking for?" Lori asked.

"Would you mind if I look through Mrs. Eubanks' desk?"

"I emptied her desk. If you can tell me what you're looking—"

"Just some notes. She was working on a story that I'm investigating."

"You don't keep notes?"

Detective Stone's eyes flashed hard as he stared at her. "She might have uncovered something I missed. If I could look through her notes or flash drives—"

"I'd need to verify you're a detective."

"I have a badge."

Kenneth stood behind the detective shaking his head.

Lori smiled. "Anyone can get a badge."

"How about I get a search warrant?"

"No need for that. I'll just make a quick call to the detective I know."

"This is ridiculous! I'll be back with a search warrant." Detective Stone stomped to the stairs and shoved the door open with such force it hit the wall.

Matt opened his office door with Phil on his heels.

"Who was that?" Matt asked, glancing toward the door when it slammed shut.

"He wasn't a detective," Kenneth said to Lori. "He wouldn't have reacted like that."

"I think you're right," Lori said.

"Kenneth, who was that?" Matt asked again.

"He said he was Detective Stone, that he was investigating Carrie's death, and that he wanted to look through Carrie's desk."

Matt glanced from Kenneth to Lori. "You didn't let him, did you?"

"No," she said. "But he could have. There's nothing in there."

"Lori handled him well."

"Kenneth, will you go down and make sure he leaves the building, please?" Matt asked.

"Sure thing."

Matt stopped next to Lori. "What did he say?"

"He told me he's investigating a story Carrie was working on. If he is a detective, I might be in trouble. Will you call Mitch and check?"

Matt slid Carrie's phone toward him and a piece of paper fluttered to the floor. It had a phone number and Detective Stone written beneath it. Lori picked it up and Matt called the number.

"Went straight to voicemail," he said. He punched in another number. "Hey, Mitch, this is Matt Kelley. I'm glad you're still in the office. Do you guys have a Detective Stone working there?"

Phil rested his arms on the wall between Carrie's cubicle and the one next door.

"No. Ever had a Detective Stone? No? Yeah, some guy was just here wanting to look through Carrie's desk. No, he didn't get anything." Matt turned to her. "Could you identify the man if you saw a picture?"

She nodded.

"Yeah, Lori got a good look at him. Sure, we'll come by. See you in about twenty minutes." Matt hung up.

"What's going on?" Phil asked.

"Detective Stone doesn't exist. Mitch wants us to come to the police station to see if you can identify this guy. Phil, can you come with us? Since he wanted to go through Carrie's desk, this probably involves her accident."

"Sure."

Lori put the lid securely on the last box. "These should be locked up in your office. I'll get my purse and meet you at the elevator."

While they took the boxes to Matt's office, Lori went to her desk. Since Carrie's accident and funeral, she'd forgotten all about the drug ring and story Carrie had been working on.

She grabbed the memory card out of her desk and slipped it into her purse.

At the police station, Mitch greeted them, then led the small group into his office, wheeling in an extra chair for Phil. "Can you tell me what happened?" he asked Lori.

Lori explained that she'd been cleaning out Carrie's desk when Kenneth escorted Detective Stone to the fourth floor.

"Can you describe him?"

"Thick white hair, tall, overweight, ruddy complexion."

"What did he want?"

"He wanted to look through Carrie's desk. He said she might have notes that would help him on a case Carrie . . . was working on."

"What case?" Phil asked.

Lori glanced at Mitch. She'd hoped they'd be alone for a

few minutes, but Matt and Phil were in the office that had suddenly grown very small. "Can I talk to you in private?"

"Of course," Mitch responded.

"Why?" Matt asked with a frown.

Her heartbeat picked up speed. She took a deep breath. "What I have to tell Mitch is going to make you mad."

"How mad?" Matt asked with narrowed eyes.

"That's hard to say. I've seen you mad, but I've never seen you really mad."

"Oh, I have, and—" Phil stopped when Matt glared at him.

He turned his attention back to her. "Let's hear it."

She pulled out the memory card. "Do you have a way to look at some pictures?"

Mitch plugged an adapter into his computer and inserted the memory card. Turning his screen so they could all see, he clicked to the first picture, the man with the big nose. Mitch leaned forward.

"That man told Carrie his name was Mike," she said using air quotes. "Probably not his real name. Carrie and I called him Mr. Anonymous."

"Is this the Mr. Anonymous I heard you two talking about?" Phil asked.

She nodded.

"I couldn't get anything out of Carrie that day." Phil stood up and moved to Lori's side. "Where were these pictures taken?"

"At a warehouse in Georgetown."

"Why do you have them?" Matt asked her.

She told them about Carrie receiving a flash drive in the mail and the anonymous phone calls. "The flash drive was password-protected. When she told Mr. Anonymous, he asked her to meet him at a warehouse to get a password. She went, but he didn't show."

"She went alone?" Matt asked.

The first time. Lori nodded. "Mike told her the information on the flash drives would lead to a big story."

"Flash *drives*?" Mitch asked.

She'd gotten ahead of herself so she sidestepped his question. "Mike said he was being followed and planned to get out of town but wanted the story to be printed first."

"Let's go back to more than one flash drive," Mitch said.

Lori bit her lip, knowing this part would make Matt mad. "Carrie asked me to go to the warehouse with her when she went the second time. Against my better judgment, I went, because I knew if I didn't she'd go alone. When she came out of the warehouse, Mike handed her another flash drive that she slipped in her pocket. When I asked her about it, she said Mike gave her a pair of sunglasses she left behind. On the way back to the office, I asked Carrie a lot of questions that she couldn't answer. I told her she should talk to Phil, but she refused because she didn't want to lose the story to him. She told me twice when she had enough information for a story she would talk to Matt and later tried to get me to believe she had."

Mitch clicked to another picture of the man with the big nose. "Is that it?"

"No, there was one more trip to the warehouse."

"The day you took a camera and binoculars," Matt said.

She nodded. "That's the day I took the pictures. We went at lunchtime. Later that afternoon, I happened to look out of my office window and Carrie was walking toward a dark sedan. I took that picture"—she pointed at the computer screen— "when the car window came down. He's the man who came to the office tonight wanting to look through Carrie's desk."

All three men leaned closer. "This is Detective Stone?" Mitch asked.

"Per Carrie, this man said the police had been following Mike and knew his story but wanted to protect him in exchange for information. He told her the situation was under control and that she would have the exclusive, but when she tried to get in touch with Stone, all she got was his voicemail. As far as I know she never saw Mike or Stone again."

Mitch clicked back through the pictures. "Did you see the man at the warehouse well enough to identify him?"

"You're seeing what I saw. On the second trip to the warehouse, Carrie told me the story involved a drug ring being run by a Seattle businessman."

"A drug ring?" Phil asked, wide-eyed.

"Mike told Carrie he was hiding out because he'd been cooking the books and stealing money from them. My guess is he wanted the story printed and arrests made so they couldn't go after him."

Matt cursed under his breath.

"I need to make a phone call," Mitch said, pushing back from his desk.

As soon as Mitch shut the door, Matt turned on her. "How could you have put yourself in this kind of danger?"

"I had no idea what the story was about," Lori said. "I asked Carrie several times, but she didn't tell me the truth. She must have known that if she told me I wouldn't have gone with her."

"Why didn't you come to me when you found out?"

"She told me the story involved a drug ring the day you saw us arguing by the elevator. You asked her if it involved the story she told you about that morning, and she said yes, but I suspected she wasn't telling the truth."

"You still should have told me."

"No, that was Carrie's responsibility."

Phil stepped between them. "Carrie only did what I

would have done—what *you* would have done back in the day, Matt. Lori went with Carrie as her friend. Most of us would have gone alone. At least Carrie was smart enough to take someone with her."

"Phil's right. She was determined enough she would have gone alone."

"We're talking about a drug ring," Matt growled.

"Which I didn't know at the time."

Phil put his hands on her shoulders. "If Carrie had been upfront, Lori wouldn't have gone, and you know it."

Lori could see the anger fading from Matt's eyes. She would be willing to bet in his days as a reporter, Matt was as reckless as Carrie—if not more so.

~

The steam fizzed out of Matt like the air from a punctured balloon. Phil was right. He wasn't mad at Lori, but Carrie wasn't here. Was her death caused by her rash decisions and her need for a front-page story?

"Sorry." He slumped in his chair. "With the addition of the missing flash drives, I'm afraid this has turned into a dangerous situation."

Unexpectedly, Lori reached for his hand, lacing their fingers together.

Mitch walked into the office and rounded his desk. "I just contacted the DEA office here in Seattle. Lori, can you meet with a couple of their agents here in my office tomorrow morning at nine?"

"I will, but I can't tell them any more than I've told you."

"They're still going to want to talk to you."

"Did you ever look into Steve's fears about Carrie having an affair?" Matt asked, searching for another answer.

"We don't have anything to go on but money missing

from a bank account. Home and cell phone records showed nothing out of the ordinary." He looked at Lori. "Why did you wait to tell me what was going on?"

"I had forgotten all about Carrie's story until Detective Stone walked into the office tonight," Lori said. "I talked to Carrie the Friday before her death, and she told me then that she didn't have enough information to write the story. Mike had disappeared, Detective Stone wasn't returning her calls, she couldn't get into the flash drives, so she'd reached a dead end."

"As far as you know, Carrie never got into the flash drives?" Matt asked.

Lori shook her head. "I suggested a couple of times that she should let someone else try, but she refused. She wanted this story to be published under her byline, and rebuffed me every time I suggested she get help from anyone."

Mitch leaned forward, folding his hands on his desk. "Did you come across the flash drives in her desk?"

"I gave everything I found, including a couple of flash drives, to Matt and Phil."

"Phil and I went through everything tonight. We didn't come across one we couldn't open," Matt said.

"What about Carrie's car?" Phil asked. "Or her purse, her briefcase? Were there any flash drives in there?"

"She only had a purse with her. Steve took Carrie's belongings after he identified her body. I'll go to the salvage yard that has her car in the morning and do another search," Mitch said.

"She always carried a briefcase. It wasn't in her car?" Phil asked.

"I didn't see one. I'll check with Steve," Mitch replied. "Maybe she dropped it off at home before heading to Lori's."

"Is Lori in danger?" Matt asked.

Mitch looked from him to Lori. "Did anyone see you with Carrie at the warehouse?"

"Not that I know of. There was no one around. The second time we went, a car pulled in and turned around, but Carrie had parked at an angle so I could see the warehouse more clearly. The angle of her car would have prevented whoever was in the other car from seeing me."

"The only encounter you had with the fake detective was tonight?" Phil asked.

"Yes. Carrie didn't want anyone to know I was with her when we went to the warehouse, so she parked facing away from the building both times. I never got out of the car."

Phil put his hands on her shoulders again. "What if she mentioned your name to the guy at the warehouse?"

"Why would she? He wanted to remain anonymous."

When they left Mitch's office, Matt walked Lori to her car since they'd all driven separately. "I'm going to follow you home."

"Matt, that's not—"

"You can argue all you want, but I *am* going to follow you home."

He shut her door after she slid behind the wheel.

"Do you want me to follow too?" Phil asked.

"No." They both turned to watch Lori turn out of the parking lot. "I just want to make sure no one's hanging around outside."

"I know you're mad, and I understand why you're worried, but don't let this mess things up between you and Lori. She went in blind. You know she wouldn't have gone if Carrie had told her the truth. She would have told you if she'd known the story involved a drug ring."

"I know. I'll see you tomorrow."

Phil waved and climbed into his car.

Matt was only two minutes behind. The whole ride his

mind circled the danger Carrie had placed Lori in. A drug ring. Was there anything more dangerous?

When he pulled into her driveway, she was standing on the sidewalk.

"My back door is ajar," she said when he climbed out of his car.

CHAPTER 19

"Mitch is sending the police," Matt said shoving his phone in his pocket.

"Maybe I scared whoever it was off when I pulled into the driveway."

"Or they left before you got home. Stay here," Matt ordered, before going to her front door, which was locked tight. "He didn't get in this way."

He took her hand and they circled around the back of the house. Only her office door stood open, but from where they stood, the lock looked intact.

"How'd they get in?" Lori asked.

Matt led her around the other side of the house. Lori spotted the broken basement window first. "That's how."

Two police cars pulled into the driveway and Mitch stopped at the curb. "Stay out here while we check the house," he said, taking her keys and going through the front with two officers. The other two went around back.

Mitch appeared on the porch minutes later and motioned for them to enter. Matt was surprised that nothing was disturbed until they got to Lori's office, which had been turned upside down.

"I guess we know what they were looking for," Mitch said.

Matt's mind spun with scenarios of what might have happened if Lori had come home alone after work like normal.

"One of the basement windows is broken," one of the officers yelled up the stairs.

When Mitch headed down the stairs, Matt followed, leaving Lori trying to straighten the mess. "Okay, Mitch, this is real. Lori's in danger."

"I agree." Mitch stopped at the bottom of the stairs and glanced past Matt. "Do you trust that she doesn't have the flash drives?" he asked, his voice low.

"She has no reason to lie. She's not a reporter, so she'd have no reason to chase a story."

Mitch pointed at the window. "Does she have anything we can put up there?"

"Let me look around." In the laundry room, Matt found a cardboard box. "I'll tape this up there tonight and get a piece of glass ordered tomorrow."

"I don't think Lori should stay here tonight," Mitch said.

"She'll stay with me."

"No."

He and Mitch turned around. Lori stood at the bottom of the stairs, shaking her head.

"You're not going to be stubborn about this, Lori."

"I'm not going to your house and put *you* in danger. I'll go to a hotel."

Walking over to her, he wrapped an arm around her waist. "I won't get any sleep if you're in a hotel."

"The police are ready to leave," she said to Mitch. "I told them it doesn't look like anything is missing."

Mitch turned to Matt. "She's right, Matt. If she's being watched, it might be best if you both go to a hotel."

"I have security cameras and floodlights all around the outside of my house, and my phone will alert me if anyone crosses the property line." He patted Lori's waist. "Go pack a bag, darlin'."

~

The rumble of thunder stirred Lori, but when Matt tightened his arm around her, she snuggled against him. He reached over and picked up his phone. One o'clock and he had yet to close his eyes. His thoughts jumped from wondering about the businessman running a drug ring to the warm body sound asleep next to him.

He'd cuddled up to Lori in his guest room once she got settled and never left. Leaving her wasn't an option. A sheet, blanket, and a layer of clothing separated them. After all these years, he wouldn't have it any other way—until they were married.

Another rumble of thunder echoed around the house, and Lori turned over, snuggling up close again. Matt smiled and moved a strand of hair off her cheek.

"Are you awake?"

"Yes," he whispered.

She turned her face up and blinked her eyes open. "Did the thunder wake you?"

"No."

"What time is it?"

"One."

She got up on an elbow, and he smiled at her tousled hair. She looked like a wild woman.

"Why are you still awake?" she asked in her sleepy, sexy voice.

Rolling to his back, he pulled her with him. She settled her cheek on his chest. "I don't know. Just frustrated. Angry at Carrie for putting you in this position."

"I should have told her no. Even before I knew what was involved, I felt uneasy. Hence borrowing the camera."

"Taking that camera was smart on your part. Did Carrie know you had it?"

"I never told her." She threaded her fingers between the buttons and through the opening of his shirt, touching his bare chest.

His breath caught. "Marry me, Lori."

Her hand stilled.

"Marry me," he repeated, covering her hand with his. "Marry me tomorrow or the day after. It doesn't matter. I want to spend the rest of my life with you, and I don't want to wait. No long engagement. Let's just run away and get married."

He tipped her face up with an index finger under her chin. When she pressed her lips together, his heart sank. Whenever they were together, he was like a runaway freight train, hurtling toward a curve in the track without worrying about the consequences.

"Okay."

He tried to breathe, but his lungs had stopped functioning.

She got up on an elbow, again, and kissed him. His whole body revved up, preparing for the curve ahead. When she leaned away, he could see her smile. She dipped her head and snuggled close. "I love you, Matthew Kelley. Now go to sleep."

"You're kidding, right? You expect me to go to sleep after that?"

"I expect you to tell me you love me back, and then go to sleep. If you don't, I'll kick you out of my bed."

He lifted her wrist to his lips and kissed her pulse point, then relaxed into his pillow and stared at the ceiling. Lori said okay and he was going to hold her to it. "I love you, Lori Maguire, soon to be Lori Kelley."

"That sounds lovely," she mumbled. "Good night."

He closed his eyes, realizing he was truly, deep down happy for the first time in years.

~

*L*ori lay quietly in Matt's arms, listening to his steady breathing and the peaceful sound of rain pattering against the windows. She was relieved he'd finally drifted off. She turned her cheek against his chest and he tightened his arms around her. This was where she wanted to spend forever.

The sky beyond the blinds brightened slowly, and she wondered what time it was and what the day would bring. She told Mitch she'd be in his office by nine, but she had nothing more to tell them.

When Matt loosened his hold, she slipped out of his arms and off the bed. Wandering through the house, she noted elements she'd missed the first time she was here. She loved Matt's house and the attention he gave to the details. Everything flowed so cohesively from one room to the next. In one of the bedrooms, she looked out over the front lawn, which was a vivid green from the rain.

On the way here last night, Matt had kept an eye on the rearview mirror. He took several different out-of-the-way roads and told her they weren't followed.

She heard quiet footsteps and knew Matt was searching for her. Seconds later, his arms encircled her and he nuzzled her neck.

"What are you doing up so early?"

"You were snoring."

He chuckled. "I don't snore."

"How would you know?"

"I'd know," he replied, pulling her back against him.

She almost said something about all the women he'd been with lying to him but squashed the thought. The past was the past, and that's where she'd leave it.

"Do you remember our conversation in the middle of the night?" he asked.

Lori smiled at the hesitancy in his question. "Yes."

He rested his chin on the top of her head. "It's too late to back out."

"I don't plan on backing out."

"Can we get a marriage license during our lunch hour?"

"Yes."

"And get married tomorrow?"

She laughed and turned to look at him. "Most states require you to wait a few days. I'm not sure of Washington State rules, but wouldn't you like your family to be present?"

"Not if it means waiting."

He took her hand, led her downstairs to his office, and sat at his desk, pulling her onto his lap. He tapped away at his keyboard while she kissed his neck. "We have to wait three days after receiving the license."

She kissed his temple. "We can get married on Monday."

"And take the rest of the week off for our honeymoon."

"I guess I better get a few columns ahead today."

"I don't want to wait that long. Let's hop on a plane to Vegas."

"Do you really want to get married in some cheesy chapel?" She ran her thumb over his errant eyebrows. "I bet your mom would love to see her baby boy get married."

"You can't change your mind."

"I won't." She slid off his lap. "You print the application while I take a shower."

He huffed out a frustrated breath that made her laugh as she left his office.

~

Mitch came out of his office and beckoned Lori, Matt, and Phil into the conference room. He pulled out her chair, then sat beside her, placing a file on the table. Phil and Matt set the boxes from Carrie's desk on the far end of the table, then sat across from Lori.

"Everything is there?" Mitch asked.

"Except for the files and flash drives I kept, but nothing was out of the ordinary," Matt replied.

Mitch stood and started going through the box's contents. "Are you sure you didn't find those flash drives?"

"Haven't you already asked that question? Twice?" Matt asked.

"I put everything I found in those boxes," Lori said.

Satisfied the boxes didn't hold any hidden secrets, Mitch replaced the contents and took the chair next to Lori.

"Last night someone took out the security cameras and broke into the salvage yard where Carrie's car is being held. Luckily, I sent officers over as soon as you left my office. They didn't find anything but this man's fingerprints." Mitch opened the folder and pulled out the picture. Lori recognized the uniquely shaped nose. Then he placed another picture next to the first one. "These guys, whoever they are, mean business."

Lori gasped and covered her mouth as a quiver ran down her spine. Phil stood up and pulled the pictures across the table. When Matt saw, he stood up so abruptly he knocked his chair over.

"Some fishermen found him yesterday in Commencement Bay. His name is John Cowl. He has a pretty extensive criminal record, mostly minor offenses. The coroner said he's been dead at least three days."

"Which means he probably died the same day as Carrie," Phil said. He looked at Lori. "Why are his fingerprints in Carrie's car?"

Lori shook her head, a hand still over her mouth. She was shaking so badly, her teeth chattered.

Phil cursed under his breath.

Strong arms wrapped around her. "I'm right here, Lori," Matt murmured close to her ear. He pulled her up and held her tight against him. "Everything's going to be okay."

"Maybe someone ran Carrie off the road because this guy was in the car with her. She told you he was trying to get out of town, right?" Mitch said to Lori.

"And maybe that's where the missing savings account money went," Matt said. "She was helping him so he'd give her the story."

Mitch nodded. "Makes sense, *but* if Carrie or John Cowl had the flash drives, the men John worked for wouldn't still be looking for them."

"Which means Lori's still in danger," Phil said. "This Stone guy saw Lori cleaning out Carrie's desk and thinks she has the flash drives."

"Did Carrie ever name the businessman who's supposed to be running this drug ring?" Mitch asked.

Lori shook her head against Matt's chest. "Carrie said he's a prominent businessman whose name is well known around the area."

"The DEA agents are here," Mitch said, looking toward the door. "Are you going to be okay to answer their questions, Lori?"

"Yes."

"You're going to have to wait outside," Mitch said to Matt and Phil.

"I'm staying," Matt said.

"No. You're going to wait outside. I'll be here with Lori."

"I'll be fine," she said, stepping out of Matt's arms.

"Phil, this story goes on hold," Mitch said. "If this businessman is under investigation, there may be people working undercover. I'm not going to put them at risk." He opened the door so the DEA agents could enter.

Matt squeezed her shoulders. "I'll be right outside."

"I'm fine." But she wasn't. She was so angry at Carrie—and at herself—she couldn't think straight. Would her involvement put the people she loved in danger? Was she being watched? What about her parents? Would these men think she'd taken the flash drive to Martha and Henry's house? Or Tara's? Kenneth had been there when Stone was trying to look in Carrie's desk. Was he in danger?

"Lori, I'd like you to meet Agent Jason Turner and Agent Seth Anderson. They work in the Seattle DEA office. Gentleman, this is Lori Maguire."

Agent Turner looked to be in his thirties, with dark hair and innocent eyes. Agent Anderson, who smelled like stale cigarettes, was early to middle fifties with light hair and a smile that showed stained teeth.

Lori shook their hands, and the men sat in the chairs Matt and Phil had vacated.

"Before we start, would anyone like something to drink? Coffee? Water?" Mitch asked.

Lori shook her head. "No, thank you."

Both agents declined.

"Tell them what you know, Lori."

She repeated her story for the agents, trying to remember any details she might have overlooked the first time she told Mitch.

"Why did you take a camera with you the second time you went to the warehouse?" Agent Anderson asked.

"I didn't feel comfortable with the situation," Lori repeated, because she'd already told him the reason. "I'm not a reporter. I'm—"

"You're not?" Agent Anderson asked.

"No. I write a column, but I've worked around reporters long enough to know what they'll go through to get a story. In my opinion, Carrie was taking too many risks."

"You were worried for her safety?" Agent Turner asked.

"Yes."

Agent Anderson ran a hand along his jaw. "What were you hoping to get a picture of?"

What did he think? "The man in the warehouse."

He nodded toward the boxes. "Those are from Carrie's desk?"

"Yes."

"And you didn't find the flash drives?"

"I gave the only flash drives I found to the *Star's* editor."

He studied her for a long minute. She could tell he didn't believe her.

"The editor is one of the two men sitting outside." Mitch nodded toward the door. "He said the flash drives didn't have anything out of the ordinary on them."

"We'd still like to take a look," Agent Turner said. "Agent Anderson and I have been working on this case for a year. We suspect the businessman mentioned to Mrs. Eubanks is not only running drugs and arms over the border, but he's involved in human trafficking as well." He held up the picture Lori took of Detective Stone. "This man's name is Thomas Tremblay. He works as the main muscle for the operation. He usually handles the dirty work or directs someone else to do it."

Agent Anderson's heavy index finger tapped the picture

Lori took of the man with the big nose. "The whole operation has been looking for John Cowl for a couple of weeks. He's been laundering the money for them while skimming a little off the top for himself."

"Why can't you arrest the businessman?" Lori asked.

"He covers his tail very well. We were hoping the missing flash drives would give us the information we need to finally pick him up," Agent Turner said.

"I don't have the flash drives," Lori told them with as much conviction as she could muster. "As I said, I'm not a reporter. I'm not after a story. I cleaned out Carrie's desk because her husband asked me to. I put everything in those boxes. Carrie told me she couldn't get into the flash drives, even using the passwords John Cowl gave her."

She glanced from one agent to the other. "I don't know what Carrie did with them. I hadn't seen her for several days before the accident."

Mitch leaned toward her. "Do you want to take a break, Lori?"

"No. I want to be done. I've told you everything I know."

"Are we done, gentleman?" Mitch asked.

"For today." Agent Anderson said.

~

*M*att watched Lori's expressions as she answered questions.

Phil shook his head. "How many different ways can they ask her the same freaking question?"

"As a reporter, you should know the answer to that."

When Lori looked distressed, Matt pushed up from his chair. "Okay, they're done."

"Yep," Phil replied, jumping to his feet.

Matt opened the door. "Lori's had enough for today."

"Relax, Matt. We're just discussing Lori's safety."

Matt rounded the table and pulled her chair back. "Until this is over, Lori will be with me. We'll be at work, her house, or mine."

"If Matt has to leave her for any reason, she'll be with me," Phil added.

"We'll keep an eye on Lori for now," Mitch told the DEA agents. "If something comes up, we'll let you know."

"We'd like to come to the newspaper office and take a look at Mrs. Eubanks' desk."

"Any time I'm at the office is fine," Matt said to Agent Anderson.

After the agents left, Mitch turned to Matt. "Can I follow you to your office and take a look at the flash drives you have? I know they aren't the missing ones, but I want to make sure all bases are covered. I'll keep these boxes locked in my office until Mr. Eubanks gets back in town."

"I'll meet you in my office in fifteen minutes," Matt said to Mitch. "But Lori and I have to leave by twelve thirty." Nothing was going to get in the way of applying for a marriage license today.

He, Phil, and Lori walked into the sunlight.

"Did they tell you anything we don't already know, Lori?" Phil asked.

"Detective Stone's real name is Thomas Tremblay. He's the muscle for the businessman's operation."

"They didn't give you the name of the businessman?"

"No, but they suspect he's also dealing in arms and human trafficking."

Phil groaned. "Carrie, what did you get yourself into?"

Matt opened the passenger door and waited while Lori climbed in, then he went around to the driver's side. "See you in a few, Phil," he said before he closed his door.

"If I'd told you about Carrie, she might be alive."

"Don't go there, Lori. She made the choice to go to that warehouse, and you're right, she would have gone alone. And maybe she did. How else did John Cowl end up in her car?"

She clasped his strong hand. "Would you have assigned someone else?"

"I would have assigned someone to help her, but I wouldn't have given her story away. Believe me, I remember what it's like to be a young reporter just waiting for that first big story that will put your name above the fold."

When they got to the office, the DEA agents were waiting in the lobby, and they rode the elevator to the fourth floor together. Matt mouthed twelve thirty before he led the agents to Carrie's cubicle. Lori nodded and headed to her office.

She barely had time to sit before Phil appeared in her office door. "They just flipped Carrie's desk upside-down, thinking she might have taped something to the bottom. I heard them say they want to look in your desk next."

"I don't know how many times I can tell them I don't have the flash drives."

Suddenly she remembered the times both she and Matt had come into her office to find Carrie sitting at her desk. She glanced at Phil. "Are they coming?"

He glanced over his shoulder. "Not yet."

She opened her top side drawer where she kept her flash drives in a case. Unzipping the case, she counted. All her color-coded flash drives were there. She flipped the flap that separated another layer and gasped when something fell into her lap.

"What?"

"Keep watch." Unfolding a heavy piece of paper, a key dropped into her hand.

Lori,

I'm so sorry I got you involved in this mess. I had no

idea what I was getting into. I wish I had listened to you and talked to Matt or Phil.

At first I thought it would be a great story, one that would finally push me to the top, maybe even win an award. Now I know I'm in over my head. Detective Stone is following me. I'm going to get Mike out of town tonight. I just wanted someone to know, in case something happens, this will help with the answers. Give it to someone you trust with the police department.

Tell Steve I'm sorry about the money and I love him.

Carrie

CHAPTER 20

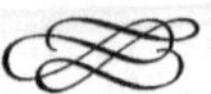

$\mathcal{L}$ori held up the key for Phil to see.

"What's going on in Carrie's cubicle?" Theresa asked.

Phil jumped and turned on her. "Don't sneak up on people."

Theresa stared at him like he'd lost his mind. "What is your problem?"

"There's just a lot— Don't you have a story to write?"

She looked him up and down. "I could ask you the same question."

"Lori and I are busy with . . . something important."

"Uh-huh." Theresa walked into her office. "Why are they searching Carrie's desk?"

"I think they might be looking for this." Lori held up the key again.

"Looks like some kind of locker key." Theresa held out her hand. "Where did it come from?"

"I found it. What kind of locker?" Lori asked.

"Well, it has numbers on it, so maybe the bus station or the airport?"

"The airport doesn't have lockers," Phil said.

"The employees have lockers. I saw them when I did a story about—"

"Can you get us into that area?" Phil asked.

Theresa was looking at Lori with narrowed eyes. "Where did you get the key, Lori?"

"I found it in my desk, along with this." She held up the note.

Theresa read the note with Phil looking over her shoulder.

Phil snatched the key from Theresa's hand and they exchanged a look. "I'll drive," he said.

"Wait." Lori jumped up and grabbed his arm. "We should tell Matt."

Phil leaned out of her office. "Mitch just got here. He, Matt, and the agents are going into Matt's office."

"Probably to look at the flash drives I found in Carrie's desk."

Theresa grabbed Lori's arm. "Let's go."

Lori felt like a thief sneaking past Matt's office, which ended being unnecessary since his door was closed.

"Maybe we should take the key to Mitch," Lori said when they reached Phil's car.

"Let's see if we can find out what this key is hiding, and then we'll take everything to Mitch, whoever that is," Theresa replied.

"Mitch is the detective investigating Carrie's accident." Phil opened the back door for Lori. "We should try the bus station first. It's closer than the airport."

Theresa held out her hand and Phil dropped the key into her palm. "What is this key hiding?"

"My guess is the flash drives John Cowl gave to Carrie."

"Who's John Cowl?"

Lori told Theresa everything that had happened since

Detective Stone, aka Thomas Tremblay, came into the office last night."

Theresa looked at her from the front seat with raised brows. "You've been busy."

"Whoever trashed my home office last night knew I was at the police station, which means I'm probably being watched."

"Let's not go straight to the bus station," Theresa said with a shiver. She pointed. "Stop at that fast food place."

"Good idea," Phil said, glancing in the rearview mirror.

Phil parked and they went inside. They ordered soft drinks and fries, which they ate at a table by the window while keeping watch.

"What do you think?" Lori asked.

"I haven't seen anyone I'd be worried about," Phil said, his gaze on the door.

"Even that grandma over there looks suspicious to me," Theresa whispered. "Let's go to the bus station, and I'll go in. None of these goons know who I am. Phil, you park the car down the street and follow me in. I'll see if I can find the locker. Lori, you stay here."

"Oh, yeah," Phil said, rolling his eyes. "That's a great idea. Let's leave Lori here alone, so if someone did follow us, they can simply stroll in and grab her."

"Okay, Lori can't stay here alone. We'll take you back to the paper and you can wait for us there."

"Oh, great plan. That way when the two of you get murdered, I can feel guilty and awful for the rest of my life for involving you. I don't think so."

"Lori, be reasonable—"

"No. We'll all go in and take whatever we find straight to Mitch. He, along with the DEA agents, think I have those flash drives, so if you guys come with me, you'll see that I never had them and will be able to tell the agents what you saw. You can tell Mitch I found the key and we all went to the locker together."

"That's not a good idea either," Phil stated, shaking his head. "Lori, you can't go. If the bad guys don't get us, Matt will. I think I'd rather take my chances with the murderers. I'd stand a better chance of coming out alive."

"Yep," Theresa said. "I'd rather take my chances with the bad guys than with Matt."

"This is stupid," Lori said, throwing her hands in the air. "We're being as stupid as Carrie. Let's take the key and the note to Mitch. That's what we should have done in the first place."

"You're right." Theresa nodded. "That's what we *should have* done, but—"

"But this is going to be a huge story," Phil interrupted. "If these guys are this desperate to get the flash drives, there's got to be something extremely incriminating on them."

"You both sound like Carrie," Lori said. "She died for a story she never even got to write."

Phil put his arm around Lori's shoulders. "We'll all go find the locker and take whatever we find to Mitch."

Theresa nodded and they both looked at Lori.

Lori took a deep breath and exhaled while thinking the same things she thought while waiting for Carrie to come out of the warehouse. *All this for a story.* When she nodded reluctantly, Phil leaned forward and kissed her forehead, then rubbed the spot. "Don't tell Matt I did that."

Theresa stood up. "We'll take whatever we find to Mitch. I'm sure he'll let me have the story."

"Excuse me?" Phil asked.

"I mean us."

"Yeah, I'm sure that's exactly what you meant. You don't even know Mitch."

Once in the car, Phil drove around several blocks to make

sure they weren't being followed and then found a parking spot at the bus station. They made their way inside. Lori looked behind them several times.

"Just act normal," Phil said, taking her hand.

"This *is* acting normal when I know someone might be following me, Phil."

The lockers were at the far end of the station, but Lori could tell even before they looked for the corresponding number on the key that they were in the wrong place. "The keys don't match the one we have," she said.

"What's the number?" Phil asked, taking the key. "We're already here. Let's make sure."

He went around the corner, then returned, shaking his head. "Where to next? The airport?"

"Does the train station have lockers?" Theresa asked.

Phil slapped his thigh. "We should have gone there first. It was closer."

"It's not the train station," Lori said.

"It could be—" Theresa started.

"It's not." Lori took the key and turned it over in her hand. "Carrie would pick a place she's talked about. I bet this key fits a locker at her gym."

"You're right," Theresa said, shaking Lori's arm. "Carrie talked about going to the gym several times a week before work."

"Problem is, I don't know which gym she used."

"I do," Theresa said. "I went to a spin class with her once, hated it, and never returned."

In the car, Theresa gave directions to a gym only blocks from Steve and Carrie's house.

Walking through the doors, Phil and Theresa headed to the membership desk. Theresa told them on the way over that they had to be buzzed into the locker room of this very private gym. Lori wandered toward the women's locker room while Phil and Theresa tried to convince the man behind the desk that they just needed to check a locker.

"I can't let you in without a membership," the man said.

"We don't want to use the facilities. We need to see if—"

"I can sell you a membership."

"Sir, you don't understand," Theresa said, batting her eyelashes. "A friend left something and—"

Three women walked out of the locker room, surprising Lori. Without thinking, she slipped through the door and hurried down a short hall, hoping the desk attendant wouldn't notice she was gone. In the locker room, she searched for the number. Finally, in the far corner of the bottom row, she found the match. She put the key in the lock and turned, holding her breath. The door swung open. Lori reached in and pulled out a small gym bag. Another group of four ladies headed for the door and she slipped out with them.

Theresa stood wide-eyed when Lori emerged. She pinched Phil, who was still arguing.

"Ouch!" Phil glared at Theresa while rubbing his arm. "What are you doing?"

"We should just go. *Now.*"

"Okay." He held up both hands. "You don't have to call the police, we're leaving."

Lori was halfway to the car before Theresa and Phil caught up with her.

"What's in the bag?" Theresa asked, looming over Lori as they hurried along.

Lori climbed into the back seat and pulled the zipper open. Inside was an envelope addressed to Steve, three flash drives, a piece of paper with one word—possibly the password—and a pocket-sized voice recorder.

"Let's get back to the office," Phil said.

"No. There will be too many people around. Lori's house is closest."

"Wait," Lori said, looking from Phil and Theresa. "We agreed to take whatever we found to Mitch."

"We will, but aren't you curious to see what's on those flash drives?" Theresa asked.

"No, I'm not. I don't care what's on them."

"Let's see what we've got, *then* we'll take it all to Mitch," Theresa said. "Or we could call Mitch and tell him to meet us at your house. That way we can all see what's on the flash drives."

"That's a great idea. We'll tell Mitch to meet us at your house," Phil said, agreeing with Theresa.

"You're both insane," Lori sighed, suddenly very tired of this whole ordeal. She pushed the envelope with Steve's name on it back into the bag. "Someone broke into my house yesterday, remember? Someone is probably watching it, and if they are, it would be too dangerous."

"She's right. We can't go to her house," Theresa said.

Lori looked at her watch. "Matt is going to kill me. We were supposed to get a marriage license at twelve thirty." She pulled out her cell phone. Eight missed calls and three text messages. All from Matt.

"A marriage license?" Theresa asked, her voice an octave higher. "Matt proposed and you didn't tell me?"

"I've been kind of busy being questioned by DEA agents and racing around town to find something we're supposed to be turning into the police." Her phone buzzed with a new message. "He's going to kill me right before he kills both of you."

Theresa tugged her phone out of her pocket. "He's called me three times."

"This is going to be bad. I've got five missed calls and two messages from him." Phil blew out a breath. "Lori's right. We need to take this to Mitch."

"Drop me off at the office first," Lori said. She pushed play on the recorder. "We might as well learn something on the way."

"My name is John Cowl. I'm making this tape for Carrie Eubanks as my confession in the business dealings with Mr. Gerald Roebeck."

"Whoa," Phil said, his eyes rounded in the rearview mirror.

"He is a Seattle businessman," the voice on the recorder continued.

Theresa turned around in the front seat, staring at Lori. "Phil. This is huge. Lori's holding our story."

"Shhh." Phil held up a hand.

The recording gave John's story in detail. He spouted names, locations, and said that the police were involved.

When Phil turned into the parking lot of the office, Lori zipped everything into the gym bag. "Promise me you'll go straight to Mitch with this or I'll take it myself."

Phil and Theresa exchanged a look before they both nodded.

"Nope, you have to say the words."

"We promise," Theresa said.

"Cross our heart or stick a needle in our eye—however that saying goes," Phil agreed.

"No stopping on the way," Lori said.

"No stopping on the way," they both agreed.

Lori passed the bag over the seat and climbed out. They pulled forward, but the red light stopped them. She took a deep breath, preparing herself to go in and try to smooth things over with her fiancé. Theresa turned in her seat and waved. Lori lifted her hand to wave back, instead, she jumped when someone grabbed her arm.

She expected to see Matt, but the hand belonged to Agent Anderson. "I need you to come with me," he said, tugging her toward the parking lot.

"Where?"

"To our offices."

"I've told you everything I know." Something poked her in the back and she glanced at him in surprise. "Is that a gun?"

"I don't think you *have* told me everything." He pushed her toward a dark sedan.

She looked up, hoping Matt was in her office and could see she needed help. Phil and Theresa had already driven around the corner.

As they approached the car, the man who said he was Detective Stone stepped out of the front passenger seat. Realization crashed over her like a tidal wave. Lori tried to jerk her arm out of Agent Anderson's grasp, but he held tight. She looked him in the eye. "You're involved in this?"

"You're driving," he said in reply.

"No."

Detective Stone struck faster than she could move. Fire and pain shot across her face, the force almost knocking her to the ground.

Agent Anderson pointed his gun at Stone. "You hit her again and I'll shoot you."

Lori lifted a hand to her throbbing cheek, the metallic taste of blood making her nauseous. She blinked her blurred vision back into focus. Her eyes watered from the pain when she slowly moved her jaw to make sure it wasn't broken.

Opening the driver's door, Anderson half lifted, half pushed her behind the wheel.

Stone climbed into the back seat and slammed the door. He leaned over the front seat and tapped his gun on the seat near her arm. "You shouldn't have gotten yourself involved in this."

"I'm not involved," she said around a swollen lip, reminding herself this man wasn't a detective.

Agent Anderson slid into the passenger seat.

She'd always heard never to get into a car with abductors, but there was literally no one around to help her. "I don't have the flash drives," she said growing desperate.

"But you know where they are," Thomas Tremblay said.

~

$\mathcal{M}$att grabbed his cell phone off his desk on the first ring. Phil's name flashed on his screen and he connected the call. "Where are you? Where is Lori?"

"Matt, Agent Anderson took her," Theresa said. "We dropped her off in front of the newspaper and—"

Matt's gut dropped. "What? Took her where?"

"We should have walked her to the door," Phil said. "We dropped her off, but before she got to the building, Agent Anderson appeared and led her to a car."

"Where were you?"

"If you'll stop yelling, we'll explain everything," Theresa said.

Matt bit back the next things he wanted to yell. He could tell Theresa and Phil had him on speaker. "Where is Lori now?"

"We're following her," Phil said. "We don't know where they're taking her."

He blew out a breath, trying to get control of his rage. "I thought you said Agent Anderson—"

"There's someone else in the car with them. They have Lori driving."

"Why would they—"

"Lori found a key in her desk. We decided—since you were in your office with the DEA agents—we'd see if we could find what the key went to."

Theresa wasn't making sense. None of this made sense. "What kind of key? What are you talking about?"

"Lori found a key—"

"You already said that!"

"Matt, you need to call Mitch," Phil interrupted. "Lori found a key and a note from Carrie in her desk when the DEA agents were searching Carrie's desk this morning. We went to see if we could find what the key fit. We found the flash drives."

Fear seized every cell in his body and froze them solid. "You're fired! All three of you are fired!"

"Great. We're all fired, but for now you need to call Mitch," Phil said. "Get him on the phone, right now! Tell him to call the DEA and ask them if Agent Anderson is supposed to take Lori somewhere."

"Don't hang up," Matt warned as he grabbed his desk phone and punched in Mitch's number. "Mitch, Agent Anderson has Lori in a car. Can you get him or Agent Turner on the phone and ask what's going on?"

"Sure. Hold on a minute."

Matt walked to the window and looked out across the city, his insides churning with alarm.

"I got Agent Turner. He said Agent Anderson isn't answering his phone."

"Phil, Lori, and another reporter found the missing flash drives. When Phil brought Lori back to the office, Agent Anderson was outside. He put her in a car, and Phil said it looks like Lori is driving. He and the other reporter are following."

"That doesn't make sense," Mitch said. "Why would he make Lori drive?"

Matt rubbed the back of his neck. "I have no idea, but something isn't right."

"I agree. Have Phil call me so I can put a trace on their position."

"Okay." Matt hung up and picked up his cell. "Theresa, call Mitch from Phil's phone so they can trace your position, then I'll call your number from my truck."

He disconnected the call and left his office. "Denise, I won't be back until tomorrow. Get three pink slips ready. Theresa, Phil, and Lori are fired!"

She wasn't the only one standing there with wide eyes. The whole fourth floor probably heard him yelling and came to find out what was going on.

Not waiting for the elevator, he ran down the stairs. The image of John Cowl with his throat slit popped into his mind as a sick feeling of panic spread through him. When he got a hold of Lori, he would never let her go. After he wrung her pretty little neck.

In all his years, no woman had ever made him so crazy. As furious as he was at all of them, he couldn't help but appreciate their spunk.

Fresh rage washed over him. *They're all fired. Every one of them!*

Once outside, he jogged to his truck and called Phil's cell from his dashboard.

"Are they headed to Lori's house?" He hoped so. He could be there in ten minutes. Matt pulled out of the parking lot, making a silent resolution. Instead of a one-week honeymoon, he and Lori were taking two weeks. The thought made him more anxious to get to her. He pressed down on the gas pedal a little harder.

"No, she lives north of the paper and we're going—" Theresa screamed.

"What?" Matt yelled.

Phil let go of a string of curses. "The guy in the back shot at us."

"Stop following so close, Phil."

"Is that Mitch on the other line?" Matt asked.

"Yes, we have him on speaker on Theresa's phone. We haven't seen any cop cars yet, Mitch," Phil said.

"Which direction are you going?" Matt asked.

"We're in a residential neighborhood, going east," Theresa said.

"Mitch, you think they're headed to Steve's house?"

"Possibly. I'll send cars there. Stay back, Phil," Mitch said.

Matt turned right at the next corner. If they were headed to Steve's, he was ten minutes behind.

CHAPTER 21

$\mathcal{A}$ gunshot exploded and Lori screamed.

"What are you shooting at?" Anderson yelled.

"That tall skinny guy is following us!"

"Don't shoot again. Every neighbor around will be calling the cops."

Lori looked in the rearview mirror and almost burst into tears of gratitude. Theresa must have seen Agent Anderson leading her to a car before they turned the corner.

Stay back, Phil, but please keep following.

"Where are we going?" Lori asked, her voice shaking.

"Just drive," Tremblay snarled.

The road ended at a T. "Left or—"

"Left," Anderson said.

"Where are we going?"

"Shut up," Tremblay commanded. "You have been nothing but trouble from the minute you became involved."

"I was never involved. You assumed I was."

"Just shut up and drive."

"Tremblay here is—"

"Don't use my name!"

"She already knows your name."

Tremblay smacked the gun on the back window. Lori jumped. Her nerves were so on edge, she felt like she'd shake apart, body part by body part.

"Turn left at the corner," Anderson said. "Stay off the main roads."

"What does it matter? That guy is still following us," Tremblay bellowed.

Agent Anderson blew out a breath. "Mrs. Eubanks shouldn't have gotten tangled up with Hook."

Lori slipped fingers into her left pants pocket, wiggled her phone out as much as she dared, and pushed the record button. Their words might come out garbled, but if she could get a confession . . .

"Hook?" she asked.

Anderson pointed to his nose. "The idiot your friend tried to help."

"Both of you stop talking."

"We had to get rid of her," Anderson added, as if Tremblay hadn't spoken.

Lori swiped the sudden tears that blinded her eyes.

"If you'd just left the flash drives out where we could find them instead of hiding them."

"I told you I didn't have them."

Anderson tipped his head toward her. "Didn't, but you do now?"

"No, the police have them." Which was a lie, but if they thought the police already had them, maybe they'd let her go. "Carrie left a note and a key to a locker in my desk, but I only found it this morning while you were searching her desk."

"I told you she didn't have them," Tremblay growled.

Anderson pulled out his cell phone, scrolled to a number, and put the phone to his ear. "It's me. The police have the flash drives. Yep. Where? Okay. We should be there in an hour." He stuffed his phone back in his pocket.

Phil was still following but keeping his distance. At the next stop sign, she looked at Anderson.

"Left. We're going to the airport." Anderson turned to look out the back window.

"The airport is south."

"Harvey Airfield is north."

"In Snohomish?"

Neither answered her question.

"So, you killed both John Cowl and Carrie?" Lori asked.

"They left us no choice," Anderson said.

"And Agent Turner."

Anderson laughed. "Nope, Turner is squeaky clean."

Tremblay pointed his gun at Anderson's head. "One more word and I'll be taking the plane alone."

Lori's mind raced. She had a little under an hour to do something. Since they'd divulged so much, they weren't going to let her go. She swallowed her tears back. At least when the police found her body, they'd have a second confession.

"That woman behind us has been on the phone the whole time," Tremblay grumbled. "She'll have the police at the airfield before we get there."

Lori was now following Lake Washington's shoreline. She knew of two places where the road ran close to the water. Maybe she could flip the car. Neither of the men had fastened their seat belts.

Anderson's phone buzzed and he pulled it out and read a message. "We're going to take a left in Lake City."

"That's the wrong way," Tremblay said.

"We'll never get out at Harvey Airfield. Jeter said a plane will meet us on the water."

Okay, she was out of time. About two miles farther, the

road cut close to the water. She couldn't think of any other option. She pushed the accelerator down a little harder, hoping they wouldn't notice. *One more turn. Don't rush. Don't alert them. Stay calm.*

Her heart was pumping so hard her chest hurt. She took the last curve and a deep breath.

"What's that?" Tremblay shoved his arm between the front seats and pointed out the window.

Flashing lights blocked the road ahead.

"Turn left now!" Anderson yelled, grabbing the steering wheel.

Lori jammed the gas pedal to the floor just as Anderson cranked the wheel to the left, throwing both men against their side doors. Agent Anderson cursed and Tremblay's head hit the window with a crack. Using both hands, she yanked the wheel in the opposite direction, then quickly reeled it back to the left and stomped both feet down on the brake pedal.

When the car flipped, something hard hit her head and the fuzzy edges of darkness threatened her vision. The front airbags exploded and jolted her back with force. Glass shattered, the shards biting into her face and chest.

She squeezed her eyes shut and clamped her lower lip between her teeth. *Don't pass out!* her mind screamed, even as her world turned black.

~

"What?" Matt yelled when Theresa screamed.

"The car flipped," Theresa choked out.

"Where? Where are you?"

"I don't know, but the police are up ahead. They have the road blocked."

The call disconnected. Matt floored the gas pedal. He'd been traveling faster than they were, so the car had to be just ahead. He spotted them just past a bend in the road.

Phil and Theresa were out of Phil's car, and the police were already surrounding the dark sedan, which was flipped upside down. He skidded to a stop, jumped out, and ran toward the car, where a police officer lay on his belly half inside the driver's side window.

Another cop tried to hold him back, but he broke free of the grasp. Police were standing around an unmoving body on the other side of the car. Matt dropped to the ground next to the police officer and saw Lori hanging upside down, still belted in, her face hidden by her hair. "Is she breathing?"

"She's unconscious but breathing."

The blare of a fire truck sounded next to them. Matt jumped up and rushed to the front windshield so the firemen had enough room to get to Lori. From there he could see two other firemen pulling Tremblay out of the back passenger side window. He had a long gash on his scalp.

Agent Anderson must have been thrown from the car. One leg was bent at an awful angle, and a piece of metal stuck out of his side. He blinked blood from one eye as a policewoman talked to him.

Matt knelt in front of the car, surprised a cop hadn't tried to pull him away. The airbag hung in front of Lori's face making it impossible to see her. And he needed to see her. He needed to make sure she was breathing.

A moment later, the firemen were lifting her out onto a backboard.

"Lori?" He rushed to her side. "Can you hear me, baby?"

"Matt?" She reached out blindly.

He took her hand, terrified by all the blood on her face. "I'm right here, darlin'. You're going to be okay."

"Phil and Theresa?"

"They're both here. Everyone's okay."

Her hand went slack in his.

"Hold on, baby," Matt whispered close to her ear, just in case she could hear him. "You're going to be fine."

CHAPTER 22

*L*ori took her dad's arm.

"You ready for this?" he asked.

"More than ready." It had taken her and Matt twenty-five years—and three months—to get here. She couldn't wait to be Mrs. Matthew Kelley. They'd traveled a long, bumpy road, but she finally met his family last night at the rehearsal dinner, and already loved them as her own.

They'd decided on a small, close friends and family only wedding in Matt's backyard. In thirty minutes, it would be her backyard too.

The summer was just beginning, and her family had already been to two weddings. Tara and Kevin tied the knot in their backyard two weeks ago, and Tara's daughter got married the weekend after.

Her dad led her around the corner of the house. Matt stood under the arbor their moms both insisted on. In fact, their moms did all the planning, from where everyone would sit to the beautiful cake sitting on Matt's deck. Though Matt fought against a big to-do, her mom argued that Matt had never been married and deserved a special day. His mom agreed, and Lori was happy to give him the moment.

Matt asked Taylor to be his best man, which made her heart swell to beyond what her chest could hold. And Megan was her maid of honor. Her twins stood up front grinning while they watched her walk down the aisle on their grandpa's arm.

May had turned into a month of rain, which made the trees behind Matt's house, the backdrop for their wedding, a curtain of green, and the rhododendron bushes were full of clusters of flowers in shades from pink to deep rose. She was going to love living in this beautiful home.

Matt wiped a finger under an eye, which touched her heart. His handsomeness stole her breath. Their eyes met and held as she walked past all their guests.

Phil wolf-whistled, and she smile. No day would be complete without Phil making her blush.

She and her dad reached the front of the rows of chairs, and he kissed her cheek before releasing her hand. When she passed her bouquet to Megan, Matt took her right hand. Never taking his eyes from hers, he lifted her wrist and kissed the pulse point. Matt would always keep their life together interesting.

She believed things happened for a reason. She wasn't sure why they weren't able to be together twenty-five years ago, but she knew they were supposed to be together now. He would always be her peanut butter.

The music faded out, replaced by a recording of Matt at the piano, playing "A Thousand Years." She didn't have to do much begging for him to agree.

While their vows were spoken to the beautiful music, everything but Matt disappeared. She took note of every detail from him stroking the pads of his thumbs over her knuckles to the look in his vivid blue eyes to the smile that played over his face.

Today her world expanded beyond her and her children. It would be hard to give up small pieces of her independence, but she would for Matt. He needed to know he was taking good care of her, so she'd let him. She knew he'd do the same for her. Because of an absent husband, she'd learned to be independent out of necessity, all the while longing for someone to share her life with. She believed she and Matt would slide into contentment, joy, and true companionship quite easily.

As the last notes of Matt's piano solo faded away, they said, "I do."

"You may kiss the bride."

Matt took her in his arms and kissed her gently like she was infinitely precious, his awed expression lasting long enough to bring tears to her eyes.

Then his wicked grin appeared and she was back on level ground, being swept away by congratulatory hugs and well-wishes. Even so, she would remember that split-second look on his face forever. They were going to have an amazing life together.

~

Standing to the side, Matt watched his new bride as she moved around the yard. She'd come out of the accident with a dislocated shoulder, very bruised ribs, multiple lacerations, and two black eyes. Businessman Gerald Roebeck, along with thirty-two others, were arrested. Agent Anderson and Tremblay both recovered from their injuries and were now behind bars.

Matt would never forget the terror he experienced when

he saw that mangled car. He'd spent the night in the hospital, unwilling to leave Lori's side.

"You look deep in thought."

He looked down at Lori's beautiful daughter. "Just watching your gorgeous mom."

"She is pretty spectacular." She leaned her shoulder against his arm. "I love your parents."

His mom was flitting around the backyard, making sure everyone had a drink and a plate of food. "She's excited to add two grandchildren to her growing brood."

"She's already invited us to a family reunion next month."

"I hope you'll come. We have great family reunions. Wakeboards and tubing and wave runners and paddleboards. Campfires with roasted hotdogs and marshmallows."

"Sounds like fun," Taylor said, joining them. He draped his arm around his sister's neck. "It's nice to see Mom so happy."

Matt glanced across the lawn. Lori was talking with his two sisters. After twenty-five years and three months, he finally got to introduce Lori to his family. And they loved her, just like he knew they would. "I plan on making her happy for a long time."

"Can I ask a personal question?"

He noticed the hesitancy in Megan's voice. "Sure."

"Have you ever been married before?"

"No," Matt answered, looking into her brown eyes, not minding the questions if it made Lori's kids comfortable with him. He'd only been around Megan and Taylor a few times since they'd come home from college for the summer. It would take more than that to build a relationship of trust with them.

They would live in Lori's house until they went back to school for their senior year. He and Lori had decided to keep the house for them to use, at least for a few years. It felt nice to be making big decisions with someone—a first for him.

"Did you ever come close?" Taylor asked.

"Once," Matt replied, looking toward his bride again. "A long time ago, I was very close to proposing."

"Was it before my dad?"

Matt smiled down at Megan. "Yes."

"Hey, Lori!" Tara yelled from across the yard. She was standing next to Phil, and both were grinning. "Tell us about the game of strip pool you played."

Quiet fell over the crowd while they turned as one to Lori. She blushed crimson and turned an emerald-eyed glare on her sister and Phil.

Taylor was the first to respond with a booming laugh. "Who had to strip for you, Mom?"

Phil and Tara turned to face Matt.

"Thanks, Phil," he said.

"Matthew Kelley!" his mom exclaimed, fists on her hips.

His oldest sister put an arm around Lori's shoulder. "Oh, my gosh. Please tell me someone took a picture."

Faith raised her hand. "I did."

His whole family flocked to take a look.

Taylor patted his back. "Didn't she warn you, Matt?"

"Yes, but she cheated."

"I didn't cheat any more than you did," Lori said. She turned to Taylor. "And yes, I warned him twice."

"You didn't believe her?" Taylor asked.

"What can I say? I wanted to see your mother naked."

"Matthew Kelley!" His mom stomped toward him. "I can't believe you said that in front of my new grandchildren."

"I'm sure Lori wouldn't want me to lie in front of her kids," he quipped.

"I find it extremely funny that you admitted, in front of

my grandmother, that you played strip pool because you wanted to see my mom naked."

Matt leaned toward Megan. "Between you and me, I wouldn't have let your mother take off another article of clothing. She was as naked as she was going to get."

"What did you get her down to?" Taylor asked.

"She still had her jeans and one of those thingies." Matt pointed to the camisole peeking out from under Megan's dress. "She had one on under her sweater. That was as far as I would let her go."

Megan squeezed his arm. "Are you that chivalrous, or was it because you didn't want Phil to see my mother without clothes?"

"Oh man, you caught me." Matt laughed. "I guess if we're being honest, I might have let the game go further if Phil hadn't been in the room."

It was Megan's turn to laugh. "I like you, Matt."

"Yep, you're an okay guy," Taylor added.

He grinned at Megan and Taylor, who both looked so much like their mother when they laughed. "I like you guys, too."

Tara was laughing so hard Phil had to support her. "Can you believe our conservative little Lori playing a game of strip pool, Mom?"

"No," his new mother-in-law said, shaking her head at Lori. "What possessed you—"

"I buckled under pressure." Lori glared at Phil and Tara. "Besides, Matt was a little too sure of himself, and Faith wanted to see him naked."

Faith raised her eyebrows and nodded. "It was a very exciting game. I wish I'd put money on it."

"Did she get you down to nothing?" Mike, his older brother hollered across the yard.

"She left the room before I pulled my briefs off." Matt

ducked his mom's attempt to cuff him upside the head and headed toward his wife.

"Thanks, Tara and Phil. That was a super fun moment to add to my wedding memories," Lori said. "I should have known I could count on the two of you."

Matt's dad tugged Lori into a hug. "Too bad Matt doesn't have a pool table. You two could start your honeymoon with a rematch."

Lori wrapped her arms around his dad's waist. "There aren't going to be any rematches."

"I'll have a pool table as soon as we move Lori's things into the house." Matt pulled Lori out of his dad's arms and wrapped her in his own. "*After* our honeymoon."

~

*L*ori kissed Matt's neck as he pulled her closer. "Do you have any idea how happy I am?"

"I think I do," she replied.

She snuggled as close as an airline seat belt would allow and gazed up at him.

"What?" he asked.

"Just looking at my husband." She ran the tip of her finger down his nose. "I've always loved your profile. You're as handsome as you were in college."

"It's a good thing you think so, because these"—he lifted her hand and kissed the rings on her finger— "say you're stuck with me now."

A flight attendant came over the intercom telling the passengers to prepare for landing. After a short shuttle ride to their Caribbean resort, they would finally be alone. Lori's heart leaped with anticipation.

She turned her face into his neck and breathed him in. "I'm going to love being stuck with you."

"You're revving my pulse up," he said, deep and quiet.

"I must be doing something right."

"Oh, darlin', you're doing everything right."

"I love you, Matthew Kelley." She pulled his head to hers and kissed him. "I can't wait to start our life together."

"You're making me crazy, woman," he said looking into her eyes. "Do you think you're safe because we're on an airplane?" He kissed her like she was the last drop of water in a parched desert.

When they came up for air, she whispered, "I know I'm safe anywhere you are, sweetheart. Do you love me?" She gasped for breath when Matt nipped her bottom lip.

"Even more today than I did yesterday—if that's possible."

"Matt?"

Matt smiled. "What, darlin'?"

"I can't breathe when you kiss me like this."

"I know, baby. That's why I kiss you like this. We'll breathe later."

If you enjoyed *Endless Love*, I hope you'll continue reading! The other books in the Second Chance Romance Collection are *When You Love Someone* and *Rhythm of Love.*

To keep up to date on new releases join my newsletter at TinaNewcomb.com.

Following is an excerpt from *Rhythm of Love.*

CHAPTER ONE

Kenzie Rivers stared at her father. The energetic, horseback-riding, hay-hauling, always-smiling man who raised her was too quiet.

His hair, habitually windblown, was slicked down too neatly, his cheeks too smooth-shaven, his expression too rigid, and his lips too . . . pink. Although his brown suit was the right choice, the decision between the traditional tie or the sterling silver galloping horse with the inlaid turquoise bolo had been harder. She'd finally decided on the bolo, which was also the right choice.

The part that was all wrong—the casket. The interior fabric washed out his usually tanned complexion making her perfect father's skin look sallow and waxen.

A hand touched her waist. She knew without turning that it was Kyle. Her brother resembled their father so much, with his dark hair and chestnut eyes, she was almost afraid to look at the living version.

"Hey, baby girl, people will start arriving in about fifteen minutes."

She swallowed a fresh wave of tears. "Dad would hate to

have all his friends file past, looking down at him. He would hate this."

Waylon Rivers would rather everyone celebrate his life at the ranch, with a backyard barbecue, lots of music, and dancing.

"People want to pay their respects. Are you going to be okay?"

Kenzie nodded.

"I asked Mr. Stewart if someone could wipe off that gaudy pink lipstick. The makeup lady is on her way." Kyle squeezed her waist. "Are you sure you're okay?"

Frustration, anger, and pain leaked through her tiny *I'm fine* fissure. "I've never had someone close to me die before, so I'm not exactly sure how I should feel or act. Am I doing it wrong?"

"It's okay to cry, Kenz," he said, ignoring her harsh tone.

She glanced up at her brother's handsome face, now etched with sympathy. And concern. "Have you?"

"At the hospital."

"You were with me the whole time."

"No. While you were in the hospital chapel, I sat in my truck and bawled like a baby."

In all of her twenty-four years, she'd only seen Kyle shed tears once, and that was on the day their mother drove away.

Rubber-soled shoes squeaked down the carpeted aisle, growing louder with each step. Kenzie cringed until the sound halted next to her.

"Mr. Stewart says you're unhappy with your daddy's makeup." The gray-haired lady, her curls as tight as corkscrews, peered into the casket. "What's the problem?"

"If you could just wipe off the pink lip color," Kyle said.

"He needs some color on his cheeks too," Kenzie added. "He looks yellow. My father worked outside every day of his life. He even had a tan during the winter months."

The lady squeaked closer and set a makeup case on their father's chest, then pulled out a white towel and tucked it inside his loose collar. "We don't want to get your daddy's white shirt smudged."

She pulled another tissue out of a box, dipped the tip in a small pot of something that looked glossy, and wiped at the lipstick.

Kenzie wanted him to grin, leap out of the casket, and shout, "Gotcha!"

He didn't.

Dizzy, she backed into a chair. She couldn't bear to watch the lady swiping and brushing at her dad like he was dead. Waylon had been a force of nature all their lives. He was resilient and kind and funny, and the backbone of Rivers Equestrian Ranch. He'd taught her to be strong and said the ranch and her brother needed her unique womanly power. Funny thing, she didn't feel powerful. At the moment she was a quivering mess.

She ran a hand over her burgundy skirt, her dad's choice for her funeral attire. "Do not wear black," he'd instructed. "I want you to wear that pretty, flowery blouse with the skirt you bought for Easter Sunday. And tell Kyle to wear his blue suit and that bright tie you gave him for his birthday last year. That's how I want you both dressed for the occasion."

Not *my funeral*, but *the occasion*.

The woman stepped back from the casket. "How does that look?"

Kenzie stood and moved next to her brother.

"He looks better." His lips were a more natural color now and bronze tinted his face. "He looks better," she repeated before glancing at Kyle.

He nodded.

The lady pulled the towel away and tucked everything back in her case. "You kids have a nice night."

Kyle and Kenzie stared at the lady as she squeaked her way back down the aisle, leaving behind a parting comment that was ludicrous enough to be laughable.

Tall, lanky Jeremy Knight passed the woman on his way down the aisle. He'd cut his shoulder-length, sandy-colored hair shorter than she'd ever seen, and his brown eyes, usually twinkling with mischief, conveyed as much sorrow as she felt.

"How are you guys? You okay?" He ran a finger under his collar, his Adam's apple bobbing when he swallowed. "Sorry. Stupid question. Man, I hate the quiet in this room." His eyes darted to Waylon, then back to them. "So does your dad. I can tell by the look on his face."

The comment made Kenzie smile. Jeremy and Kyle had been friends since they were toddlers, and he and his parents were like extended family.

Minutes later, Kenzie stood between her brother and Jeremy while people filed through the room, expressing their condolences, hugging, kissing, shaking hands.

Dove Hill, Tennessee was a small town, population eight thousand, and most people within fifty miles knew Waylon Rivers. Either Jeremy or Kyle had their arm around her, supporting her through the endless evening while they talked with friends and neighbors, people they'd known all their lives, and people who did business with the ranch.

The next day was a blur for Kenzie. She scanned the gathering at the church, hoping to see the one face who could shore her up through this. His mom and dad were there, but she didn't see him. After the moving funeral service, during which many friends got up to share memories of her father, and the equally emotional graveside service, there was still no sign of Nick Marshall.

Everyone converged at the Rivers' ranch following the

service. Jeremy had tables and chairs delivered from an event rental party place in Nashville, so people had plenty of places to sit and visit under the shade of huge trees.

A Nashville catering company delivered barbecued brisket, pulled pork, and fried chicken. Fresh buns and sides of potato salad, baked beans, and coleslaw filled the tables, along with veggie trays and separate bags of chips. Neighbors contributed platters of cookies and brownies, cakes, and pies.

The ranch house and surrounding yard overflowed with people consoling and reminiscing, story after story told and retold.

After two hours, Kenzie escaped down a path, past Kyle's small house, through the pecan grove, to a big shed almost hidden behind a wall of dogwoods that had already dropped their spring blossoms.

The day smelled fresh, like new growth and sunshine. The sky was too beautiful, the temperature too perfect for a funeral. Her mood called for black clouds and booming thunder, followed by a torrential downpour.

Bypassing the big sliding doors, she walked around to the side door and stepped inside. Kyle, Jeremy, and Nick, along with all three of their fathers, had turned this old building into a practice space for the band Kyle and Jeremy had started in junior high school. Nick joined a year later, and the other three members joined a few months after that. And they still practiced here every Tuesday, Thursday, and Saturday.

Knight Rivers band—named after Jeremy Knight and Kyle Rivers—had only lost one member over the years, when Nick left just three months earlier to pursue bigger dreams.

Wandering around the inside of the building brought back so many memories. Over the years they insulated the walls, added windows, heating, and air for comfort. Her dad even built a small kitchen in the back that he kept stocked so the boys had food when they were too busy practicing to eat.

She grew up loving music as much as the boys did, and she'd spent hours and hours in here. Kyle taught her to play the guitar, Jeremy taught her to play the drums, and she taught herself to play the piano.

She started writing songs at fourteen. Total fluke, a pop singer heard one of her demos and bought the song and sang it all the way to number one on the charts. That was the beginning for Kenzie. Since then she'd written jingles and sold songs to music artists who specifically asked for her work. A couple of songs even found their way onto movie soundtracks.

All that changed six months ago, when her dad suffered a severe stroke and his health deteriorated quickly. She still wrote for top artists, but rarely left the house while taking care of the man who had taken care of her most of her life. Until two weeks ago, when Waylon came down with pneumonia and, in his weakened condition, couldn't fight it.

She sat at one of three keyboards and plunked out a tune she'd been working on. The haunting melody seemed appropriate for the occasion.

The door swung inward on squeaky hinges, and she looked up to see Jeremy standing in the opening, backlit by the setting sun, which cast him in a golden glow, like an angel swooping in to rescue her from the path of darkness she was headed toward.

"What are you doing out here alone, sweet pea?"

"Escaping, same as you. Or are you here to check on me?"

He sat down at the drums, picking up a pair of sticks and twirling them through his fingers. The beaters, as he called them, were as much a part of Jeremy as his hands. "Kyle's worried about you."

She knew her brother. No matter how often she told him

she was okay, he'd continue to check. He'd looked after her since the day their mother left with *the nice insurance man.* Kenzie was four and Kyle eight when he became her surrogate guardian. *I'll take care of you, baby girl. Daddy will take care of the horses, and I'll take care of you.*

Kenzie plunked another few keys. "You can tell him I'm fine, Jer."

"You've been through a lot the past six months. Your father's stroke and then Nick leaving."

Nick.

Even though the band he was playing with was in nearby Nashville, he hadn't come yesterday or today. The worst days of her life, and Nick, who was less than an hour away, hadn't been here for her. That he missed her dad's funeral hurt more than him leaving in the first place—which wasn't fair of her. The opportunity he'd been offered was too big to pass up.

Kenzie got up and walked to a window. From here she could see the pristine horse stables—painted right before her dad had his stroke—and the pastures beyond. After several days of rain last week, the grass was such a vivid green it looked unreal—like someone had painted it a shade richer for her father's last days.

She sensed Jeremy's approach. He put his hands on her shoulders, squeezing lightly, letting her know she had a support system at the ready.

"I'm sorry about Waylon. We're all going to miss him."

She reached up and linked their fingers. "I know."

He turned her around so she faced him. "I'm sorry about Nick, too. He shouldn't have left like he did. And he should have been here today."

She wanted to defend Nick, say she understood, but if the tables were turned, she would have moved heaven and earth to be here for him.

His leaving cut deep. That he asked her to come, even though he knew she couldn't, had deepened the wound. She would never leave her dad when he was so sick. After all the years Kyle had taken care of her, she'd never leave him with the responsibility for the ranch and the care of their father, too.

Nick knew her hands were tied. He also knew she'd never ask him to stay because playing bass guitar with a rising country star's band was his dream come true.

The tears that refused to come since Nick's departure and her father's death flooded her eyes. Jeremy drew her close and held tight. She hated crying in front of people, but the sobs came without warning, shaking her.

"Go ahead and cry, sweet pea. Let it out. You've been holding it in for too long." Gently rubbing her back, Jeremy stood unwavering and let her soak his shirt. Once she settled into shuddering breaths, he tipped her face up and dried her cheeks with the pads of his thumbs. "You think you're done?"

Kenzie could count on Jeremy as much as she could count on Kyle. He'd always be there for her, just like she'd been there for him when he buried his wife and their unborn daughter after a drunk driver ran a red light and hit her as she crossed a street.

Her smile wobbled at the corners. "You can now report to Kyle that I cried. He'll be so ecstatic."

He chuckled and kissed her forehead. "Do you feel better?"

"No, but *he* will."

"Anytime you need an ear"—he lifted his wet tie—"or tissue, just give me a call. I'll be here in minutes."

She tried to swallow around the tears that spilled over a second time.

"Oops, you're not done yet," he said with another chuckle. He kissed her cheek.

She swiped under her burning eyes just as he aimed for her other cheek, but their lips met instead. And neither of them pulled away. It started as a gentle brush of lips and an inkling of wonder that turned deeper in a split second.

This is wrong, ran through her mind as she got up on tiptoe and wrapped her arms around his neck. He pulled her tight against his chest. She could feel his heart pounding against hers, and she lost herself in a moment of comfort, of not feeling so alone.

The hinges on the door squeaked, and they wrenched apart to face Nick.

ACKNOWLEDGMENTS

Thank you to my Beta Readers, Jeanine Hopping, Chris Almodovar, Holly Hertzke, and Marnie Giggey. Their input is invaluable. I appreciate all of them for giving their time, patience, and talent.

Thank you to my editor, Faith Freewoman. She battled the word *was* like a Demon for Details.

Thank you to proofreader Julia Allen for catching my missing or extra commas and rewriting a sentence or two, so they'd make more sense.

A special thank you goes to my cover artist, Dar Albert, for her understanding and patience with me. We (she) changed the cover four or five times because I couldn't quite find the right image to portray Lori and Matt.

Another special thank you goes to my kids for their support. Love you all!

Thank you to Richard and Stefan Newcomb, who keep my web page current—one less thing to worry about.

And a huge thank you to my husband, who takes care of all the behind-the-scenes work. Love you bunches!

Finally, thank you, dear readers, for reading, reviewing, sharing, and letting me know you like my books.

xox

Tina

ALSO BY TINA NEWCOMB

The Eden Falls Series

Finding Eden

Beyond Eden

A Taste of Eden

The Angel of Eden Falls

Touches of Eden

Stars Over Eden Falls

Fortunes for Eden

Snow and Mistletoe in Eden Falls

Rumors in Eden Falls

Second Chance Romance Collection

When You Love Someone

Endless Love

Rhythm of Love

Second Chance Romance Collection

ABOUT THE AUTHOR

Tina Newcomb writes clean, contemporary romance. Her heartwarming stories take place in quaint small towns, with quirky townsfolk, and friendships that last a lifetime.

She acquired her love of reading from her librarian mother, who always had a stack of books close at hand, and her father who visited a local bookstore every weekend.

Tina Newcomb lives in colorful Colorado. When not lost in her writing, she can be found in the garden, traveling with her (amateur) chef husband, or spending time with family and friends.

Follow Tina on:

facebook.com/TinaNewcombAuthor

instagram.com/tinanewcombauthor

bookbub.com/authors/tina-newcomb

goodreads.com/tinanewcomb

pinterest.com/tinanewcomb

9 781947 786509